MAKE ME CHOOSE

Bayshore #4

Ember Leigh

ABOUT 'MAKE ME CHOOSE'

CATCH FLIGHTS, NOT FEELINGS.

So says Weston Daly, the playboy backpacker I keep running into around the globe. And I, for one, am sick and tired of tripping over his windblown chestnut hair and that impossible heartbreaker grin every time I leave the country.

First Amsterdam. Then Portugal. And now? Aruba.

He's Instagram-famous and too gorgeous to trust. I've hated him since the day I met him, but on this trip, I have to play nice, even though he makes it impossible. It's our best friends' wedding...and I'm the official photographer.

The more this man smiles through my viewfinder, the harder it is to remember why we've always butted heads. Before I know what I'm doing, paradise takes on a new meaning, and it involves Weston Daly's tongue.

His profile might say that he stops for nobody, but when we're together, time itself freezes. When I receive the offer of a lifetime, Weston wants something that throws my whole world into disarray.

And worse yet? He plans to make me choose.

contents

DEDICATION

This book is dedicated to my twenties, which were spent in a constant flux of readying to buy a plane ticket and having just returned from somewhere.

Also dedicated to all of those seat-of-your-pants choices we've all made in life that everyone says are bad ideas but end up being really fucking good ideas.

AUTHOR'S NOTE

This book takes place on a real island, but liberties were taken with the geography and, er, *inhabitants* therein.

Just wanted to throw that out there for anyone who's been to Aruba recently and is wondering what I'm smoking.

CHAPTER ONE

NOVA

Is this farts or is this joy?

Inside my head, I sing this line to the tune of The Clash's "Should I Stay or Should I Go?" The plane I'm on is just now cresting the northern ridge of Aruba, offering me a pristine view of the island below. My stomach lurches again—this is definitely joy. Because, motherfuckers, *I'm about to be on Aruba!*

It's the same every time I travel. Nervous belly in advance of a new locale. Possibly a foreign tongue awaiting me, though according to my research, I may be hearing plenty of English. This constituent country of the Netherlands (thanks Wikipedia) was not exactly on my Top Ten Next Destinations list, but when my bestie from another chestie told me she was getting married on this twenty mile long hunk of Caribbean goodness (thanks again Wikipedia), you know I put in my vacation request to my supervisor before we'd even ended the Skype call.

My knee is bouncing as I look out the plane window. All I can see is the turquoise water of the sea and the frayed edges of the island giving way to white sand beaches, which is the mathematical equivalent to *one week of paradise.*

And holy crap, I need the getaway. Travel is in my blood, but I can only afford to donate said blood on strictly scheduled vacations and long weekends crammed around the edges of an uninspiring full-time job. Besides, if I ever tried to do something wild like *travel for more than two weeks at a time,* I'm pretty sure my family would have a collective heart attack and stage an intervention.

That's how my family is. They don't travel. Hell, they don't even leave New York State. The wildest thing they've done so far is name me Nova, which came from my father's brief obsession with the movie *Planet of the Apes.* There's the one fun factoid about my life.

The plane banks as it aligns with the runway. One week. Seven full days of Aruba magic. I'm only assuming it will be magic, of course, since I've never been here before. This is my first destination wedding, which either means it will win the best week of my life until I die at age ninety, or some sort of disaster fit for a decently performing rom-com.

I peer out the window, trying to spot which beach my best friend and her fiancée are getting married on. Amelia and I met our sophomore year at Purchase College in southeastern New York. She was a free-spirited art major who loved to travel, which is how she met Rhys Henry Bradford III, her British other half. They figured they'd bridge the distances between their respective countries by heading to an island that felt energetically equidistant from both their hometowns.

I definitely can't complain once the plane touches down and I catch that first whiff of sea breeze. The plane unloads in the middle of the runway, because island life, and the humid air feels like a salve to all the stressors and dissatisfaction I left behind in upstate New York, which I have categorized into three main areas:

1. I am a 25-year-old drowning in debt

2. Who lives with her grandmother in a small shack behind her parents' house

3. And uses her high-falutin' fine arts degree to...take senior high school portraits.

Of all the items on that list, my grandmother bothers me the least. Because my grandma is the fucking best.

But if it seems like things couldn't be more pathetic for a woman my age, I assure you, they get worse. I also haven't had sex in so long, I technically qualify as a virgin again. Yep, that's a thing that can happen.

I don't expect Aruba to change any of these things about me. No, I just expect a most-expenses-paid *escape*. Because that's the American Dream, isn't it? Quietly pay your bills your entire life and be happy with your one-to-two week getaway to a beach.

After I step onto the tarmac, an ocean breeze blows every last bit of my thick, red hair across my face. As I struggle to see the blue sky again, a familiar, feminine voice cuts through the air.

"NOVA!"

My best friend Amelia is jogging toward me, her arms open, pure joy written on her tanned face. Before I know it she's wrapped me in an oxygen-stealing hug, shrieking with laughter in my ear as she says "You made it, you made it," over and over again.

"Amelia! I can't believe they let you this close to the plane without a boarding pass!" We're laughing and hugging, and I'm already full of so many #vacayvibes I can hardly stand it.

"Yeah, well, I sweet-talked the luggage handler, and he said I could find you if I moved quick," she says with one last squeeze around my waist before we pull back to look at each other. If the sculpting world had a Hollywood, she would be the It Girl. She's even dressed like an incognito celeb, with a baseball cap pulled down over a low white-blonde ponytail.

"You should be an international spy," I remark as she grabs my hand, leading me toward the lone terminal. "Sculpting is the perfect cover for your next career of espionage."

She tosses her head back and laughs. "What makes you think I'm not already a spy?"

This is how it is with us: easy, fun, a little ridiculous. Exactly the sort of interaction I've never been able to strike up with the opposite sex. And trust me, I *wish* I could just be into women and call it a day. If only I didn't love the D so much. And the rolling hills of a nice pair of biceps. And the gruff bass of an unexpected "hey, babe." And, you know, about a million other things that go into the butterflies and frustrations of dating a man.

With any luck, I'll find that elusive man before I die.

We whoosh through the baggage claim, and she talks with the luggage handler on the way back in as if she's known him for years, not minutes. That is one of Amelia's superpowers: she can become anybody's best friend in minutes. My lime green luggage wobbles past us on the rickety conveyor belt a moment later.

"Let's go find our *driver*," Amelia says with a mischievous giggle once I've got all my things. This destination wedding is off to a great start. Ocean breeze: check. Private escort to the resort: check. I can't keep the silly smile off my face as I follow Amelia onto the sidewalk of the airport arrivals lane. There's a sleek black van waiting for us that looks like it could double as a party bus or an FBI vehicle. The side door slides open, and Rhys hops out, shooting me a smile fit for the British rag-mags. This is pure party.

"Nover! You made it!" His British lilt on my name never fails to delight. I laugh into his solar plexus (he's like seven feet tall) as we embrace. "Can I help with your bag?"

"I'd love that," I say. "Not gonna lie, I packed eighteen times more clothes than I'll need, so it weighs as much as an iceberg."

From inside the party van, there's a little snort. Rhys goes to the back of the van to load my bag.

Amelia says, "So, I forgot to mention…" but I can't hear her after a certain point because the person who snorted at me has now revealed himself.

First thing I notice is the hair—longish, chestnut brown tresses that are caught between stylishly windswept and bedhead. And then I notice the broad shoulders, dark tee pulled tight over the afore-mentioned hills of biceps. And once he comes to standing on the sidewalk, I barely notice that two others are following, because I can no longer focus on anything that isn't *this man*.

Because the man who stepped out of the van isn't just a casual hottie.

He's none other than Weston Daly.

The man who's made my heart flutter since I first met him four years ago. The living definition of tall, tan, and handsome. A vagabond who has never noticed me even a tenth as much as I have noticed him.

And this marks the third time *around the world* that he has come to haunt my vacation.

"…and Weston, Elliot, and Keko came along, too!" Amelia is finishing up. My gaze is hopelessly riveted on Weston, and I can't tell if my face looks like petrified shock—something you'd find on one of those mummies accidentally preserved by the eruption of Mount

Vesuvius, no doubt—or blatant chagrin. His icy blue eyes return my surprise-volcano-eruption stare, and the smirk that curls at his lips says volumes without him uttering a word.

"Good to see you again, Nover," Elliot, the other Brit, says. Keko, the final member of their groomsmen bro squad, waves at me. I met both of them during a trip last year to Portugal, which marked the second time I spent too many consecutive days with the gorgeous—I mean, *completely irritating*—Weston Daly.

Weston hasn't greeted me, and I won't be the first one to budge on that front.

"This is great," I manage to say, smiling brightly at Amelia. I hope she can read the strain in my eyes as *Oh, you didn't fucking tell me that Weston Daly was coming*, because that's exactly what those near-burst blood vessels are trying to convey.

It's been a year since I saw him last. Each time we've met up has been an accident—a misfortune, really—and I should have expected he'd be here too.

Because when I say he haunts my trips, I mean it. He's like a ghost I just can't get to cross over to the next dimension. It doesn't matter how many times I chant "You're free." Weston continues to appear at all my international getaways.

Rhys comes from around the back of the van. "I bet they charged you triple for that beastly thing."

It's only beastly because I need to justify all my last-minute thrift store purchases by wearing outfits outside my comfort zone at least *once*. But I'm not high maintenance, no matter what the bulging weight of my luggage suggests. Really, all I need to travel is a few days' worth of clothes, my cameras, and my travel talisman.

The talisman is important. It's my good luck charm whenever I leave the country. I've never been robbed as a result. I know this doesn't stand up to the scientific process, but I don't care. It's a gorgeous necklace that protects me and has mystical powers, surely. Even if it can't convince Weston to stop tagging along on my itineraries.

The boys are all clambering into the car, leaving the middle bench seat for Amelia and me. Once the van lurches into motion, the driver nodding his greeting to me through the rearview mirror, I feel vulnerable. Weston is sitting directly behind me, and the fact that we haven't technically exchanged a greeting but *have* stared each other down is weighing on me.

He's holding out, but so am I. And I feel like he knows that I know that.

Reggae music floats through the van while Weston's existence sizzles behind me. Amelia and Rhys start recounting a funny story about a passenger on their plane from England who insisted on gherkins to the point of requiring an emergency landing in Boston, and I'm trying to listen while also spying on Weston without actually turning to look at him. This is a hopeless task.

"So...no hello?"

The bass rumble of Weston's voice near my ear sends goosepimples flaring up and down my spine. I catch a waft of his scent—sandalwood and spice. If he were anyone else, and we were *anywhere* else, I'd be taking my panties off by now. But no. Despite how intolerably *good* it feels to have his hot breath graze the back of my neck, I will not give in to him.

"Sorry?" I turn slightly, feigning confusion.

"Just was wondering if you'd ignore me for the rest of the day or the entire week."

I suppress an annoyed sigh. "There was no ignoring. I greeted you with my eyes."

"Oh. Did you *smize*?" he asks, which makes me laugh. *Almost.* "I must have missed it."

"Don't let it keep you up at night," I say, heat and curiosity curling through me.

Because Weston is *exactly* the type of guy that I have dreamt about for a lifetime and never once considered a possibility. Confident, attractive, impossibly put together men? They never go for someone like me. If I had a warning label, it'd say "Fat and Sassy". And then in much smaller font, right below, it would say "And incredibly unsure of herself; please tell me I'm funny".

But Weston can do whatever he wants in this life, without reassurance. He's *that* attractive. I've watched with my own two eyes as he sought out and dominated cute backpacker girls in our shared hostel in Amsterdam, like they were doltish gophers and he was an incredibly dapper coyote. He floats around the world unperturbed and totally at ease. He eats confidence for breakfast.

And if he weren't so annoying, I'd sort of look up to him. Because that confidence breakfast is what I've been missing since college graduation. Except this guy is the *last* person on Earth I'd ever ask for advice.

"...and then we can go surfing!" Amelia wraps up, clapping her hands together.

"Surfing," I repeat, pretending I've been listening.

"The lessons will be free," Rhys insists. "If you've never learned, now's the time."

Bless his accented optimism. "I'm not a big...swimmer."

Though I am big and I know how to swim, I don't make a habit of flinging myself into waves that could drown me. Rhys doesn't need to know the details, though.

"Well you could at least sit on the beach with us," Amelia suggests, just as the van runs over a jagged pothole. I slide out of my seat—that's what I get for not buckling—and crumple into a pile against the front passenger seat. I catch the annoying twinkle in Weston's eye as he tosses his head back and laughs.

What a confident and sexy way to start off my trip. If Weston eats confidence for breakfast, then I must eat puffed embarrassment. I grimace, collecting myself onto the bench seat of the van. It's not like I came down here to bang random hotties—it's not my MO—but Weston reminds me of how not his type I am. And yes, part of me would pawn a lung to be his type.

I stare out the window while the van merges onto the highway outside the airport. Palm trees buttress the road, and cotton candy clouds dot the pristine blue sky. We make a few turns, pass an astonishing number of deep purple flowering bushes that I can only gawk at, and then we pull onto a one-way street that immediately bleeds into white sand beaches and resorts.

My heart stutters as the asphalt turns into a neat cobblestone driveway. My fingers twitch, wanting my camera, but I'll have plenty of time for that. It's what I came here to do, after all. Take pictures of everything as my best friend's *official* wedding photographer. But for right now, I want to simply absorb these perfect early moments.

The driver pulls the van under the palm-frond-bedazzled overhang of a sandstone resort while Rhys and the rest of the group bicker about what time they should start drinking.

Sometimes, when I'm feeling itchy for a trip but don't have the money or time off (which is often, with how much debt I have), I scour the internet for reviews of faraway resorts and destinations. I've noticed that some resorts aren't truly *resorts* like you might expect. You could slap a cow barn onto a Motel 6, label it a wedding venue, and register the whole thing as a resort, technically, as a certain establishment in Florida attempted, according to Google Maps.

But this place?

This is a resort with a capital *Ritzy.* There is a swimming pool in the foyer *just because,* which also doubles as a glass-topped atrium. I stare at the clouds through the ceiling as Amelia leads me toward the front desk, which looks to be carved from volcanic rock. I can't tell if I'm in a fantasy, the future, or a Salvador Dalí painting come to life. Hopefully it turns out to be all three.

"I can't believe you're getting married in Aruba," I tell her as we wait for my room key. The guys disappeared as soon as we crossed into the foyer, and I'm reminding myself I don't care where Weston is.

"It sounds ridiculous," she admits.

"You're going to be Rhys's *old lady,*" I remind her, craning my neck to take in the ever-changing wonders of the resort once we're checked in and she whooshes me down a wide hallway bedecked with Grecian columns. I'm on the lookout for melting clocks, Dalí-style.

"That means I'd have to join a motorcycle club," she corrects me.

"No, *he'd* have to be in the club. Unless you've been hiding your loyalty to the Viper Sculptors MC all these years."

"Viper Sculptors MC. Where we sculpt a bitch, *and* cut a bitch!" She snort laughs, which only makes me laugh harder in return.

Suddenly the hallway we're in opens up to a sprawling patio, leading out to so many things that yank at my attention I don't know what to absorb first. There's a pool shaped like a skinny kidney. A gazebo draped in vining orange flowers. Signs point to a spa area, promising even more treasures I can't quite fathom.

And then there's the boardwalk. Amelia leads me, her flip-flops a'floppin', along the wooden walkway that crisscrosses the resort. My wheeled luggage goes *clack-clack-clack* behind me. Everything is lush and fragrant and oh-so-beautiful.

We pass a fountain with teal water. A statue dripping with pearls. An honest-to-god tiki bar. And then the boardwalk gives way to white sand, the type of sand you only see in commercials, with palm trees towering above us and the most fascinating series of thatched-roof huts sprawling out along the border of the beach.

"This is where the bridal party is staying," Amelia says in a reverent whisper. I'm considered the bridal party, even though I'm technically the photographer and not a bridesmaid. She wanted me to be both, but I wanted to give her the gift of eternal photos more. Besides, how can the photographer include herself in all the bridal party pictures? Selfie sticks aren't exactly a beacon of professionalism in the photography world.

She gestures toward the huts, and I drift toward them at her side. Each one is a different tropical color. Bright orange. Vibrant yellow. Relaxed green, if that's even a color. My wheels get stuck in the sand, but I don't care. I abandon my luggage. Who needs changes of clothes anyway? Not me. Not when I'm here, in Aruba, about to behold my own personal *Crayola hut.*

Laughter and low voices register with me, but I'm too laser focused on the prize to notice who else is out here in this dreamy transition between resort and full-fledged ocean beach. The waves create a mesmerizing soundtrack as I pass Amelia in our sandy trek to the huts. I'm pretty sure she told me which one was mine, but I don't need to confirm. I can hear it calling to me in the salt-tinged breeze. *My fated teal vacation home.*

More laughter, and then the vinyl *thud* of a ball.

"Nova—" Amelia begins, just as I swing around to look at her.

A ball whizzes past my face. Something white and high velocity. My breath evaporates, and I freeze.

And that's when I find out where Rhys and the guys went. They headed straight for sand volleyball. Except now they're all shirtless, and I feel like I just stumbled onto the set of an Abercrombie & Fitch shoot.

And then I spot him. Again.

Weston Daly.

Except this time, he's shirtless and his body might as well be sent from God himself as a little care package he wanted to bestow upon humanity.

"Did you have to get in the way of our game?" He saunters toward me, the lines of his abs practically yanking me by the earlobes to make sure I notice them. Dark swim trunks cling to sculpted thighs in the same way a koala hugs a bamboo tree. His chestnut hair pairs too well with the dimple in his left cheek, and the outrageous glint of his ice-blue eyes.

My breath disappears. I can't stand this man. Yet I have never *not* wanted to jump his bones.

"Oh, Jesus," I spit, annoyance flooding me.

"First you barely acknowledge me, then you get in the way of my game?" Every step closer feels like a threat, and I can't explain why. He's too beautiful. He's too virile. He's too much of everything I've ever wanted.

And I hate him for it. Because he's never wanted *me*.

"Your *ball* got in the way of my *path*," I explain to him.

"Excuse me, Princess Nova." Weston bows exaggeratedly. "Continue on your way. I'd hate to have to cross your path while I get my volleyball."

"You don't need to be ridiculous." To Amelia, I say, "He's gotten more ridiculous since last time, hasn't he?" And he has. Our tense stand-off in the van should have been my warning. He was only gearing up to unleash the full brunt of his attack: shirtless, using all his muscles, looking like *this*.

Weston has an intolerable smirk on his face, hands propped on his hips. And it only makes his biceps pop even more. And when he speaks again, I can *feel* the scrape of his bass voice inside me.

"Even though you're the more ridiculous one, I'll overlook it this once," he says. "Because we're about to spend the next week together, *neighbor*."

There's something about the word *together* that excites me. Ignites me, even. But I squash it. Tamp it down, because I learned everything I need to know about this man the first day I met him. He might be hot enough to send my ovaries into shock, but luckily I can see right through his sexy, sandy smirk.

Weston Daly isn't just out of my league—he's in a league I don't want any part of.

One populated by beautiful drifters and callous playboys.

And I learned long ago just how far away I need to keep men like him.

CHAPTER TWO

If you've seen one beach, you've seen them all. Personally, I've seen a fuck ton. And the one I'm on now, though great, is about what you'd expect for a blissed-out-paradise beach.

This saying applies to almost anything in life, depending on how jaded you want to be. After eight years of on-again, off-again travel, I can attest that this outlook firmly applies to the following: beaches, big cities, slums, greenhouse tomatoes, international airports, and, though I know it invites criticism, butthurt redheads.

Guess where the *ever-so-lovely* Nova Henderson falls on my Scale of Predictability.

"Weston! Come on, mate," Rhys implores from near the volleyball net. All our friends, plus a few new friends we just met on the beach, are waiting for me to rejoin them. The volleyball is safely tucked under my arm as I watch Nova resume her angry stomp toward the huts.

I don't know what the fuck I did to get her to hate me so much, but here we are. We've been nipping at each other's heels like a couple of rival wolves for the past four years. It doesn't matter how much time goes by between our unfortunate reunions—she always shows up with just as much distaste as before.

Which is a shame, really, because there are a few things I appreciate about Nova that have nothing to do with the way she treats me.

One of those things is shifting underneath her flowy skirt as she sprays sand behind her, heading straight for *my* hut.

"Hey," I bark, just as her hand lands on the doorknob. But she doesn't hear me. Or maybe she doesn't care. But this is unacceptable. We've been around each other for thirty minutes and she's already barging into my fucking hut?

Amelia is jogging in the sand behind her, calling Nova's name. But the redheaded bull doesn't stop. She storms into my hut like she owns the place, and I race that way, beating Amelia to the front door.

"What are you doing?" I demand.

Nova is in the center of my hut. She turns to me with narrowed eyes, hands propped on her hips. She's the type of woman that has historically both attracted and repulsed me, for very different reasons. But right now, it's an unnerving mixture of the two.

You see, Nova and I bump into each other around the world. I figured I'd be seeing her here, but there were two other trips around our tiny globe when I ran into her and absolutely did not expect it. Each time—one during the trip to Amsterdam that brought Rhys and Amelia together, the other a completely unexpected shared itinerary in Portugal—is its own brand of complex. Because being around her is equal parts irritating and awe-inspiring.

She attracts me because of her brain and because she's got the badonk-a-donk.

But she repulses me because she acts like she'd rather be anywhere else in the world than near me.

"Can you just let me enjoy my precious first moments in my new home?" she asks, with a look that suggests she's had to explain herself various times to no avail.

I snort. Nova's refined her game plan, because this seems like an entirely new approach to annoying me. "*Your* new home?"

"Yeah. Amelia said that the teal hut was mine—"

"I never said that," Amelia pipes up from behind me, where she's sticking her head through the doorway. Watching us like she might have the cops on speed dial.

"This is *my* hut, Nova." I say it slowly, hoping that spelling it out for her will let it sink in faster. Confusion clouds her pretty, green eyes. Yes, I'm enjoying this. Every last second of it. Because it's like Nova walked right into a trap that I didn't even realize I'd laid.

"You said I had the teal hut," Nova tells Amelia over my shoulder.

"No, I didn't! I didn't even tell you which one!" Amelia squeaks.

A defeated burst of air passes her lips, and she clutches her forehead in her hands. I can't even hide my victorious smile. *I win.*

Try as I might, competition is in my bloodline, and this type of victory isn't just nice, it's being handed to me on a fucking silver platter.

"Yours is the next one over," Amelia goes on.

"Oh, *God,*" Nova groans, avoiding my gaze as she storms past me. "That means I'll have to hear the entire female population of Aruba file through this front door."

My smile melts away, a frown replacing it. Well I guess it's more than clear what she thinks about me. She's only partially right, though. A week isn't enough time to bang the entire female population of Aruba. Additionally, I'm not interested in banging the *entire* female population.

Just a slim fraction of it.

"Sorry, what was that?" I deadpan, following her and Amelia back out onto the beach as Nova heads for the neighboring hut. "I wasn't really clear on what you thought of me."

"Rotating teal door of night visitors," Nova clarifies, pushing open the door to the fuchsia hut next to mine. "Violating noise ordinances with your sex groans."

I grimace. "Got it." The door slams shut a moment later, her and Amelia swallowed inside. The entire sand volleyball game has stalled, since I still have the ball tucked under my arm.

"Christ, mate, you ready yet?" Rhys asks.

I grit my teeth as I head back to the game. Goodbye relaxed sand volleyball match. Now all I'll be thinking about is what else I could have told Nova. And some other things, like how fucking sexy she's gotten over the past year and a half that we haven't laid eyes—or insults—on each other.

"Good thing she's not your girlfriend." One of Rhys's best friends—sorry, best *mates*—from Bedfordshire, Elliot, is watching me with a smirk. "You wouldn't be getting any tonight."

"Real funny." I toss the ball to Rhys so he can serve. Every inch of me wants to turn around and see if Nova might come back out of her fuchsia hut, but I refuse to engage with her any more than necessary. So yes, even eye contact is off-limits for the rest of the week.

I don't beg for sex, much less for someone to like me. If Nova wants to hold a grudge that spans half a decade, so be it. I'll just have to remember to send her a postcard, addressed to I Hate Westonville, population 1.

Aruba isn't huge, but I won't have any problem staying out of her way.

The volleyball goes *thunk* as Rhys launches it to the other side of the net. After a few volleys and one graceless tumble into the sand by a guy who says his name is Wino, we snag another point, which means we win the game.

"Fuck yes!" Rhys bounds toward me, his fists in the air. We jump and touch chests mid-air, like the frat brothers we never were. Elliot joins our bro huddle, followed by another friend that Rhys and I met during the trip that brought us together, Keko. We're an international brotherhood. I represent the USA, Rhys and Elliot rep the UK, and Keko is the representative for South America, since he was born in Chile.

This is how most of my social circle looks. I've got more friends in Europe alone than some people will meet in their entire lifetime. I could couch surf from California to Croatia if needed—which I almost did by accident once. This destination wedding in Aruba marks the tenth country I've visited since last year, when I officially started the vagabond-or-bust lifestyle. And there are so many other places left to see. But the next stop on my itinerary, after a quick rest in Bayshore post-Aruba, is Thailand.

The one, the only: Chiang Mai. Not only that, it's going to be the fucking *spark* that will ignite my sagging social media influencer career. Because it *has* to be.

I told myself I'd use this week in Aruba to stop thinking about my downward spiral into obscurity. What started out as an explosive following two years ago during a vacation featuring amazing, adventure-focused photos has petered out into a stagnant following of 300,000 followers and declining. I haven't gotten bids from any awe-inspiring companies that want to continue putting money into my bank account.

They were supposed to be chasing *me,* but now I am chasing *them.* I submitted an influencer pitch to a big name in adventure travel—Cliffhangers Gear—weeks ago to see if they would pick We-ston Wanders to represent their brand across Thailand, Morocco, and more. Now I just have to wait and not go crazy predicting the demise of my location-independent lifestyle.

"Hey, you guys busy?"

A soft, feminine voice causes us all to turn toward the water. A tanned blonde with a wide-brimmed hat is peering at us, gnawing on her bottom lip.

"Uh, no, not at all," Elliot says, his chest inflating.

"Can you help me with something?"

This is the quintessential in for any macho bachelor to score. But despite what Nova thinks about me—not that I care—I'm not looking to score. The scores find me.

Elliot is practically tripping over himself as he hurries toward the blonde waif, Keko following in his tracks. I miss what she tells them, but Keko is waving for us to follow. Rhys follows reluctantly behind me, as though he can tell that following a single blonde onto the beach is inherently risky.

"What could she need help with?" Rhys asks, just as there is a very poignant *oink* and some sort of wild hog emerges from the cluster of palm trees and bushes nearby. The blonde shrieks, and then suddenly Elliot stumbles backward, flat on his back. He might be paralyzed with fear, but I can't quite tell. Rhys and I rush toward them, the sand spraying behind our footsteps.

"What the fuck?" Rhys demands once we reach Keko and Elliot, who is now vertical again. The blonde is gripping her wide-brimmed hat and laughing into the sun like this is a swimsuit ad, or maybe secret auditions for a candid camera show.

There are gruff shouts and the occasional girlish squeal as the wild hog runs in circles, stops, huffs at something in the sand, and then wanders back toward the crop of bushes. Amelia's voice pierces the air next.

"I'm pretty sure that was a fucking pig!"

"Wild hog, honey," Rhys calls out. Nova pokes her head through the doorway, and immediately our gazes lock. As Rhys would say, *bollocks.* I wander toward Keko and Elliot through the warm sand, where the blonde is showing them something on the inside of her hat. Her hair flows behind her like white glittery ribbons in the sea breeze. I should definitely focus more on what's happening over here, as opposed to the joy-sucking redhead fifty feet behind me.

Maybe that should be my motto for the whole damn week.

"Oh, you have friends!" Keko exclaims a moment later, looking over at me with that devilish brand of excitement glinting in his eye. His pitch-black hair is plastered across his forehead in a hilarious windblown sweep. "Well yes, you should have them come over. It turns out we have friends too."

"The more the merrier, I always say." Elliot's laying the British charm on thick now, adding in a half-bow. His British accent got thicker since he started talking to the blonde.

"And what about you?" The blonde heads my way, a dimple flashing in her tanned cheek. I catch the lilt of her accent—something Scandinavian I bet—as she blatantly checks me out. I'm shirtless on a beach, sure, but you'd think she might try to gawk less at my pecs. Even if they are pretty killer.

"Uh, yeah. I'm a friend." I flash her a grin, the type of smile that I know girls eat up.

See, I'm part of the Daly family. This shit is second-nature to us. I can pick a woman up with five words and a well-placed smirk. I could make this blonde my Aruba girl faster than Keko could ask her where her friends are from. My brothers are pussy hounds, and they shaped me in their image. By the time I hit adolescence, my oldest brothers Dom and Grayson had already perfected the art. All I had to do was sit back and lap up the lessons.

Yet none of them realized that I'd become the resident expert. That's what world travel taught me, at least.

"You look a little weird," the blonde says, narrowing her eyes playfully. She wants me—it's written all over her face. She zeroes in on me like a laser beam.

"Was that a compliment?" I tease. She's making this too easy. I can have her putty in my hands within five minutes.

But do I want to? Undecided.

She laughs, trailing the wide-brimmed hat behind her as she heads back toward Keko and Elliot. She shouts something in Finnish or Norwegian as she walks back up the beach, gesturing for us to follow. This is definitely the type of situation where I would follow. But a deadpan voice cuts through my evening beach reverie.

"You know, she looks like the type of girl who's going to lead you to your untimely demise."

I turn and find Nova and Amelia behind me. Nova has her long red hair pulled back in a ponytail, and the breeze is plastering her dress to her full figure. All of my comebacks dissolve on my tongue as I behold her. The year and odd months apart has done her good, but I can't put my finger on what exactly has changed. She's fresher, somehow. Probably snarkier. And sexy in a way I don't remember noticing before.

"Like, you know those movies where some pretty girl lures unsuspecting tourists into an organ-harvesting trap," she goes on, when my silence must have convinced her I didn't understand. "I've seen it happen in the jungle before. The beach is another popular location. You just might want to watch out."

"I'm staying back, mate," Rhys says, because of course he would. He's about to get married to his own beach blonde. "Not because of the organ harvesting, mind you."

"That wild pig didn't seem to be a good sign either," Nova adds unnecessarily.

I glance at the retreating figures of Keko and Elliot. I should follow them because it's what I do. It's who I am. Follow the trail for the biggest adventure. Always hop to the next experience, the next woman, the next flight.

"You sound a lot like someone who has insider information about the black-market organ trade," I tell Nova.

"No, no. Not personal experience," she clarifies. "Not yet."

I stifle the snicker that wants to escape. I must not confirm Nova's funniness to her face. After all, we're in a stand-off, even if neither of us exactly know why.

"Well, thanks for the advice. I'm going to go sacrifice my kidneys now." I tip an imaginary hat to Nova, Rhys, and Amelia, and then begin my sandy trek along the shoreline toward my friends.

Even though there's a weird yank in my gut telling me to stay back.

It's not because of the organ harvesting. It's because of Nova.

But hell if I'll listen to anything she has to tell me. If I listen to her, then I run the risk of getting to know her. And if I get to know her, I might really like her.

And that doesn't fit into my five-year plan. I don't want to fall in like with her, or with anyone. My life is set up to achieve my specific goals: constant travel, a fascinating life, and finally obtaining that elusive success that every single fucking person in my life—and especially my family—has achieved except for me.

In order to do that?

I need to catch flights, not feelings.

CHAPTER THREE

NOVA

Warm, late-evening sunlight bathes me in a golden pool of perfection. I have not moved from this spot on the charcoal gray chaise longue in twenty minutes, because *I am in Aruba.*

"Nova, babe. Let's go."

Amelia's super-chill voice breaks through my sunlit reverie. Sure, I might have left late spring in upstate New York, but compared to this island getaway, my little hometown not that far from the Canadian border might as well be in the icy throes of winter. I heave a long, contented sigh, grinning up at my best friend.

"Can we move here?"

She snorts. "Trust me, Rhys and I have already started checking out property here."

"Thinking a second home?" Rhys is one of those ambiguously wealthy people. Come to think of it, so is Amelia. In fact, pretty much everyone in their bridal party is well-off without seeming to work much. I feel like the lone blue-collar plebe who's just trying to prove to the elites that I'm like them. I would never admit to Amelia how long it would have taken me to save up the funds for this trip—which means I'm extra grateful they bought my ticket for me. She told me that footing the bill for my flight and room was still cheaper than bringing out a different photographer for the wedding, which allowed her to shoot two birds with one camera. My words, not hers.

"Well, just trying to get a feel for the markets in different places," she says breezily, in the same way a tastefully wealthy fifty-something might comment on designer watches. "We can't decide where we want to settle yet."

"I love that you guys can even consider anything that isn't on your parents' backwoods property," I say as she leads me toward our next scheduled activity. I was given a bridal party itinerary upon arrival, but it's already been swallowed up into the exploded luggage in my fuchsia—*not teal*—tiki hut.

Amelia sends me a sympathetic look. She knows how much my parents dislike the idea of me venturing past the New York state lines. "What are they gonna do when you get married and, I dunno, want to move out of their backyard?"

"I'm not sure they'll let me," I say ruefully, squinting into the painfully beautiful scenes as we stroll along the boardwalk. I don't add that it's unlikely I'll ever get married. Something must have happened generations ago to curse me in the romantic interest department, and I don't know enough witches to undo the spell. *Yet.*

"Get married or move away?"

"Move away," I clarify. "They definitely want me to get married. I think they're arranging my wedding as we speak."

Amelia snorts. "Wait, did I miss something? You weren't dating anyone, last I knew."

"I'm not dating anyone. That's the thing." I run my finger along the stitched seam of the little purse slung across my body. "But they *really* want me to date Jimmy."

"Jimmy?" The name sounds dull on her lips, which part of me wants to read as a sign.

"We went to high school together. We've always been friends, but we've been hanging out more. So obviously my parents think we should get married."

Amelia snorts. "Right."

"I think they're terrified that their dating-challenged daughter won't have any other opportunities to become a Mrs.," I say. "Which, joke's on them, even if I do get married? I'm not changing my last name."

"You guys should create your *own* last name," Amelia gushes.

"Who, me and Jimmy? No, we just play pool together. I'm never going to, you know, play with his other balls."

Amelia grips my arms as the laugh rockets out of her. "What's wrong with his balls?"

"I don't know. They're probably fine. I plan on never knowing the truth about them. I'm just not physically attracted to them. I mean him."

Admitting this seems sacrilegious somehow. How could a woman like me, with so few dating prospects, turn down the first man in my post-college life who has shown a real, long-term interest in me? I must be an ingrate. I must be demented. I must be unforgivably stupid.

That's what society tells me. And my family sometimes hints at this with less harsh words. But dammit, I want to at least feel a flutter of sexual attraction to a man before I commit my life to him.

If only I could put Weston's abs on Jimmy's body. And probably Weston's face, too. At *least* his insanely blue eyes. But also those powerful thighs, which look amazing in damp board shorts that get plastered to his legs. And his collarbone. For some reason, the man has a sexy collarbone.

So basically all of Weston's physical appearance in place of Jimmy's, and *then* maybe I'd consider forever with him. As long as Weston's personality didn't somehow get attached to Jimmy's body, too. Because that would be a dealbreaker. Weston has already drawn the line in the sand, literally and figuratively, in the five hours I've been on this island. He's already chosen some beach blonde over me. Even though I do not want him to choose me, *I desperately want him to choose me.*

"That's the thing about relationships, right? You can be with the greatest guy in the world," Amelia says, "but if he doesn't light your fire, then you're just dating your brother."

"Jesus. I never thought about it like that, but thank you for making it creepy."

Amelia giggles exactly in the way a mischievous fairy might. Even though I am profoundly disgruntled with my life back home, right now, everything seems right in the world. This is the power of a best friend. And, you know, a beach paradise.

"Maybe you'll find some outrageously sexy man this week," Amelia says encouragingly. "Love is in the air, you know. Rhys and I will leave the island married, but you could leave the island engaged."

"Ha! If only this resort's boyfriend menu was half as good as their cocktail menu."

My phone dings with a new message. Of course, it is Jimmy. Because I'm sure he could feel me not wanting to be with him from a thousand miles away.

JIMMY: I miss you already. Is that weird?

No, it's not weird. Because I also miss my friends when they're not around. But Jimmy means it with an extra level of romance baked in. He's been giving me moony eyes and lingering hugs the past few months. I know he's trying to be a gentleman, to take things slow. But part of me wishes he'd stop beating around the bush so I could just squash this thing. The other part of me is whispering that nobody else will ever want me like he does, so I should just say *yes* and run with it.

I don't know which truth to abide by: the truth that tells me I'm exactly as ugly and small-town as I've ever believed, or the truth that tells me I should hold out for an amazing life I've only ever dreamt of in secret.

So far, all signs are pointing to the former. Especially my parents. The debt load that my family carries isn't just crushing, it's glacial: an enormous harbinger of a financial Ice Age, which is definitely going to take forever to leave. I have to help out, because how could I not? I'm not going to let my gram starve, even though she eats like a bird and sometimes just chooses Budweiser for dinner. The least attractive part of the whole Jimmy concept is that I think my parents want me to be with him more because of his job. He makes *great* money in his union job, which would mean more income, and a faster road to shoveling ourselves out of debt.

It's practically a debtor's arranged marriage, and if I go through with it someday—a thought that makes me shudder—then so help me God, they better make a Netflix special about my story.

"At the very least, I want this week to be *fun* for you," Amelia goes on as we breeze toward a tiki temple in this elaborate maze of beachy huts and outposts. "I know how hard it's been for you back home since we graduated. Honestly, I just wish you could come travel with Rhys and me."

Isn't that the dream? Getting away for more than two weeks every other year. If my finances would allow it, then my parents would disown me for spending my money frivolously. It feels like a brutal cycle. But if I suffocate my dreams just so that I can pay my bills, I might snap one day and shove my car loan booklet into Dad's woodchipper. I don't know where the happy medium is.

For now, I'll continue to sacrifice my time while I try to figure it out.

Amelia pauses at the tiki hut where a big cream-colored sign says *BRIDAL INTIMACY.* My brows shoot to the heavens.

"Oh, is this the first item on tonight's agenda?"

"I know the name sounds weird, but it was one of their highest-rated activities. Apparently this intimacy coach is world famous, and she made a cool group bonding class for the wedding parties that come here."

All of these things sound slightly nerve-wracking but overall pleasant. And as Amelia pulls open the wooden door, an additional layer of pleasantness wafts through the air in the form of exotic incense, something between patchouli and religious temple. Low hums fill the dimly lit hut, and it takes me a moment to realize that it's music playing...and that the hut is nearly filled with participants.

"Welcome, welcome." The soothing voice of the instructor immediately sets me at ease. Her curious tonality alone is worth international fame. She probably sounds tenth level chill in the middle of a hurricane, too. "You're just in time. Sit anywhere you like. We have the beautiful blessing of combining two wedding parties this evening!"

So *that's* why there are so many people in here. I'm the first from Amelia's side to arrive on the island, and the bridesmaids aren't showing up until tomorrow night. From then on, wedding guests will be arriving daily until the big rehearsal dinner on Friday night, followed by however you say *the big Saturday event* in Dutch.

I sink onto an empty mat, anxiety licking through me. The hut is just shrouded enough that I can't tell who is who without squinting and peering, but who wants to be the person that inspects the attendees in a chill group class? I'm supposed to be unruffled. So I will be ruffled quietly, while looking at no one.

"Since we're all here in the spirit of solidifying the futures of two people into one, for two different blessed couples, it seemed fitting that our session this evening would focus on drumming up heat."

I glance around, wondering if Senorita Chill's words are making anyone else distantly nervous. Does drumming up heat mean melting into a sweaty puddle?

"Since so much of a wedding is focused on logistics—preparations and flower deliveries and cake arrangements and all of that—I wanted us to take an evening where we could focus on the sensual side of what brought us all here in the first place."

Actual sweat breaks out on my forehead. The sensual side of what brought us here? It seems like she wants us to watch Rhys and Amelia have sex, which I am *not* down for.

"Through a focused and intimate group coaching session, the plan is for all of us to channel our love and respect and admiration into a vortex of support for the two couples about to be wed this weekend."

Phew. Some of my muscles relax. *So no group sex.*

"Let's start by pairing up," Lady Chillax says, and all my relief re-hardens into terror. Elementary school trauma is real, and every school in the nation has that one kid who was always picked last in gym class. Well, that's me. My unofficial name is Nova AlwaysPickedLast.

While I'm sitting as rigid as a tree trunk, our instructor lights a few more votives, allowing me to catch the features of the people around me. Murmurs spread through the expansive hut as people begin assessing their intimacy mate. I am too meek to even move. I want to shrivel into my mat and express my adoration for Rhys and Amelia some other way.

"If you are stuck without a partner"—I think she's talking directly to me now—"let me know and I'll find you someone. We have an even head count, so everyone will get a partner."

Great. This feels a lot like my love life, now that I think about it. Just sit here petrified until someone else swoops in to match me off. Maybe this is the sign I'm looking for that I should suck it up and marry Jimmy. Then I can bait Amelia into my own love-and-honor vortex in a different tiki hut in upstate New York.

"Is everyone paired up?" Her voice is the equivalent of the warning beep of a kitchen timer. *Time is almost up.* I had one task, yet I have accomplished nothing except critically analyze my love life. I begin to raise my hand, and the instructor whooshes toward me.

"Here we are," she says, gesturing for someone else to come my way. "Last two. If any of you are unfamiliar with your partners, please introduce yourselves. This intimacy exercise is perfectly appropriate for friends, lovers, and even strangers."

Her words are not consoling, even less so as my new "partner" emerging from the shadows of the well-scented hut turns out to be Weston Daly himself. Everything inside me groans. But a very specific part of me is excited. I choose to ignore that part.

I don't catch Weston's expression as he sits beside me, but I do catch his defeated sigh. He doesn't look at me—I'm sure he's less than thrilled to have to be near me. I just wish I could let him know I'm *even less thrilled* than he is.

"Don't get excited," he tells me in a low voice. "This was her idea, not mine."

"I'm shocked you even needed a partner," I tell him as the instructor weaves her way through paired off couples headed for the front of the hut. "I thought you had a new beach girlfriend."

"Let's begin by facing our partners," the Princess of Sensuality oozes. "Sit cross-legged. Let's gaze into each other's eyes."

I grimace, doing as she says. This is going to be rough. Not because I don't want to look into my partner's eyes, but precisely because I *do*.

"Just because a woman exists near me doesn't mean she's my girlfriend," Weston mutters as his gaze snaps up to meet mine. Our knees brush as we settle into place, and heat is pouring off him like he's the goddamn sun. I swallow hard, the sustained eye contact rendering my insides numb.

"I don't care," I manage weakly.

"You're the one always bringing it up," he says, his gaze hardening. The corner of his mouth twitches. "Are you jealous, Nova?"

The instructor lets out a low hum, encouraging everyone to do the same. I glare at him before snapping my eyes shut and following the instructor's lead. Even after we've all hummed and hoo'd our ways through something like a meditative exercise, I'm still sizzling over Weston's words. I have calmed down approximately none.

"Let's open our eyes...reach up toward the sky...and then one partner sit with your back facing the other."

At least I don't have to look at his impossibly handsome face. Now I just have to ignore the encroaching heat of him, which I can feel growing nearer as he positions himself behind me. His long legs extend out on either side of mine. I can't tell if he's two feet or two inches away from me, but as far as my body is concerned, he's nibbling on my earlobe.

"Scoot closer," the Sultana of Sensuality says. She's making a slow path between couples as she peers down at all of us, occasionally offering adjustments. She pauses above us, and then gently corrects Weston's form so that his chest is pressed to my back.

Great. I squeeze my eyes shut, trying not to enjoy this. He shifts behind me, clearing his throat. Every part of me wants to warn him not to get a hard-on, but he would probably laugh. I'm sure I would appear in the very last of his fantasies. Probably not even an emergency fantasy.

"I can't believe you think I'd be jealous," I say, trying to refocus on how ridiculous he is. Our back-and-forth already seems outdated, but there's still some outrage simmering inside me. "Jealous of those girls? Seriously?"

"Let's breaaaaaathe together." The instructor wants us to breathe in and out in sync, so we can feel the rise and fall of each other's chests. It's weird, but whatever. Weston and I fumble through it.

"Oh, come on," Weston says, his bass rumble closer to my ear than it's ever been before. My thighs go tense. *Fuck.* This might be the most erotic thing that's ever happened to me, and Weston doesn't even technically want to be near me. "You think I meant that you were jealous of them? I meant you were jealous of *me.*"

It takes a moment for his true meaning to penetrate the thick fog of lust that the heat of his thighs are inspiring. He shifts behind me, and goosepimples flare across my lower back. I didn't know I could even get goosepimples down there.

"Oh." I scoff quietly. We might be arguing, but we're in a chill class. We need to *Zen argue.* "You mean you think I'm into women."

"Now, for the partners who are sitting behind, with your chests touching your partner's backs, place your palms gently on the tops of your partner's thighs." Our teacher hums contentedly as her gaze sweeps across the classroom. "There we go. Yes. We want to conjure that intimate fire power. While we do this, let's think about sending it to our brides and grooms today."

Weston's palms appear on the tops of my thighs, and I almost faint. I gulp, thankful he's not somehow taking my blood pressure at the same time. Though I can't rule that out as an upcoming activity. I'm supposed to be directing my thoughts toward Rhys and Amelia, but all I can think about is the heat pouring out of his palms. The rough scrape of his hands against my skin tells me that he works with his hands. At least a little. Which, you know, doesn't interest me at all.

"Fire power?" I mutter. "This isn't *Super Mario 3*."

A burst of air grazes my ear lobe as he snort laughs. I am officially turned on. If only he would slide those hands between my legs or wrap his thick biceps around me, I could die happy. Which is a strange thing to think about a man you cannot stand.

"You need to quit talking," he scolds me, his sexy rumble scraping through me. My eyes flutter shut. I feel like this is not what Madam Fire Power had in mind: dissolving into desirous puddles of want for a hot jerk. "This is serious."

"Pff. Like I should listen to you. You think I'm a lesbian. You have no idea how much I love dick."

Weston is notably silent after this, which of course makes my face and ears so hot you could toast bread on me. Thank God this hut is dim. Now Weston won't be able to see how embarrassing it is to accidentally talk about my sexual preferences. He doesn't care. We're not alike, he and I. Nowhere near the same level. So I just need to stop.

I'm mentally berating myself as the instructor encourages each couple to lean forward, then lean back. Lean forward. Lean back. It's like we're in a weird eighties video about dry humping. It is, at the very least, a boring soft-core porn. Just when I'm wondering whether it's the quiet embarrassment or the continued touching of Weston's groin through my lower back that's going to kill me first, our instructor claps her hands gleefully.

"Now partner two, turn around so we can press our backs together. It's time for a team effort."

Weston's heat leaves me, and disappointment trickles through me. It shouldn't feel that good to have this person pressed against me. It sure as hell hasn't felt that good with anyone else.

Could it ever feel that good with Jimmy? Maybe I just haven't tried hard enough.

My thoughts disappear as Weston's firm back presses against mine. It's time for the team effort. And though I wish Lady Love Language meant sex, I have a feeling it's going to be something much less satisfying.

CHAPTER FOUR

This intimacy class is going to get me into trouble.

I should have insisted on choosing literally anyone else as my partner. Hell, if I'd known that I'd have to be within zero inches of Nova's luscious booty, I would have skipped entirely. This isn't fair. I dislike this person. I shouldn't have to be aroused by her, too.

"I want each couple to come to standing," the instructor says simply. Her voice sounds like an adult voice actor's attempt at sounding like a kid. It's mesmerizing and a little weird. She instructs us to interlock our arms.

Confusion ripples through the room. I scoff. This lady is nuts.

"It *is* possible. But you have to work together," she goes on, probably responding to all the telepathic cries of *what the hell*.

"I could never work together with you," Nova mutters. I roll my eyes, even though she can't see me. Still, I trust she can feel my eyeroll energy.

"Gonna have to," I snap. "Unless you want to fail out of yoga."

"You can't fail at yoga."

"Most people can't, but *you* can."

She lets an annoyed *tsss*. "You have no idea what you're talking about. This isn't even yoga. This is *intimacy*. Which you also fail at."

"Here we go," the instructor prompts. "One...two...three...STAND."

I don't know what I'm expecting, but what happens isn't it. How do you stand from sitting while wrapped up in another person pressed against your back? You don't. Nearly the entire room erupts into some version of laughter or grunts. Nova and I are no exception. She crumbles against me, and we both topple to the side.

"God, Weston," she complains.

"That was all you."

"Yeah, right! You're the man, aren't you supposed to lead the way?"

I send more eyeroll-energy her way. "Come on. Let's stand."

We try again and fail miserably. I can't figure out what the trick is. But to our left, a couple pops to their feet. And then on the other side of the hut, Rhys and Amelia spring to standing. Their triumphant smiles make something beat wildly inside me. I need to win at this. Call it the Daly Competition Response, but I wasn't born to lose. We *cannot* be the last two sitting.

"Nova," I tell her through gritted teeth. "Get it together."

"I'm perfectly together," she quips. "You're the one losing your shit."

Her response is high-grade annoying. I grunt and heave again, but we both fall sideways. My heart is racing—like desperate fight or flight mode here—and I almost can't see straight with how badly I need to stand up so that we're not last. There were a few things my upbringing instilled in me, and graceful losing isn't one of them. Even when this is clearly not a competitive sport.

"Come on. On the count of three. One…two…" Before I reach three, Nova launches. Irritation spreads through me like wildfire.

"I said on the count of three!"

"I was preparing my thighs," she shoots back.

"That doesn't even make any sense. You either use them, or you don't. And you clearly aren't."

By this time, we're attracting attention. Rhys and Amelia are grinning wryly over at us, our arms interlocked at our sides like the weirdest sort of prisoners. We're trapped here with our own permission and doomed to live here for the rest of our lives, because there is no way in hell I'm leaving this hut without winning this challenge.

"Okay. Listen. If you would just *calm down* and work with me here," she starts.

"You're one to talk," I spit. "You're preparing your thighs. That shit should have been done weeks ago."

She twists a little so that I can see her glare. "What I do with my thighs—"

"How you guys coming over here?" The instructor squats down to smile warmly at each of us in turn. The chill version of *shut the fuck up, you two.*

"Everything's great," I say.

"This is quite the challenge," Nova says. "If this man were actually my husband, we'd be divorcing afterward."

The instructor's laugh flutters through the air like a melodic butterfly. "Go on. Try again. I believe in you."

Well, isn't that quaint? I don't believe in Nova, that's for damn sure. I grit my teeth and brace for another failed attempt.

"Okay. Let's both push on the count of three," I tell her.

"Right."

"Not on the count of two, like last time."

"I would never," she says.

"One...two...three." This time when we try to launch to standing, the instructor is encouraging us. But Nova's side doesn't come through. She slips and we both crumble to the floor once more.

But now, all the rest of the couples are standing up, milling around, chatting with each other about how hard it was. We're the last couple sitting. Something dark and hot flashes through me, and the instructor just squeezes my wrist.

"Good try, guys! We're going to move on now." She breezes away, asking for everyone to come to the front of their mats. My arms drop to the floor, and I scoff.

"Wow. Great work, partner."

Nova twists to look at me. "You are a really sore loser."

She's not wrong. "You are a really sore team player."

"You know it doesn't matter, right? This is supposed to be a fun activity. This isn't life or death, Weston. You can get over it now."

I don't know how she's able to cut to the core of me like that, but she does. Still, it's annoying. And I choose to reject her logic. "You apparently have no drive to succeed. Maybe you're okay with living like that, but I'm not."

Nova is strangely quiet as she moves away from me, coming to her feet at the front of her mat. I go back to my own, my entire body tense as I wait for a response from her.

But it doesn't come. Her mouth is a thin line as we are led through another series of gentle movements. Except now I can concentrate less than ever. Somehow, all I can hear are my brothers in my head. Mocking me for losing at an intimacy class. This counts as one thing among many that I will never admit to my family.

I suffer through the rest of the class, completely unable to unwind the taut muscles across my back since Nova failed to hold up her end of the deal. In the deepest, farthest recesses of my mind, I know that she's right. But I wasn't raised to listen to that voice. *Second place is just the first-place loser.* That saying is practically the Daly birthmark all five of us sons were born with. Except my brothers don't have the misfortune of actually being the one who came in last.

My mind wanders down a dark path as the instructor eventually asks us all to sit cross-legged with our eyes closed. The whole point of this next year is to finally burst into the stratosphere of success after I unequivocally failed in the largest way possible two years ago.

It's the number one thing I'll never tell my family about, which sits just a few spots above this class.

If I can't turn the money I inherited from grandma into a real, live career born from traveling, influencing, and drawing, then I don't know where else to turn. I've been running away from failure for the past two years, and for all the miles under my belt and followers commenting their support, I don't think I've advanced an inch.

I'm twenty-six. I'm going to Thailand after this, but really, I have no idea where I'm headed. There should be a fucking light at the end of this tunnel. But all I've got to show for myself is an abandoned graphic design career and a series of plane tickets to exotic destinations. The pictures I post are fire, but behind-the-scenes is a different story.

All three of my older brothers have found success. Even my younger brother Maverick has a career as a mechanic, even though his going into a trade as opposed to college *almost* got him disowned. But it's okay, because nobody could fall as low in the Daly family as I have.

Each day that passes, I can actually *hear* my father's sighs growing louder and more disappointed from however many thousands of miles away. He won't accept my career as legitimate until I can prove I'm making six figures a year. And sure, that's an arbitrary fucking standard—one that I want to reject. But no matter how much I tell myself my life has meaning and who cares what my dad thinks, I can't shake this shit. Because he created me in his image. And damn, it stings to be the one kid that your dad can't get excited about. The one son who has both the *aimless* and *lost* labels.

But at this point, I can't remember if he put those labels there or if I did.

When the class is finally over, I'm the first out the door. I am so ready to forget about the class and just how warm and soft Nova's thighs were under my palms. I've never been so simultaneously annoyed and turned on by the same person. So the game plan is to toss back enough whiskey to ignore her for the rest of the week.

Rhys and Elliot catch up with me down the boardwalk, where I've paused to stare out at the horizon. The sunset is exploding in streaks of burnt orange and crimson. It's actually too pretty for words.

"Feeling relaxed, mate?" Rhys asks me, slapping me on the shoulder.

"More or less," I tell him, even though relaxed is the last thing I feel. I can't tell if I need to have sex or put my fist through a wall. The lines are blurring more and more. The acid ache inside me has no known relief. It's not gonna be through relaxation classes. It's not gonna be through fucking—though I've certainly tried that route plenty. Plane tickets used to help, but now they just twist things up more. And the fact that I can't figure out a remedy just makes it burn worse.

"I think it's time for shots," Elliot announces. The humid breeze filling my senses is inspiring somehow. Sultry and promising. Reminding me that with my best friends at my side and the ocean surrounding us, I'll be able to move past whatever this is.

Even if it happens on the heels of alcohol.

Keko joins us a moment later, slinging his arm around my shoulders. "I'm ready for a full Aruban night, *hermanos*."

Rhys leads the way toward one of the five restaurants inside this enormous resort. We have a table for six reserved on a huge wooden terrace looking out toward the ocean. A slatted veranda crisscrosses overhead, twinkle lights already lit as the sunset makes its slow trek toward dusk. Our table is arranged so that every seat is looking toward the ocean. We all have front row seats to the best show on earth.

Rhys sits down, saving a seat for Amelia. The rest of my buddies take their seats, leaving one open spot to my left. Realization clicks into place as soon as Nova arrives.

"Do you have to be my partner everywhere we go?" I ask as I settle into my seat.

"I'll gladly trade seats with anyone else," she offers sweetly, unslinging a camera from around her neck. She sets it on the table with a soft *thud*. "But if you really can't handle sitting next to me for a meal, might I direct you to the empty table over there?" She's gesturing toward a lone table in the corner of the patio.

"I think I can survive dinner," I shoot back. "But so help me God if you show up in my hut tonight like you did earlier today."

A weird heat spreads through me as soon as I say the words. Yes, a part of me *does* want her to show up in my hut. But no talking allowed—only touching. And kissing. God, I'm more curious than I want to admit about what those pretty, pink lips might taste like. She is a sun-kissed redhead, which is officially my new favorite look.

Not like I'll admit that to her.

"I will *never* make that mistake again. Trust me." She shudders exaggeratedly. "I'm too scared of what I might find happening in your hut to *ever* open that front door."

"Not sure why you're so afraid of sleeping and showering, but okay." I idly straighten the silverware at my place, trying to look as bored as I can. "That tells me a little bit more about you, I guess." Which is false. She smells like honeysuckle and vanilla and the sweet tang of femininity, a scent that will haunt me until the day I die.

"I would like to continue knowing as little about you as possible." She sends a sweet smile that is comically at odds with her words. It's a struggle to remain unaffected. But I am nothing if not born to compete in any challenge invented.

Rhys snorts from the end of the table. "You two have gotten *bitier*."

"I think she just likes to argue with me," I say, crossing my arms as I lean back into my chair. "Some women like walks on the beach. Other women like picking fights they know they'll lose."

Nova snorts, and I catch her lips curling up at the corners. The server arrives to take our drink orders, which temporarily pauses our back-and-forth. We all pick our poison, and then we're given the green light to head to the buffet. Keko and I buddy up, making a beeline for the inside of the restaurant where the long line of steaming pans awaits us. And the bounty is truly glorious: there's pan-seared salmon, roasted asparagus, colorful quinoa dishes and all manner of grilled meats. I take one of everything, which means I've got a plate bursting with food by the time I head back to the table.

I waste no time digging in. Everything is delicious, and Keko, Rhys, Elliot, and I exchange grunts as we ingloriously inhale our food. Nova and Amelia arrive last to the table, their plates arranged carefully with bird-sized portions of food.

I frown at Nova's plate. She selected approximately one whole grain biscuit and three wimpy stalks of asparagus. "That's all you got?"

"What? You've even got a problem with my food?" She sighs as she slides into her seat. "There is no pleasing you."

"You don't have to please me, so strike that item off your to-do list." I stab the thick sausage on my plate and take a big chomp.

"Thank God," she mutters. "It would be an impossible task anyway."

I derive a sick pleasure from our needling. I act like this with *no one*—and I mean absolutely zero humans—in the world. Especially with members of the opposite sex. To the world at large, I am easygoing and laidback Weston who gets along especially well with women. And to be fair, I am that person *normally*.

Yet there is something about Nova that annoys the shit out of me. And something else. I just can't entirely figure out what the something else is. I'm pretty sure it's something I should run away from.

I'm just incapable of entirely running away from her.

I chew happily, and the table cheers when the server returns with our drinks. The bloated sun is just about to sink past the horizon. I jerk my chin toward the spectacular sight in front of us.

"Are you really about to let this sunset pass by without taking a picture of it?" I sip my whiskey on the rocks. Smooth. Perfectly aged. I take another sip to verify the perfection of it. "That camera is just a prop, huh."

She sets her fork down and narrows her eyes at me. "Did it occur to you that I might want to simply *enjoy* the sunset?"

Everyone else at the table is buried in different conversations, so our haranguing is just for us this time. "So the camera is for taking pictures of the food you didn't eat."

She sighs loudly. "I'm the wedding photographer. I need my camera on hand at all times."

"Right, but being the photographer means actually taking pic-tures."

I take another bite of sausage as she grabs the camera. She holds it up and snaps a picture of me without consulting the viewfinder or digital screen or anything. Then she sets it down. "That better?"

"Come on. It'll turn out like crap with that amount of emotional investment."

She shakes her head. "Nah. It's all about the subject. And let me tell ya—that was a pretty poor subject."

"Let's see it." When she doesn't immediately comply, I nudge her. The whiskey is burning hot through my veins. "Come on. I wanna see it."

"You're so obsessed with yourself." But she turns it on and scrolls to the image previews anyway. My unamused face fills the screen, blurry and oddly backlit.

"See. You didn't fuck with the aperture enough."

She snorts, sending me an incredulous look. Her green eyes look like gemstones, and for a moment, I can't force myself to look away. "Are you kidding me? You're trying to mansplain to me right now."

"No, I'm trying to help." Lie. I'm mansplaining, because it makes her react like *this*.

"You just fucking mansplained *to a photographer* that I need to adjust aperture. I can't believe you." She stabs an asparagus spear, shoving it angrily into her mouth. "You are actually the most an-noying person in the world."

"Most annoying? You're one to talk. Outrageous."

"Ridiculous," she shoots back.

"Flagrant."

"Shameless," she says.

"Ludicrous."

It looks like she's trying to fight a smile now. "Preposterous."

Across the table, Rhys and Amelia share a private smile before looking our way. "Your feud has definitely gotten more interesting over the years," Rhys comments, which makes my next retort dissolve on my tongue: *ostentatious.*

"We're just preparing for a thesaurus competition, apparently," she mutters, before ripping into her dinner roll.

I try to squash the smile threatening to overtake my face as I return to my food as well. Bantering with Nova shouldn't be this fun. She's an annoying redhead who just happens to be hot.

But the most tiresome thing about her is the fact that despite how much she dislikes me...I still want to know more about this buxom, irritating bombshell.

CHAPTER FIVE

I wake up at eight the next morning to the sound of ocean waves going *hushhhhhh* against the shoreline. For a scorching moment, I'm confused. But then reality sinks in.

I am in an insanely comfortable king bed in my own private hut on Aruba.

I stretch out, grinning up at the domed thatch roof. Man, this is the life. There is exactly nothing on my to-do list for the day except for whatever fun, relaxed, wedding-related activity Amelia has planned. I'm basically making no decisions. Amelia and Rhys have already made all of them for us, and they are all equally fantastic. I am just being ushered along from one delightful thing to the next.

Except for my less-than-delightful companion, *Weston Daly,* who insists on being unpleasant at every turn.

I frown, but it doesn't stay long. My mind drifts to him, recalling the ghostly remnants of whatever dream I'd been indulging in before waking up. Weston had been there. Of course he had been. He's the unwelcome dinner guest in the cafeteria of my brain. When my subconscious takes over, watch out—Weston butts to the front of the line, demanding more chicken nuggets. He's annoying in real life and even in the recesses of my skull.

Which means I need to work harder at ignoring him. I'm hopeful that we got all our arguing and nitpicking out yesterday. After the group got drunk and wandered to the beach after dinner, we fell into a quiet disregard for each other. That's how it needs to stay. Just mutually pretending the other doesn't exist.

I yawn and reach for my phone on the bedside. A text message is waiting for me.

JIMMY: Morning, beautiful. How's the ocean today?

I frown at the words for a few moments. Not because I don't like thinking about the ocean, but because Jimmy is beginning to circle me like a vulture.

He's never called me "beautiful," at least not to my face. We've always been the sort of friends who just pretend the other one has no genitals. But apparently, somewhere along the line, Jimmy realized I have genitals. Even though I would like to continue ignoring his.

NOVA: Super large. Very wet. Potentially fatal.

JIMMY: LOLOL. Always a way with words.

I think back to my word battle with Weston, a strange ache forming inside me. The rest of Weston's personality aside, he's got one admirable trait. I like a man I can have a word battle with. Someone who turns me on with both his appearance *and* his mind. Come on, I'm not fully shallow. Brains matter. It's just, so does the packaging.

I roll out of bed and stumble toward the bathroom to wash my face and my brush my teeth. Just as I'm ready to contemplate my wardrobe for the day, Amelia's sing-song voice wafts through the door.

"Nooova. Are you up yet?"

"Up, yes. Dressed? No."

"We've got yoga at nine," she says through the door, which helps me choose the sturdy sports bra I'd been eyeing. I've got some jugs, and they have no qualms about flopping all over their owner. "Followed immediately by mimosas."

"You know the way to my heart, love." I toss on a flowy tank top and some loose linen pants. Perfect beach yoga attire. I fling open the door and hug my best friend. Because it's been nine hours since I last saw her, and I miss her.

"Good morning," I say, just as I spy Weston ambling out of his hut next door. Shirtless. Yawning and scratching idly at his perfect chest.

All of my muscles go taut with awareness. I can barely rip my eyes off his tanned shoulders or the way his back muscles ripple as he props his palms on the back of his head and stares out at the ocean. My Ignore and Forget Plan is already unraveling.

"Nova, are you okay?" Amelia looks concerned as she pries me off of her. "You look like you just saw a ghost."

"No, no. Yes, fine. No ghost." I swallow hard, finally jerking my eyes off Weston and back to Amelia. "Yoga, right? Tell me it's girls only. I don't want men seeing me at a class in the light of day."

"You were at a class with men last night."

"Yes, but we were in a darkened hut. And we were sending our sensual love vibes toward you and Rhys, which is very different." I grab my phone before locking the hut. Amelia and I begin a slow walk through the warm sand, coming up on Weston's hut. There's no hope of ignoring him now. He's got bleary eyes as he looks our way, jerking his chin into a nod.

"Morning." His voice is raw, gritty. Pure *just-woken-up* man. I steel myself against the wave of desire that crashes through me. It's not fair.

"Morning, Weston," Amelia purrs. "Did you sleep well?"

He grunts, running a hand through his hair. "Not exactly. Keko and Elliot and I made some new friends last night."

Disappointment pings through me. It's probably a reference to sex—I'm sure he hooked up with someone last night. I force myself to watch the sand as we head for the boardwalk, even though I'm dying to peer inside his cabin and see if there's an unexpected bedmate in his tiki paradise.

"Well we're going to yoga right now if you want to rejuvenate your morning," Amelia offers. I jab her in the side with my elbow.

Weston laughs a little, his gaze sliding back to the horizon. Once we hit the boardwalk, I say, "We don't need to invite him to everything, right?"

Her laugh lilts through the air. "Trust me—he won't come. Those boys aren't the yoga types."

I am only distantly relieved. Though I will never be fully relieved, because the memory of his six-pack is not something I will soon forget. "So what else is on deck today? Do I need costume changes?"

"Well, the rest of the girls are arriving this morning." *The girls* refers to the bridal party, which includes our other best friend from college, Laney, and Rhys's two sisters, who have since become extremely close to Amelia.

"And dinner is on a sailboat," she goes on, excitement brimming in her eyes. "I think we should get our best yachting attire ready for that one."

"You're lucky I brought my designer anchor with me."

"I hemmed silk sails specifically for the occasion," she says in her best haughty, transatlantic voice, which makes us both break into laughter. Right near our side of the resort, a different teacher—with a far more normal voice—has laid out yoga mats facing the ocean on a cement patio lined with potted flowers.

Amelia and I do gentle stretches on our mats closest to the instructor while a few more women trickle in. The class begins with all of us facing the ocean while the instructor leads us through a mental exercise about imagining gulls and the swell of our equanimity. I'm not entirely sure if I'm doing it right, since I envision gulls going bloated until they explode. But hey—there's probably no wrong way to do it. Unless you're somehow doing it with Weston.

On a long exhale, we all bend forward with our legs spread wide. I peek at the world through my legs—and I gasp.

Weston is behind me.

He can't see me, of course, but he's been behind me the whole time. That sneaky sneak—why would he come to this yoga class? He probably just wants to pick up some new girl. Maybe he's already tired of whoever he took to bed last night. And really, isn't that how it goes with men?

By the time we come to standing at our mats, I have completely lost all my chill. Weston is behind me, which means that he has a front row view to my *enormous ass* every time I bend or move. I can only take comfort in the fact that he surely does not care about my ass, or any part of my body. Therefore, he won't notice it. Right? Right.

The instructor is unaware of my racing heart as she guides us through some familiar poses, and then into weirder poses. Weston's unseen presence behind me burns like I'm standing too close to flames. Once we've been guided into squatting, twisting, and making prayer hands, I'm feeling a little gassy. Like all this bending and early morning movement has got something else moving too.

I spend each eternal second focusing on the fact that I will not, under any circumstances, fart. This is a truth I know so intensely that nothing else can be true. I focus on tightening my gut, on clenching my ass cheeks secretly, on having a quiet, intense conversation with my intestines.

Please do not pass gas in public. Not now. NOT NOW.

When we're told to whoosh to standing, my efforts to retain my internal rumblings fail. A fart squeaks out of me, and every muscle in my body goes rigid. It's the only thing preventing me from melting to the ground in a puddle of mortification. I stand in a daze, wondering if anyone heard it. Maybe the waves of the ocean drowned it out. Maybe it was a trumpet. Maybe it flew directly into Weston's mouth.

I don't even register the rest of the class, I am so hung up on my public farting incident. I have certainly never farted in the middle of a yoga class, and I have *definitely* never farted straight into the face of the hottest man I've ever tried to hate.

When class wraps up, I ignore the smiling and sweaty-faced Weston and breeze toward Amelia. "That was so fun and relaxing. Let's go get breakfast now. I'm starving. I feel like I could digest an entire pineapple just by looking at it."

That is an exceptionally weird thing to say, which I realize when Weston scoffs off to our side. He's dragging his forearm across his forehead, which shouldn't be allowed when it makes his biceps bulge like that.

"You'll need more than a pineapple after that class," Amelia says, then sends a bright grin toward Weston. "I can't believe you came! Did you enjoy it?"

"It was a rootin'-tootin' good time."

I can't even hide the scowl that creeps over my face. I would glare at Weston, but that would be confirming the fact that I know that he knows that I farted. Instead, I glare at the nearest palm tree.

"I'm sooo sweaty," Amelia says. "I think it's the humidity more than anything that killed me."

I'm nodding, herding Amelia back toward the boardwalk and away from Weston. "Humidity is strong. Extremely humid. Can we do mimosas now?"

"I love mimosas," Weston says.

Everything inside me groans. "That's cool. I'm sure they have some for you somewhere else in the resort. Amelia? Can we?" I jerk my head toward the boardwalk.

"Why are you being so weird?" Weston asks me, point-blank. Post-yoga-fart directness is on par with violating an accord of the Geneva Convention. *We all silently agreed that this would never be acknowledged, OR ELSE.*

"I'm hangry," I say simply, offering him a fake smile. "Low blood sugar problems. Thanks for being so sensitive about it."

It's not entirely false, but it's also not entirely true. My phone buzzes from inside the huge pocket of my linen pants. I swear to God, if this is Jimmy calling to ask about the ocean...I'm tense as I fish it out, and then all the air leaves me in a relieved whoosh. No. It's not Jimmy. It's just Gram.

"Graaaam," I say, and before I know it, I could cry. I don't know why. My grandma is practically my mom, and we live together, and I just farted in some guy's mouth. I need my Gram.

"I'll make this quick." Her smoker's growl is both familiar and hilarious. "You get kidnapped by pirates yet or what?"

Laughter rolls out of me. If there's anyone who can bring me back to center, it's my grandma. I would have brought her along as my plus one, but she's deathly afraid of the pressurized cabin part of air travel. "Not kidnapped yet. But I'm working on it. I hear the Bermuda Triangle is nearby."

"Nah, the Bermoota Triangle is overhyped. It sucks up airplanes but not much else. If you're looking for a real good time, I think you should go for the pirates. Or maybe a shark."

Gram is both inspiration and cautionary tale. She is the only one in my family pushing me to see the world, live my life, and have a helluva time doing it. But she also serves as a reminder of what can happen when I ignore my impulses and curiosity. I'm convinced that she and I are the same person, separated by fifty years. Except I was raised in a world where I could access cheap plane tickets, and she was raised in a world that kept her pregnant and in the kitchen.

"Are we talking, like, a love affair with a shark?" I ask, trailing behind Amelia and Weston as they lead the way toward breakfast. "Or something else?"

"Sweetcakes, that's what you're there to figure out." A rickety laugh escapes her. She stopped smoking years ago, but still sounds like she smokes a pack a day. "Everything okay down there? You alive and everything?"

"Yeah, I'm alive and everything."

"Good. I'll tell your mom. She's convinced you've already been brainwashed by the cults."

I snort. "What cults? I'm at a destination wedding, for God's sake"

"I don't know, just general cults. They're everywhere. That's what she says, at least. You eating and everything?"

"Plenty." Even though it's a lie. I have so many options around me, but this rumbling stomach of mine is my own fault. I was too embarrassed to eat in front of Weston last night, which is a nervous tic from high school that I just can't get rid of. Hot guy in sight? Oh, must pretend I don't rely on food in any way, lest he think I'm a chronic overeater due to my natural girth. Being a woman is the most exhausting thing out there. Being a woman of *size* is even more fun.

"Okay, I'll tell your mom. She's so worried. Your dad is too, but I just tell him to shut up."

I smirk. My dad is her youngest son. I'm thankful to have Gram on my side when it comes to travel, but she's the only one. Sometimes, I feel like we're a misfit pair destined for some sort of feel-good family movie. *Nova & Gram Take On the Haters.* Complete with action-packed meadow adventures and all.

Up ahead, Weston and Amelia have paused at the junction of the boardwalk, waiting for me. I ask Gram to tell my family I miss them and then pocket my phone.

"You joining a cult?" Weston asks. Weird that he listened in on my phone call, but whatever.

"No. I mean, not willingly. Are we ready for breakfast?"

Weston breaks off, claiming he needs to go find Elliot for something, leaving Amelia and me to breakfast by ourselves. It's not like I miss the presence of Weston, but something definitely feels different without him. I wouldn't go as far as saying that I enjoy when he's near, but he does lend something when he's around. A solidness. Stability, somehow. Which is weird, since he's an aimless drifter who apparently wipes his ass with twenty-dollar bills.

But Gram herself said that I should go for a pirate or a shark if I wanted to have a good time. Which makes me wonder: which one is Weston?

And more importantly, should I even find out?

There's about 0% chance Weston would even notice me in a room full of naked women, much less want to spend an evening with me. Furthermore, I don't want to spend an evening with *him.*

Except I do.

Which makes me worry about something just a little bit more serious than what Gram had foreseen.

Weston is the type of man capable of plundering bodies and mauling hearts...which makes him both pirate *and* shark.

CHAPTER SIX

WESTON

Tss. Tss. Tss. Tss.

The synthetic bassline pumping out of the sailboat's speakers is the auditory equivalent of a party drug. There is something familiar and comforting in the upbeat techno, something that makes me feel like I've drunk way more beer than I really have.

Or maybe it's just the rhythmic rocking of the boat. The way the entire fucking ocean is bathed in velvet red and goldenrod as the world's most perfect sunset gets underway. I don't know. I sip my cocktail—I can't even remember what it is, other than it contains orange and mint. The rainbow is alive and breathing all around me, and I haven't even taken drugs.

Nova's sharp laugh distracts me for the fifteenth time in the past hour. She's sitting across from me on a long row of bench seats, legs crossed, in a romper that hugs her curves in a way I'm not sure is strictly legal. Every time I look at her, I think about what it might be like to pin her to the nearest surface. Press my body up against those curves. Bury my face in the tantalizing cream of her cleavage and ask her to call me *preposterous* one more time.

This has to be the party-drug bassline and the alcohol talking. *Has to be.* Because any thoughts about actually making a move on Nova are about as preposterous as the idea of visiting the moon for tomorrow's activity. We've known for four years that we don't get along, even if we don't entirely know *why*. There's a reason we've never hooked up. If we were able to somehow lock lips, I'm sure I'd discover fangs inside her mouth.

"Okay, okay. I need to be the photographer," Nova purrs, encouraging Amelia and Rhys's sisters, Eleanor and Harriet, to crowd together on the bench. She snaps a few pictures, consulting her digital screen in between shots. She climbs onto the bench then, kneeling as she takes the picture from a different angle. The wind billows up the shorts of her romper, revealing the back of her thigh, and she gasps, a hand shooting out to corral her clothing.

"Frisky weather we're having," she says with a laugh, just as the end of her ponytail lifts and whips over her shoulder.

"Mate, you need a napkin?" Elliot's voice at my ear jostles me from my stupor.

"For what?"

"You're drooling."

I smirk, trying to focus on anything else. I watch the captain for a few seconds, where Rhys is having a spirited conversation with him about something nautical and gesturing out to the ocean with both arms, his cocktail sloshing.

"You could just go hit on her, you know."

"I have no idea what you're talking about."

"Nova."

He's drunk, so he's being loud. I shush him, delivering a well-placed jab in the ribs for good measure. "I'm interested in photography. I'm watching her work."

"Mm-hmm. I'd say you're interested in *the photographer*."

He's right. Except the photographer isn't interested in me. She makes it abundantly clear whenever I'm within four feet of her. Even though part of me has a sneaking suspicion that Nova likes what she sees whenever she looks my way, I doubt her redhead pride would ever let her indulge. I've seen the way she gets flustered when I'm shirtless. The way she clams up if I look at her a certain way.

She's not immune. But she's fighting it.

Maybe I've been imagining how silky soft her legs might be for too long, or maybe it's the natural hypnotization of the bassline. Whatever it is, the decision scorches through me. *Just try it.* If Elliot is calling me out, I'm doing a bad job of hiding it.

"Wouldn't that just be lovely," Elliot goes on, throwing his head back to shout into the ocean breeze, "if everyone could hook up except me?"

Poor guy has been striking out with the ladies recently. I pat his shoulder consolingly. "You really think I have that much of a shot?"

"Mate, she talks a fierce game, but don't be barmy. Go after her."

Elliot is right, even though I'm not exactly sure what *barmy* means. I come to standing, wobbling only briefly before I adjust to the rhythm of the sailboat. All those years on friends' sailboats in Briggs Bay in Bayshore have taught me a thing or two about sea legs. I head to the bench where Nova is examining the camera again. The rest of the girls have wandered up to the bow to join Rhys. They're looking out at the horizon, wind blowing through their hair.

Nova stiffens as I sit beside her. "Please, no more helpful photography hints."

"Oh, come on." I settle into the cushiony back of the seat, resting my arm on the ledge behind her. "I only give out a few hints here and there. Otherwise I'd have to charge you."

She laughs, but this time, it doesn't sound sarcastic. "I'm sure your advice rivals what I learned from all the experts and leading artists in college."

"Well, some of them had to consult me before teaching you." I sniff. So she went to school for photography. I already knew that she and Amelia shared an alma mater. I just wasn't sure what she'd studied.

"Be real with me. You don't know a thing about art."

I feign a shocked face, but deep down inside, I'm gleeful. She knows nothing about me. *Nothing.* And I cannot wait to rub how wrong she is in her face. "You are such an under-estimator. I have a full-fledged art degree, thankyouverymuch."

She snorts, flipping her ponytail back over her shoulder. "Yeah, right."

"I am right. I even spent a semester as a photojournalist."

She eyes me suspiciously, but I'm not seeing that. All I can focus on is the plump pink of her lips and the line of her cleavage in that low-cut romper. She runs her thumb over the buttons of her camera, and then says, "What did you go to school for?"

Oh my god. She actually asked me a question, instead of just assuming something about me. Time to uncork the champagne.

"Why are you looking at me like that?" she asks.

"I just can't believe you showed interest in my life."

Confusion mingles on her face, along with something unreadable. I can't tell if I called her out or hurt her feelings. Or maybe something else entirely. She's as much of an enigma to me as I am to her.

"I got my degree in graphic design," I say.

I don't miss how her eyes lift up, something warm washing over her features.

"Oh," she says. "That's...interesting."

Seems like she might say more, but she's biting her tongue because of who I am. Honestly, this little game is fun. She wants to put me in a box? That's fine. I can escape. I brought pliers.

"Probably weird to you, since according to you all I do is fuck strangers. But no, I actually got a degree in something other than women."

Her eyes narrow to slits again.

"And yes, I *also* hold a degree in great sex."

"Ha." That acid edge is back in her tone. "There we are. Just when you start to act like a normal human being, the truth slides out of you."

"Like a mutant giving birth," I add.

She dissolves into laughter, giving me an incredulous look. "Oh yeah? Is that how the truth comes out of you?"

"Each and every time." God, it's so fun to just spitball with her. "Tentacles flying everywhere. Remember the alien birth scene in *Men In Black*? Kinda like that."

"Wow. A classic nineties movie reference. Now your street cred is really soaring."

The deadpan in her voice just makes me want to try harder. "I've got a few other tricks up my sleeve that could make it soar higher."

This time, only one of her eyebrows arches. All the way up to the clouds. "Oh?"

Now we're flirting. This is where I feel most comfortable. That wild and free dance that can lead to nothing or everything. With me though, it leads to everything...with a time limit. It's the whole *catch flights, not feelings* philosophy. Know enough to engage; stay distant enough to be able to walk away.

And I officially want to engage. I lean into her, the side of my arm sizzling where it's brushing against hers. "I can show you later. Once we're back at the tiki huts. We can involve the camera a little too."

The frown tugs at her lips. That's not exactly the reaction I expected. She huffs and turns away from me, breaking the seal of our arms.

Okay. Flirtation scheme not going according to plan. Time to pivot.

"Fine. I won't hit on you."

"That was you hitting on me?"

I scratch at the back of my neck. "You really know how to make a guy question his game plan."

She doesn't look amused, which means my Rico Suave self-esteem is plummeting to the molten core of the Earth. "Telling me you hold a degree in great sex and then referencing a freak alien birth? If those are your pick-up lines, I'm scared to see how you get down in the bedroom."

I smirk. She has a point. "You figured me out. I have alien sex. Secret's out."

She giggles. "Stop."

I can't tell if this is one step forward and two steps back, or just three steps backward altogether. The higher she builds this wall between us, the softer my buzz grows, exposing the glaring clarity of the situation. I'm chasing Nova. She is not reacting like any woman I've met anywhere in the world. And I officially have no idea where to go from here.

"Fine." I sigh, leaning back against the bench. I run my hands through my hair, counting the seconds of my exhale as I stare up at the cloudless pink sky. I tried to get to know her, and I failed. This was my lesson: stick to the philosophy. Plenty of hot girls out there are the equivalent of low-hanging fruit. Ego boosters. Cuties who just want a night. Backpackers looking for a memory to take home with them and nothing more.

Women like Nova are complex, interesting, annoying, and untouchable. So I'll give her what she wants.

I won't lay a finger on her.

Even though I want to.

CHAPTER SEVEN

NOVA

This trip has taught me one crucial lesson. I need to update my resume. Why? Because I have a new professional tagline.

So dense that any future employer will expend unnecessary working hours explaining seemingly obvious situations.

It didn't even occur to me until Weston retracted his bid to hit on me that *he was even hitting on me.* I am not just dense, I have a nut of dark matter inside me that is absorbing all my awareness and reason. I have been paid so little—and such detrimental—attention throughout my late adolescent years, that I literally cannot tell when a sexy man is trying to make a move on me.

Because even though he said the words, I still cannot believe he was hitting on me. There's no way that's true. I've been hit on twice in my life—the first time my junior year of high school, which turned out to be an evil ruse by the popular guys that destroyed my self-esteem for the rest of my life; and the second time in college, which was my ex telling me one night at a group movie, "Hey you're cute, y'wanna date?" approximately one year before we broke up because he was flirting with prettier girls.

All other experience with flirtation has been gleaned from movies, and it's my understanding that there is a lot of coy smiling and batting of eyelashes that accompanies it. Weston didn't bat his eyelashes *once*. Case closed.

Besides, he's too hot for my blood. His attention reminds me of the last time I got excited about *the hot guy* showering me with attention. My junior year of high school taught me that if a man at Weston's level is paying attention to me, it's for some ulterior motive. In Weston's case, he probably just wants to fuck. But there could be more—way more—to it than I even realize.

Ten years ago, there *was* way more to the situation than I realized. Garth Warren was *the* hottest guy in my school. I'd been in love with him from afar since fifth grade. One day, one of his friends cornered me before lunch to tell me that Garth had his eye on me. He pretended to be interested in me long enough for me to spill my heart out and fill the margins of all my notebooks with his name, which he promptly shared with the entire freaking world. I was labeled a clinger. A stalker. A desperate wannabe. A grade-A loser. After I realized I'd been the butt of a school-wide joke, one that also brought my weight and chubby face into the taunting, the embarrassment was crippling. I failed my driver's test and cried for a full two weeks after it all came crumbling down.

And the effects of bullying don't just magically disappear, even after ten years. It is a gift that keeps on giving—well into your adult life. *Thank you, Garth.*

Weston doesn't make my prolonged, reflective silence weird. In fact, the whole thing doesn't feel half as awkward as it should. At least there's that. Finally, though, he speaks.

"Want me to take a picture of you?"

I shake my head. "Not really."

"You're the photographer. You're always taking pictures of every-one else."

"I don't need any more pictures of myself."

Weston tuts, interlacing his fingers over the waist of his board shorts as he relaxes back onto the cushiony back of the bench. "I just think you should have photographic evidence."

My gut shrinks to a knot, imagining all the different things about me that are less than photogenic right now. My hair. My belly rolls. My thighs. My weird ankles, that aren't technically cankles but also aren't regular ankles either. "Of what?"

"This killer outfit you've got on."

His words prompt an avalanche of emotion. I am torn between adoration—*wow, you've paid me a compliment, thank you, you are male number four in my entire life to do so*—and suspicion—*he doesn't mean it, this is just a joke, a man like him could never be attracted to you.* The operating system of my brain freezes with the high-energy demands of sorting through all the potential meanings and mines buried within his words.

And you know what wins? The same thing that always does.

"I don't need you making fun of me," I tell him, turning away from him.

Weston sighs again, resting his palms on the top of his head. Then he hops to his feet, coming in front of me. He gets down on one knee, holding his thumbs and index fingers together to make a square in front of his face. He squints one eye, and then makes a *click* sound with his mouth.

Lowering his hands, the smirk on his face is sexy enough to make me forget what I was ruffled about. If only Weston could look at me like this all the time. Like I was the only thing he could see right now, the only thing he cared about. There's a finality in his gaze, something that tells me this is no joke.

But of course, I can't just flip the switch. Not after so many years of believing myself to be the inherent, secret butt of the joke.

"That one's just for me," he says, and comes to his feet. He mimes admiring the photo and tucking it in his pocket, and then he wanders away.

And all I can do is watch him go. I'm unsure if I want to grab him by the wrist and beg him to stay, or take a blood vow to never speak to this man again until we cross paths in some other part of the world two years from now.

Because his interest in me is both a compliment and a threat. I pine for his attention as much as I am suspicious of it. This double standard is as exhausting for me as it is for anyone who has ever had to listen to me complain about it.

I decide to get lost in taking pictures. Rhys and Amelia are kissing on the bow, and I seize the opportunity to be useful and productive. I hurry toward them as much as the alcohol buzz and boat-rocking will allow and snap some excellent pictures of them against the burning red backdrop of the sunset. Elliot and Keko join in then, followed by Rhys's sisters and my other bestie, Laney. My smile stretches ear to ear as I catch their hilarious antics on my camera. Weston hangs back, laughing off to the side. I finally wave him toward the group.

"Get in there," I tell him. He almost seems reluctant. Like he'd rather be on this side of the curtain with me. But maybe that's my moony brain, imagining things that aren't truly there. I don't know what to believe anymore. I am clearly not a good reality detective.

I snap rapid-fire photos of our group in various stages of smiling and posing. I guide them through a few staged pictures while the captain heads back to shore. We're racing against the clock, as the sun has nearly touched the eternal horizon of the Atlantic Ocean. We are in ethereal primetime right now, and soon the claws of dusk will take over. I snap approximately three hundred pictures of the group and then Amelia shouts out,

"Take a selfie!"

"I can't with this camera, it's too big," I tell her.

"With your phone! Just so you're in it," she insists.

"Yeah, we've got to get a picture with you in it," Rhys adds.

"Use my phone if you don't have one," Laney offers, hopping from foot to foot.

"Selfie, selfie!" Weston begins the chant, and soon everyone else joins in.

Grinning, I fumble to find my phone in the pocket of my romper and then line it up for the picture. Everyone pulls a funny face, and I resist my photographer impulses and just take one. Once *that's* over, everyone is cheering and jovial and triumphant. Because not only did we just witness an amazing sunset in great company, we did it on a sailboat.

The captain maneuvers us up to the dock we left from three hours ago. This sailboat ride was our first foray beyond the walls of the resort, and honestly, part of me wants to ditch for a couple days and just get lost in real Aruban life. I am so insanely curious about the rest of this city, not to mention the entire rest of this island. Even though I'm sure no brighter and more comfortable fuchsia tiki hut exists out there, I am willing to leave it behind in the name of research.

The sailboat glides up to the gently bobbing docks where our dinner-and-drinks adventure began. As my sandals touch the wood of the dock, I forget how to use my land-legs. I wobble. And then my sandal catches on the slat of the dock, and I stumble.

Gracelessly. And straight for the edge of the dock.

I don't even have time to scream or gasp or do anything other than stare at my watery fate.

And then strong arms are around me. *Really* strong arms. Like safety belt with biceps. Weston snatches me up against him, leaving me staring at the choppy water of the inlet.

All I can think in my head: *OH. MY. GOD* and *HE. IS. WARM.*

"Nova," he chides, easily guiding me back to standing. "Careful."

"Oh my Goddd," Laney exclaims drunkenly, her dark hair blowing across her upper lip like a windblown mustache. "Did you almost fall off the dock?"

Her exclamation causes concern to ripple through the group. I clutch his arm even after I'm stable and steady on my own two feet because I can't stop thinking about what almost happened. *You almost fell face-first into the water. You almost ruined your most expensive piece of work equipment.* And, perhaps most perplexingly: *Now you know just how good Weston's arms feel around you.*

I'm braindead. It's official. The pressure from his thick fingers against my ribcage has rendered me stumbling and mute. And I'm still clutching his arm, as if my body refuses to return to my life pre-Weston, now that I know what it feels like to have crossed over.

Everyone has gathered around me on the dock now, fawning over my near-fall, sending sincere and drunken thanks to Weston for saving my life. As we shuffle further down the dock—still clutching Weston's arm like he's my home health provider and I'm his most geriatric patient—everyone is sharing stories of the moment they saw me trip.

Rhys: "I about shat a brick, mate!"

Elliot: "I swear to God, I saw it in slo-mo. I could even see the pixels."

Laney: "I just froze, because what about your camera? And your freaking cute romper?"

It's oddly heartwarming that everyone cares so much about my well-being and clothes. This feels distantly like a parade, where the cause for celebration is the fact that I'm dry. I'll have to draw the line at lifting me up on their collective shoulders. I might be relieved, but not relieved enough to cause another accident or two. Knowing me, I'd probably fart directly *on* Weston's face if we did that.

Once we reach the parking lot of the charter business, Weston looks down at me, something warm in his gaze. His eyes drop to my hand still clutching at his arm.

"You think you can make it on your own?"

I hurry to drop his arm. "Sorry," I mumble.

"Didn't say you had to let go."

His words sizzle in the air between us, but I don't get much time to dwell on them. Keko and Elliot have wandered up ahead, already striking up a conversation with a group of girls who were waiting at the designated pick-up point. The resort is sending a car to pick us up in roughly ten minutes, which in *single guy striking up conversation at the bus* stop terms, is equivalent to an hour.

"No *way* you're a graphic designer," Elliot is saying to the trip of pretty girls wearing bikinis under transparent shifts as the rest of our group walks up. "You know, my good friend Weston is too."

Weston immediately drifts toward the conversation, having been thusly summoned. I am curious to know more. Way too curious, in fact. I have a long list of questions for him, beginning with *Can I see your portfolio* all the way to *Do you prefer Adobe or Corel?*

I drift between eavesdropping on the guys' conversation and listening to Harriet and Eleanor recount some hilarious story about Rhys from their collective childhood involving picking his nose after having dipped his finger in cayenne pepper. Laney snorts repeatedly, murmuring "Oh my god, that's funnyyyy."

Amelia appears at my side, slinging her arm around my shoulders just as Elliot shouts over at us in his thicker-than-usual British accent, "Oy! What about the club tonight?"

Amelia squeals with excitement. Laney's face lights up like she just spotted a rainbow. Everyone else in our group cheers. Weston's gaze meets mine, which delivers another gut punch. Chestnut hair tousled, his simple gray tee straining at the biceps. Ice blue eyes focused directly on me.

If Weston is the mothership, I am the confused farmer being swept up in his tractor beam. I can't look away. He's both magnetic and fearsome. In alien terms, I can't tell if this is a friendly probing or a premeditated attack.

Everything bright inside me wants it to be friendly, but everything dark inside me knows that this attraction is laced with danger. I should turn away from the tractor beam. Politely decline the probing.

But those ice blue eyes are more manipulative than I bargained for. After all, I'm not immune to the excitement. A night out! Thumping music! Continued drunkenness! Isn't this the American dream? I didn't fly all these miles to sit in my tiki hut and contemplate whether or not a cockroach was secretly hiding somewhere, waiting to brush its wings over my face while I sleep (which, let's be real, it probably is).

But more than that, I am dizzy with curiosity and empowerment. Weston waved a white flag today. One that was embroidered with ever-so-slight sexual attraction. Can I even say he's attracted to me? I'll never verbally say any of this, that's for damn sure. If I speak it, it might dissolve like sand through my fingers. And there's something about this chance—this possibility—that I want to tuck away and protect.

I don't know where it will lead. I'm not even sure I should head down this path.

But I'm tipsy, and I'm feeling frisky. And hell if that isn't the most dangerous combination on the face of the Earth.

CHAPTER EIGHT

Alone in my teal tiki hut, I'm psyching myself up for the night out. I couldn't give a shit about going to the club. That's another thing that if you've seen one of, you've seen them all. I've always been more partial to lounges with live music and some artisan beer—or even root beer—but hey. When in Aruba.

The voices of our friends reach me through the thin walls of the tiki hut. Outside, our group has congregated on the boardwalk. Torches illuminate the path and the grove of palms. Amelia is heading toward Nova's hut, and I remind myself not to care.

I remind myself to get excited about the prospect of meeting random girls and hooking up and getting drunk.

I remind myself that right now, Aruba, and soon, Thailand.

Isn't this what it's about? I'm living any twenty-six-year-old's dream. I'm a fucking Instagram influencer. I travel the world and make people jealous. Everyone wishes they could have my life.

Except I know the truth of the situation. That my bank account is slooowly dwindling. That nothing truly awaits me in Thailand as of right now—nothing more than bustling streets, new friends, and plenty of amazing pictures. And yes, those are all great things to look forward to. But when those things become normal, then what am I truly traveling to experience?

I call it the nomad's dilemma. Maybe I should just call it Weston's Dilemma, though. I'm trying to carve out my own success in life, chasing big goals and dreams just like all those inspirational bull-shitters say we should. I'm #chasinglife, bruh.

So why do I just want to sit on the beach and watch the waves for a few months?

You'll be doing that in Thailand. The thought sits heavily inside me. Maybe the problem is that I haven't heard back from Cliffhangers Gear about my pitch, and each day that drags on feels like a concrete rejection. If I could even get one green light—from Cliffhangers or any other company I've been reaching out to over the past few months—then I might feel like I had a direction in life again. Because if I have a project to look forward to, then I have more financial security. Then I have *purpose* again.

Right?

Maybe the alcohol is getting to me. Being semi-drunk for most of the day is taxing. Disorienting. I'm on day two of the wedding festivities and ready to tap out. Weston can't hang—apparently I'm not fit for the party lifestyle the way I was in college.

I just need to teach my brain that.

"I said, *I know, girl!*" Nova's voice reaches me, causing me to spin around. She's on the boardwalk chatting with Amelia, looking fifty times sexier than the last time I saw her, which is approaching the event horizon of sexiness. She's in a floral high-waisted skirt and a low-cut top that shows every inch of that cleavage I'm dying to know for myself. Her red hair is pulled back in a smooth, high ponytail, big hoop earrings glinting in the firelight.

I blink, a hard *thud* registering in my chest as I'm sucker punched by lust again. Operation Leave Nova To Her Own Devices is not off to a great start. I'd march her right back into that damn hut and cancel club night if I knew she felt even an iota of attraction to me.

Nova and Amelia come this way, already lost in their own world. It's not wise to keep looking at Nova, so I turn my back to her, following Rhys as he leads the way to the front of the resort where taxis are waiting for us. Everyone begins to pile into the cars: Rhys and Amelia and Harriet; Keko and Elliot and Eleanor. The last taxi is for the leftovers: me, Laney, and Nova.

It's not ideal, but the ride shouldn't be long. When I try to get into the front seat, the driver tuts at me and points to the back seat. Fine. I hold open the door as Laney scoots inside. Nova eyes me as if this might be a trap.

"Go on," I encourage.

"I'll sit up front."

"He won't let you." I jerk my chin toward the driver who has settled into the front seat and started the engine. "I already tried."

She sighs, ducking into the car. I fill the last space and shut the door, the driver immediately zooming off. Nova gasps, hand shooting out to grab the back of the passenger seat. Our sides are touching, the soft heat of her leg pressed to mine. My vision goes blurry for a moment as the scent of her overtakes me. She is peonies mixed with grapefruit and something so feminine I have to force myself to ignore it.

"Sorry guys," she says.

"For what?" Laney asks, nuzzling into her friend's side.

"For getting my ass all over you."

I shift beside her, allowing said ass to butt up against me. I don't mind it. Not even slightly. I'd fucking live here if I could. No, scratch that. Nova would be in my lap. Facing me. That booty-full derriere filling my hands. Her red hair splaying over her shoulders.

Apparently I should have taken the down time in my tiki hut to jack off, because I'm getting hard, and this is ten seconds away from being awkward.

"I don't mind your ass on me," Laney quips.

"Me neither," I say.

Nova narrows her eyes at me. "Don't start."

An incredulous laugh pops out of me. Her admonishment to not start is the perfect impetus to, in fact, start. I don't even know what I'm starting. I just know that she inspires it, time and time again, even when I'm trying to ignore her and focus on anything other than her sparkling wit and bodacious curves.

"I wasn't aware you were in control of who gets to start," I say.

"I'm the official taskmaster. Everyone starts and stops on my watch," she deadpans.

"Is that photographer privilege, or just Princess Nova privilege?"

A smirk tugs at her lips. "I hate that you call me Princess Nova."

"Well you better get used to it. I wasn't committed to it before, but now that you hate it, it's mandatory."

She snorts. "Figures."

Her phone vibrates in her hand, and she flips it over to assess the glowing screen. My eyes follow the light—I can't help it—and I see a new message alert from someone named Jimmy.

I don't catch the whole message, but I sure do catch the opening line: *"Hey beautiful."*

My gut twists into a knot as I move my gaze toward the dark Aruba night flashing past us beyond the taxi. Laney gasps. "Oh my god. You never finished your story about Jimmy!"

I am listening to Nova's reply with every cell of my body. Because if it turns out that she's been taken this whole time, then I misread this situation *real bad*.

"It's nothing—" Nova starts.

"Pff! Don't tell me it's nothing. You said there might be wedding bells next month."

I grimace at the window. Awesome. So I've been fantasizing about a girl who not only was never available to begin with, she is actually considering *marriage* with someone. That's the opposite of what I'm after. My dream girl starts out with *available* and *definitely not engaged* as qualities, so this rules out Nova once more. And the more I think about it, I'm not sure how she ever got ruled back *in*.

"No, no. Zero wedding bells," Nova says. I can feel the nervousness pouring off her. "I'll tell you all about it later, I promise."

Right. When I'm not there, which means she can tell the truth. I'm no homewrecker. A few of my brothers might cop to that level—thinking about my little brother Maverick here—but fuck if I mess with stuff like that. I don't want to ruin some guy's life. I don't dabble in shady shit, not even for a night or two of fun.

The taxi stops in front of a large warehouse-looking building on the beach. We tumble out, Rhys suddenly appearing out of nowhere to pay our driver. I fumble for my wallet, needing to beat him to the punch, but Rhys is handing over bills before I can get there. I punch him in the shoulder instead.

"You asshole," I tell him, which prompts a sly grin from him.

"Whatever. Let's go party."

"I'm going to buy all of your drinks tonight," I warn him.

"Like hell you will." Rhys slings his arm over my shoulder, and we strut up to the front doors of the club, where thumping music leaks out. Inside, the place is a confusing mess of human bodies and strobe lights and a distinct smell of cheap cologne. Rhys abandons me, and I head straight for the bar. I'm still thinking about Nova, which I'm not excited about, so my plan is to get lost in the sea of people and see what happens.

The bartenders are busy, hopping between clubgoers who line the edges of the bar like adoring fans at a rock concert. Except we're adoring the alcohol they have tucked away back there.

Friends begin to appear in different spots along the edge of the long, curved bar. Rhys shows up about midway down, Amelia's blonde bun bobbing behind him. And then Nova arrives at the other end of the bar.

Her smoky eyeliner and glittering green eyes serve as a reminder. Somewhere between the yoga class and the yacht, I became *deeply* invested in getting her on my good side. But when her gaze finally lands on mine and we lock eyes across the sprawling bar, the electricity that lights me up from head to toe is a warning.

She's got a situation. I'm not trying to get involved. Because I never get involved.

Not with her. Not with anyone.

Still, I can't look away from her. We've locked eyes like *Guinness World Records* is keeping track. Whoever looks away first loses. There's something happening between us right now. I can't say exactly what it is, other than I'd rather get sucker punched in the head than look away from her right now.

I guess I'm disappointed. That's the heat and heaviness circling through me. I got way more excited about her over the past twenty-four hours than I fucking realized, and that's the first step on a path I know I shouldn't be following.

So why is it so hard to course correct?

"Hey, can I squeeze in here?"

A feminine voice interrupts our stare-down. A petite brunette is at my side, batting her eyelashes at me, smelling like plums and hair product. I shift, allowing her to slip in at the bar. Our arms brush, and she hasn't stopped smiling.

"Are you here alone?"

"Came with some friends."

Her grin stretches wider. "Guys or girls?"

She's not making it too hard to figure out where she's going with this. "Both," I tell her. "We're here for a wedding."

Her eyes light up, hand shooting out to grab my wrist. "Oh my god, so am I! Wait, are you the groom?"

And just like that my doorway of opportunity swings wide open. I want to forget about Nova? Here's my chance. This girl is hopeful and bright eyed.

"Not the groom. Just his bachelor groomsman."

The brunette pushes up against me, tucking some hair behind her ear. "My name's Kitty. But you can call me Sex Kitten."

I've heard lots of pick-up lines in my time, but that was one of the more blatant ones. I wish Nova were here to overhear it. I'm sure she'd be crying laughing. I look across the bar just as Nova glances away. She was watching us—the way my gut drops confirms it.

"What's your name?" Kitty presses.

The bartender shows interest in me, and I swoop in, placing my order for a root beer. When he walks away, Kitty scoffs.

"You came to a nightclub to drink root beer?"

"I don't feel like drinking alcohol."

Kitty rolls her eyes. "We're all here to party. Could have at least asked me for my order while the bartender was here."

Sex Kitten is getting her hiss on. This is amusing to me—not irritating. "I'll share my root beer if that's what you really want."

She softens a little, sighing. "Well, listen. Do you wanna go fuck in the bathroom?"

I laugh in her face. I can't help it. This is too absurd, yet this is real life. "Sorry, what?"

"You're hot, okay? We'll never see each other again." She's dragging her pink-tipped fingernails up the side of my arm.

Once upon a time, the answer would have been *yes*. Kitty's got cleavage for days and a skin-tight maxi dress hugging a model-worthy body. But she's got *Hell, no* written all over her.

The bartender returns with my root beer, and I tip him. I raise the bottle to Kitty as I sidle past. "Night, HumpCat."

"Sex Kitten," she corrects me, just before I get swallowed up by the sea of people.

It takes me approximately thirty seconds of navigating between sweaty bodies to realize that I want to fucking leave. I've lost everyone again, yet I get the sense that I'm searching for Nova. I spot her red hair near the main doors, and I follow the swish of her high ponytail like it's a lighthouse illuminating a dark night on the sea. The door opens, and I rush to follow her. My footsteps crunch over the gravel outside, the music receding to a dull, rhythmic thump behind the closed doors.

Nova is walking toward a series of benches along the front of the building, holding a finger in one ear. Her phone is pressed to the other side of her face.

"Hey, sorry," she's saying. "We were inside the club. I didn't hear it ring."

The disappointment returns, filling my veins with lead, and yet again I'm left wondering what the fuck I'm doing here. I've been telling myself all evening to get off Nova's trail. But I can't. I fucking can't.

The door bursts open a moment later, and Rhys's younger sister Harriet stumbles out. She crashes right into me, and I catch her easily. She giggles into my collar bone. She's been shit-faced since we left for the club.

"I wondered where you went," she murmurs into my shirt.

Nova finally sits down on a bench about twenty yards away and notices us. She pauses in her conversation, her gaze raking over me. Harriet squints at her.

"Is that Nover?" The Brits can't help but add an R to the end of her name.

"Yeah." I clear my throat, adjusting Harriet so that she's more on her own two feet. I don't know what to say or do here. I'm out of my element. I'm officially chasing, and I feel caught. To Nova, I call out, "You okay?"

Nova nods, phone still pressed to her ear. I don't know how to say any of the other things knocking around inside me: *Can I sit by you? Is that your boyfriend on the phone? What if you and I left the club altogether and walked the beach for a while?*

Laney bursts through the door next, heading straight for Nova. "I told you not to take it!"

My gut takes that sickening nosedive again. Harriet is nuzzling my neck. She is so off-limits it's not funny, being Rhys's sister, and besides, I'm not attracted to her. I have no interest in anyone...except the one person who doesn't want me. I'm pushing Harriet to standing, trying to put distance between us again, while Nova waves Laney away.

Harriet stumbles away, giving a weird smile to a nearby guy. "What about you and I go dance?"

Oh no. This is not good. The guy's eyebrow lifts. "You new around here?"

"New? I invented new," Harriet replies.

I cannot let this go further. She is out of her mind drunk, so I swoop in, hooking my arm around her back.

"Harriet, I thought I told you I was calling for the cab," I say, offering the guy a tight smile. "Remember?"

"I wanna dance," Harriet insists, her lips smashed against my cheek.

This isn't good. I help her stay upright and fish my phone out of my pocket, seeing a missed text from Rhys. With one hand I struggle to type out: *Ur sis is drunk. Needs to go back. I'll take her.*

This is the out I was looking for. I just wish Nova could somehow join us.

"Listen, you need to lie down."

She snickers so hard that she snots onto my shoulder. I grimace, helping her walk toward the taxi stand. Laney is hovering over Nova, hands on her hips.

"I'm taking her back," I call out to Laney, who turns briefly and nods. I don't think she has any idea what's going on. Hell, neither do I. One of the idle taxis nearby rushes to snag our business, and I'm guiding Harriet into the back seat as gently as I can. She flops backwards, skirt hiking up to her waist.

"All right, Harriet. We're not trying to show the world." I struggle to sit her upright in the backseat, but she keeps giggling and flopping over. I finally cram myself into the backseat with her, giving the driver our destination. As the car pulls away from the club, I spot Nova heading back inside.

I'll never not help someone who needs it. But part of me wishes that I could have gotten Nova to myself for a little bit.

Because I think Nova might need some help too. She just doesn't know it.

CHAPTER NINE

NOVA

My alarm goes off at six the next morning. Why?

Because I'm a masochist. I like to torture myself on my vacation with excessively early rising in the name of art.

I am on a mission to catch this sunrise, even though I went to bed roughly four hours ago.

I fumble through the darkened hut, my limbs heavy with the aftermath of not enough sleep and too many martinis at the club. I'm ashamed to admit that I drowned the ache in my chest with alcohol, but Weston made it clear last night that whatever happened on the sailboat was a blip, a freak occurrence, a whisper that immediately faded into the ether.

In the span of one hour I saw him flirting with and hitting on three different girls. He even left with Rhys's sister. I need to feel thankful that I didn't take the bait and add myself to his list of female conquests. My knee connects with the side of the dresser and I blurt, "Fucking hell!"

This sunrise is going to be my reset for the rest of the week. I'll be in official photographer mode starting today, at least for part of the time, as Rhys and Amelia's first family-and-friends mixer is happening tonight. No better way to get myself in game mode than by getting a crappy night of sleep and hurting myself in the dark.

I finally locate the bathroom switch and blink against the sudden light. Maybe I should just go back to bed. I hobble over to the slatted blinds covering the tiny window looking out toward the beach and tug them open. The last gasp of night has everything coated in cobalt blackness, but out on the horizon I can spot the first hint of dawn.

The sky looks cloudy and intense, which promises an epic sunrise. I must go. Renewed with excitement for my mission, I hurry to pull on my bathing suit, followed by a flowy beach dress. Because what's a sunrise session without a dip in the ocean? I won't be caught dead in this bikini around anyone else during our trip, so I better make the most of the water in the wee hours. Even if it's cold—I'm in Aruba. I *must* take advantage of every last opportunity.

I gather my camera bag, eyes burning as I struggle to focus on my belongings. I slip on my flip-flops before heading out into the cool morning. Sand sprays behind me with every step, and the pure isolation out here on the beach at this hour is disorienting. I'm far enough away from the common areas of the resort to be bathed in pure, crushing darkness. The rhythmic hiss of the waves, growing louder as I near, is my only compass.

Once I reach a spot that feels like it should be my outpost, I slip off my sandals and set down my bag. I stand and let the sea air accost me, blowing at my hair, the salty breeze coating me. It makes sense why sometimes the best medical advice in the early 1800s was just *go live at the ocean for a little bit.* This shit is healing. Whether you're here during a quarter-life crisis or undiagnosed consumption, the ocean can handle it.

The first blush of dawn crests the horizon, and my heart beats a little faster. This feels like Christmas morning, honestly. I've seen so many sunrises, and some of them in fascinating parts of the world, but it never gets old. Not even a little bit. I'm feeling around in my camera bag blind, but I don't need light to see what I'm doing. I know every inch of this camera and my bag, inside and out. I deftly pop off the lens cover and sit down in the sand, waiting for the show.

It starts slow, but follows with a bang, the light cresting first in soft, lazy yellows until the fire is leaking onto the horizon. I sit transfixed just long enough to get my unfettered fill, and then I'm snapping pictures of the sky, the color show, the way the waves crest and the orange light bounces off the foam.

By the time the sun has revealed itself halfway, my camera has over a hundred pictures on it. I set it back in the bag and button it up. *My time has come.*

I tug my dress off and race toward the water. I need to act quick or I'll lose my nerve. Especially if I sit here and think about how cold the water might end up being. I brace myself for a cold blast but—oh—*oh*—it's fucking warm. It is so heaven-sent warm that I start whooping and splashing and kicking at the water. Why is this a surprise? I can't say, other than it really *is* Christmas day and Mother Earth herself has given me this perfect ocean dip at 81 degrees.

I immediately sink to my knees, bathing myself in this luxurious bathwater at six thirty in the morning. I feel more alive than possibly ever. I laugh and kick and stand up and splash again. God, everything feels good. Everything feels *right.*

As I float in the knee-deep water looking toward the orange blast of sunrise streaking the sky, I start to hum. I don't even know the music. It's just some tune that apparently exists deep inside me. I'm usually not a hummer, but here we are. I move my arms in time to this apparently ancestral song emerging from the depths of me. I watch the sky and the wispy streaks of cloud being illuminated like they're cartoons in the nascent daylight.

And I feel like a witch, sort of. Some sort of half-clothed siren, brewing mischief in the lapping waters of the sea. I came here to make art and dance in my bikini.

I dance and gaze and grin and laugh until the adrenaline wears off and tiredness is licking at me again. I slosh through the warm water, headed for the shore, feeling excessively happy.

Life is nothing if not a series of these ecstatic moments, tiding us over through the stressors and monotony and financial crises. At least I can say my cup is full now.

But I can also say that my cup-filling didn't go unnoticed. As soon as I step out of the ocean and reorient myself to the shore, I notice someone else on the beach.

Someone who looks a lot like Weston.

Sitting in the sand, elbows propped on his bent knees, grinning out at me like he just watched every last second of my private dance session.

Terror streaks through me. Why is he here? For a moment I don't know what to do. It's not like I can pretend I didn't see him. There's nobody else on the beach except him and I. He's in my direct line of sight. It would take a cartoonish level of gall to feign blindly stumbling past him and back toward my hut. Which I would actually attempt, if it weren't for all my things sitting right next to him.

I draw a tense breath and start the walk through the sand toward him. His gaze doesn't waver from me, and as I get closer I can see the bleariness in his eyes. His hair is tousled by the gentle breeze. The air is crisp and salty and pure, and as the space between us shrinks, the ache in my chest turns into a ravine.

There is something about this man. Something I can't even begin to comprehend. But the safest thing to do is ignore it.

"That looked fun," he says, his voice featuring that just-woken-up gruffness that sets the butterflies swarming in my belly.

I swallow hard, looking at my camera bag. Would it be so wrong to grab it, run back to my hut, and pretend this was all a dream? "What are you doing here?"

"Just wanted to catch the sunrise." He squints out at the brilliant wash of color. "I'm pretty glad I did."

I can't tell if he's quietly making fun of me or being sincere. I'll never truly know the difference, or more importantly, trust my judgement. I'm inclined to believe him. But whenever I trust my heart with the opposite sex, it leads to horrible outcomes.

It wasn't just the popular seniors who fucked me over in high school. It was my one and only ex, too. That boring-looking business major who I'd thought would provide a stable, secure relationship? Yeah, even he screwed around on me behind my back. I ate up his reassurances like they were candy. And then went on to eat a *lot* of candy once we broke up.

"Did you have a fun night?" I ask before I can think better of it. His gaze washes over me, making me painfully aware of my wide thighs and my big butt as I'm standing in my bikini before him. I should just go back to my hut and move on with my day. But there's something pure about this daybreak moment. Even though I feel exposed and vulnerable, I'm curious to see where this goes.

"It was short," he says, pinching one eye shut to look up at me. "And full of too many drunk girls."

Ah, yes. The charmed life of Weston Daly. "I'm sure most men wouldn't complain about that," I say, reaching for my dress. "Isn't that what you're here for?" I tug it on over my damp skin, the wet ends of my hair plastering to my chest. Weston's gaze drags back down over me, leaving goosebumps in its wake.

"I don't know about most guys," Weston says, distaste lingering in his words. "But too many drunk girls is not exactly my style."

His words ring through me like an alarm. What I really want to know is *did you fuck all the girls you flirted with last night?* But I shouldn't care. I can't care. Because Weston is not for me, and I need to not want him in the first place. It's just that whole *not wanting him* part that I'm struggling with.

"I assumed that being surrounded by drunk models was sort of your life's mission," I say, tucking some hair behind my ear as I bend down to button up my camera bag. "I know you like to party and have a good time. No judgment."

"Right," he says, the acid clear on his tongue. Maybe there's something about this early morning clarity that's got him rawer than usual. But he is *not* hiding his displeasure with me. So we're back to square negative one. "No judgement at all from Princess Nova."

"What you do with your life is your business," I say.

He snort-laughs. "Then why do you keep bringing it up?"

Aaaaand he called me out. Great. The tops of my ears go flaming hot, and I yank the zipper shut on my camera bag. It gets caught on my strap, which is odd, since I am positive that I set everything inside carefully like I always do. I struggle to tuck everything back inside and zip it up. I have nothing to say, so I say nothing.

"I don't know a single other person that casually brings up my sex life even half as much as you do," he spits. "Not even Elliot or Keko. Is there something you'd like to know, Nova?"

I straighten and sling the camera bag over my shoulder. I look up and down the beach. A few other people have scattered along the shoreline, lured out by the promise of a new dawn. Yes, there is something I'd like to know: *could a man like you ever be attracted to me, or am I insane?* I just can't force myself to say it.

Because acting like I care will make me a liar. It will prove that it's important to me, when I've spent my whole adulthood trying to convince the world—or just myself?—that I don't need a hot man's approval.

"No need for a Q&A, thanks." I run a hand through my hair, suddenly exhausted by how stupid this all is. Someone is messing things up, and I'm pretty sure it's me.

"Then why don't you sit your ass down and enjoy the morning with me?"

I have a million reasons why, none of which would ever dare pass my lips. But the truth is that my head is spinning. I need to ground myself. I need to stare at the wall of my tiki hut and figure out what the hell is going on in my loins and in my head.

It was so much easier to hate Weston Daly before knowing him. Now that he's showing me pieces of himself, I'm falling into his vortex headfirst without a second thought. And I don't like it one bit.

Because I do want to stay with him. More than anything. I slide my camera bag off my shoulder. *Watching the water with Weston.* Has anything ever sounded so perfect, in fact? As I'm looking down at him, admiring the hopeful glint in his blue eyes as he waits for my response, a movement nearby tugs at my attention.

Amelia is trekking through the sand, heading for my hut.

"Shit," I murmur, anxiety knotting my belly. We have a morning photo shoot scheduled for an hour from now, but I was fully planning on sleeping—or sitting with Weston—for at least forty-five minutes before we started.

I call out to her just as she knocks on my door. She spins around, cupping her eyes against the bright new day.

"I can't figure out what to wear!" she cries out.

I grin. At least there isn't an emergency, like she and Rhys calling off the wedding or some sort of nighttime venomous sea creature bite.

"What's the problem?" Weston twists to look back at her, and all I can see is the crinkle of his belly as he turns. Jesus, this man is pure muscle and heat. Every time we've touched, he's been warm, living steel. I can't imagine what it would feel like to run my fingers over those abs. If the sound of his voice in the morning can turn me on, I can't imagine what his voice might do to me if we were actually getting intimate with each other. I'd turn into a quivering, whimpering mess before he even took his clothes off.

"She, uh…photo." I swallow hard, trying to remember English, or anything that is not a vision of what sex with Weston would be like. "We're doing a picture."

"A picture?" He smiles up at me, a dimple flashing. Ugh, his rough bass and dark hair can *shut up* already. I can't look at this man anymore.

"Shoot," I clarify, looking out into the distance. "Photo shoot. Like a…" All I can think about is whether he'd give me that smile in the bedroom, too. "What do you call it? Bride thingy."

"And you're the professional photographer here," he says, but there's warmth in his jab. It doesn't slice as much as it amuses. For once.

"Believe it or not, I can do the job, even if I can't describe it." Amelia looks impatient, so I know I need to cut my beach reverie with Weston short. I'm not sure if I should be mortified or emboldened by what happened here this morning, so I'll just consciously avoid thinking about it for a while. "I gotta go."

Weston uses two fingers to salute me, and I begin a slow trudge through the sand.

Even amid the confusion, each step away from Weston reinforces one basic truth: I want more of this man.

CHAPTER TEN

WESTON

There's something floating in the air today. Like someone at the resort made an essential oil blend of caffeine and Adderall and set the diffuser on high. I am *amped* for no discernible reason. I soar through breakfast, chug fresh pineapple juice, and crush my metaphorical obstacles against my forehead like a pop can.

I am ready for whatever comes my way. And even though my A game is prepared for mountain climbing or solving complex riddles, what actually happens is Rhys's and Amelia's families begin to arrive on the island.

Both sets of parents arrive just before lunch, along with scattered aunts and uncles and cousins, which means lots of introductions and an afternoon full of Amelia's and Rhys's fathers. Apparently destination wedding schedules are dictated by gender, so we are tasked with entertaining the men while Amelia and her crew enter-tain the women.

This means I don't see Nova. Not even a glimpse as we cycle through the bars and the fathers get progressively drunker. Even though both families are rich as hell, nobody has ever made it to Aruba, so this is basically the fifty-something parent equivalent of spring break. The only thing missing is slipping dollar bills into the string bikinis of hired dancers.

And just like that, a gut punch of adrenaline hits me. My mind is riveted on Nova once again. That bikini she wore this morning—holy with a side of hell. I exhale long and low, looking to the heavens for reinforcement.

It wasn't just the fact that the emerald green scraps of fabric straining across her tits and over her pussy were some of the only pieces of cloth I've been jealous of in this life. It was the fact that I caught her. I fucking caught her. She was letting loose in the ocean, with gorgeous, swaying hips and red, windblown hair like the most erotic performance artist—or maybe witch—I've ever laid eyes on.

And yes, my goal was to ignore her. To let her be, to continue with my own agenda as usual.

But fuck, my agenda is boring. I could have hooked up with any number of girls last night, but that's not interesting to me. I thought this to be an unwavering fact about masculinity: *as long as there is sex potential, there is excitement.*

The endless stream of doe-eyed blondes and brunettes wandering this island proves to me my basic assumption about my own sexuality is wrong. I thought ignoring Nova would be easy. Turns out, it's the type of challenge that deserves a trophy simply for participating.

And this millennial will have failed so badly I won't even get a participation award.

How can I turn away from Nova now? She's existed as a distantly unlikeable gnat for the past four years, until she exploded into a super-fucking-rare and gorgeous butterfly in the blink of an eye.

How was I supposed to know this buxom babe is also an artistic genius and wittier than fuck? Trust me, I scoped out her sunrise pictures. Right before taking my own little gems of her gorgeous dance session.

Because I see Nova, despite how much she thinks I don't notice anything other than peripheral pussy. She's doing the things that I want to do—sitting on the sidelines, talking about weird shit, getting up at the buttcrack of dawn just for a good sunrise.

And honestly, sunrises technically qualify as 'seen one, seen them all,' but they're one of the few exemptions. Every single sunrise is unique and awe-inspiring in its own way, and Nova seems like the kind of person who gets that.

I'm not even going to get started on how painfully fucking attracted I am to her. It's a moot point anyway, because she's got that situation back home. Which is yet another reason to *stay the fuck away*.

But I can't.

So I won't.

The day blurs by in childhood stories and good old fashioned male bonding. All that's missing is going out into the field to hunt some pheasants or quail, which I'm sure we would have done had there been time and rifles available. I spend a lot of time with Amelia's dad talking about fly fishing, because he discovered that I've actually been fly fishing before, so he goes into extensive detail about his trip last fall. Every conversation I have is punctuated with curiosity about Nova. I can't get her out of my head. And it's absolutely the most annoying thing ever.

By the time evening rolls around, everyone is being herded toward a specific patio in the middle of the resort for our dinner. It's the first semiformal event of the wedding week, with both sides' parents in attendance. The itinerary Amelia gave me had this dinner marked with a star: *The Bradford and Baker Family Mixer.* Enormous white sheets swoop between trellises, and spotlights illuminate the sheets in bright blues and greens. Twinkle lights adorn nearly every other inch of the patio, and from the sheer number of servers here folding cloth napkins, I can tell this is going to be a hell of a soiree.

I still haven't seen Nova, and I'm not even trying to hide how hard I'm looking for her. Not seeing her since seven that morning feels less like twelve hours and more like an eternity. The patio is brimming with conversation and laughter. Keko appears at my side, clamping his hand on my shoulder.

"You want anything?" he asks.

"Root beer," I tell him.

He rolls his eyes. "What else?"

"If they don't have root beer in the bottle, I'll take it in a glass." I grin as he rolls his eyes harder. "And if not in a glass, then I'll take water."

"I'm bringing you whisky," he tells me, and then walks toward the bar on the patio. Which is fine. I'll drink whisky. I just want to avoid being in a drunken haze all evening. Yes, we're here to celebrate, but I like to actually remember my travels and big events. Especially when Rhys is so prone to getting sauced—he needs someone to help him remember his own damn wedding week.

I spot Amelia nearby, conversing with her aunt and uncle. Electricity sizzles up my spine. If Amelia is here, Nova must be near. She has to be. Everything inside me is tense as I wait to spot the gorgeous, bristly redhead. Keko returns with our drinks just as I spot her.

Camera to her face. Half-crouched, shooting a conversation between Rhys and his mother while they're none the wiser.

"You gonna take this or not?" Keko elbows me.

"Yeah." I don't take my eyes off her as I watch her stalk the perimeter of the party, occasionally pausing to frown down at her camera screen. She's wearing a simple black romper, but with her long red ponytail and red heels, she's got my heart racing for the billionth time today.

"Hello? Weston?"

Keko's confusion breaks me out of my spell. "What?"

"Take your damn drink." He shoves the tumbler into my hand. I focus on him long enough to clink glasses and take a sip. And then I'm back to looking for Nova.

"She's over here," Keko informs me a moment later. I follow the jerk of his chin and find Nova by the bar.

I smirk at my friend. "Thanks, buddy." I clap his shoulder before I brush past him, heading for the only girl I'm able to see. Nova doesn't see me approaching, so when I sidle up next to her at the bar and clear my throat, she gasps, a hand shooting to her cleavage. Her floral grapefruit scent wraps around me, sending desire streaking through me.

"Jesus, Weston."

"Did I scare you?"

"I about shit myself."

That's one of the things I appreciate about Nova. She doesn't try to play it too perfect. She's not acting like a doll just because I'm a dude. I can't even guess how many women get around a guy and act like they don't swear, pee, or get morning breath.

"Good thing you didn't. I hear these rompers are difficult to navigate." I jerk my chin to her outfit, grateful for the sanctioned chance to blatantly check her out again. Pink stains her cheeks, but only for a moment.

"That's your real goal here, isn't it?" she says, a coy smile on her lips. "Scare me until I soil myself."

I snort at the absurdity of it. "One goal among many. What are you doing?"

She tilts her head, looking out at the patio full of guests. "Oh, just taking some pictures."

"Need any more advice about aperture?" I can't resist needling her now. It's too fun. Too gratifying.

This time, though, she laughs. "Yeah, actually, I was hoping for some beginner tips in general."

"Okay. Here's your first one. Now listen close." I pause for dramatic effect. "You're gonna want to press the button to take the picture."

"That's a good piece of advice. Anything else?"

"After you take the picture, you're going to want to edit it."

She rolls her lips in, nodding. "You're on fire."

By this point, I'm burning with curiosity about whether she saw the photos I took of her that morning. And whether she'll give me copies of them. But before I can say anything, Amelia sweeps up.

"We got the green light from the hotel," she says in a low voice before sweeping away.

Nova looked pleased. "That's my cue."

"What's going on? Are we going to stage a heist?"

"I don't know why you think you're invited to the heist." Nova haughtily tosses her ponytail over her shoulder. "If you didn't RSVP, you can't come."

"So there *is* a heist."

Her gaze glitters for a moment, looking at me so warmly that I'm completely shellshocked for a moment. I have no voice. I have no brain. I only see Nova and live in this moment. Jesus, when was the last time someone took my breath away?

"We're doing pictures," she finally says. "And as the photographer, well..."

"You have to do the bride thingy," I finish for her.

She snorts, that pretty blush returning to her cheeks. It's easier than I thought to get on her good side. After four years and an entire seventy-two hours of struggle, that is.

Nova whisks away, leaving me in a cloud of that peony-infused magic scent. Heat sizzles through me as I watch her leave. Yeah. Need that girl. Immediately.

Nova begins herding the party toward an area nearby that is the resort's equivalent of an Instagram-ready backdrop featuring rustic knotted wood and cream silk draped anywhere that looks fitting. Laney appears at my side, a cocktail glass in hand. She lifts it in a silent toast, and we clink glasses.

"I'm so drunk I feel like this is my freshman year of college again," she says.

"So you down for a beer bong after this?" I ask her.

She snorts, pushing at my chest. "God, you're so funny." Her gaze slides down to her palm on my chest. "And hot. I never understood why Nova doesn't like you."

Disappointment slices through me. And here I thought I'd made some progress. Two days ago, I wouldn't have cared that she didn't like me. But now? Fuck, there's only one thing I want in this life and it's to make her see that I'm an okay guy.

"Does she like anyone?" I ask.

Laney snorts. "Women, yes. But men? She doesn't even like her own boyfriend."

My disappointment bleeds out and hardens into a weird breed of loss. It doesn't make sense. In five days, I'll never see Nova again. I'll never see this island again. Whatever I was going after was only destined to exist in this tiny, tenuous sliver of time. A mere gasp in the yawning stretch of history.

Why does it seem like I missed my chance?

"So she's seeing someone," I confirm, bringing my tumbler up to my lips slowly as I watch Nova direct family members to various positions in front of the knotted wood.

Laney sighs. "I don't know. I never know with her. Sometimes I think she'll be single until the day she dies."

Now I'm lost. "So she's single?"

"She's just Nova."

This is the opposite of helpful. Laney might be too drunk to adequately steer my Lust Brigade, so I'll need to move to plan B, which is to continue quietly hunting Nova until I figure out if she's single or weeks away from marriage. It could be either at this point, but everything inside me—and Nova's heated looks—tells me it's the former.

"You know," Laney says as she tips her head toward me, "you two would look *really* cute together."

I swirl the whisky in my glass. That's obvious. Nova would make any jerk look good. "Not if she's got a boyfriend."

Laney doesn't add anything, so I chalk it up to one more strike in the *Wait, She's Actually Taken* category.

"Ohhh, come on." A gruff rebuke from some man nearby cuts through air. One of the party guests—Amelia's uncle, I think—is scoffing, looking more than annoyed. Nova is watching him, her cheeks pink, while Amelia trails after the family member to calm him.

"We *are* doing the pictures," Amelia says.

"I'm starving," her uncle says. "You think I got time to wait for her to set up some useless light?"

"Uncle Larry," Amelia begins, but whatever she says to him next gets lost in the commotion around us. I move toward Nova without even deciding to. She's fumbling with the light stand she'd been working on, swearing under her breath when I arrive.

"You trying to set this up?"

She glances at me, wilting slightly. "The lock is broken on the tripod. It keeps sliding down."

"Can I check it out?"

She huffs, handing it over. Stress is creasing her face, and she keeps glancing around and then down at her phone. After a few cycles of her nervous tics, I jerk my chin toward the family members milling around.

"Why don't you go get them in their spots? This will be fixed by the time they're in their places."

She looks equal parts horrified and confused. "But the leg won't stay in place. If this light falls over and breaks—"

"No, no. I get it." I sit back on my heels and look around while I hold the broken leg of the light stand. "You see that plant over there?"

She squints in the direction that I jerk my chin. "The succulent?"

"No, the one next to it. Go grab me a few of those long fronds."

She watches me suspiciously but does as I say. When she comes back, I bite the frond and then tug at the end of it. Strong enough. And it'll have to do. Besides, this will be way faster than hunting down a server, who would then have to go find a maintenance guy, only for a half hour to pass and then learn they don't have twine or string after all.

I start winding the frond around the broken leg, and Nova nods. "Ohhh, you are good." Without another word, she spins on her heel and begins herding the family back together for the picture. I tighten the frond, tie it off a few times, and then step back to admire my handywork. It's solid. That's what vagabonding has taught me—I can jury rig damn near anything in a pinch. It's just a test of creativity.

Nova looks over her shoulder, a grin blossoming when she sees the fixed stand and my thumbs-up. Everyone shuffles into place, Amelia's uncle grumbling loudly but being compliant. Amelia looks mortified, but there's always that one family member who has to keep things spicy, I guess. When Nova gets closer, I call out to her,

"Where do you need the light?"

She nibbles on her lips while she assesses the layout. "Can you move it a little to the left?"

I move it, and when I get an even bigger grin in return, I know my work here is done. She waves me over for the picture too, directing me to stand to the left of Keko.

I sling my arm around my buddy's shoulder, basking in the body buzz of an averted disaster, a job unexpectedly well done. And damn, I hope Nova notices. I hope she sees how hard I'm paying attention to her. How many notes I'm taking about her blushes and comebacks and quirks.

Because I plan on getting an answer to my question tonight.

Is Nova taken, or is she about to be mine?

CHAPTER ELEVEN

It's almost nine p.m. when I'm making the lazy walk back to my hut. It's only me—everyone else is still partying on the patio. Dinner came in a delicious, pan-seared-fish blur. Every inch of my body is feeling satisfied and oddly sensual. I went out on a limb tonight with the heels and the romper, way beyond my comfort zone. I am a vision for Forever 21's plus size collection, if they truly fucking had one. But now, I am ready to strip down to loose shorts and take a load off.

I don't know if it's the unexpected self-image boost or the insanely expensive red wine I drank.

But there's a lot of things pumping through my veins. What's spreading farther and faster is the fact that I am unbelievably horny.

Weston doesn't help matters one bit. He is the least helpful person on the face of the planet when it comes to feeling rational and platonic. It's like he gets hotter every day spent on the island, and tonight? He had to pull the *oh let me be creative and helpful at the same time, while also possessing this glorious set of abs* card. Which was preceded by the *Oh, is your sister too drunk to function? How about I politely escort her home and make sure she makes it to bed safely like a total platonic gentleman* card, which I learned about when Harriet let it slip earlier.

I've reached my saturation point. He's driving me into my bed, forcing my hand between my legs, where I will spend the next ten to fifty minutes imagining what our impossibly hot sex would be like. I need a break from the all the people-ing, anyway. Amelia warned me that her not-so-loveable uncle would be in attendance, whose claims to fame include getting into fist fights with florists and fast food workers. Weston stepped in swiftly and discretely. Not at all what I expected from the man who got competitive with intimacy exercises, but hey, I guess we all have our quirks.

I'm sure he was just trying to be helpful, but now he's gone and made himself even more irresistible.

I hoist my heavy camera bags higher up on my shoulder. My hut is in sight—just a little bit farther in these heels. My calves are screaming from an entire evening spent in these gorgeous weapons. I need an hour to lie down, masturbate excessively, and then maybe sneak in a late-night swim while everyone is off getting tanked.

Excellent plan.

Back in the dark hut, I sigh with relief as I toe off my heels. Then I flip the switch, and golden light bathes the tiki-chic interior. My paradise home away from home. I smile as I unzip my romper and disrobe from the long day of entertaining Amelia's and Rhys's family members, shooting pictures, and trying to stop thinking about sex with Weston.

My phone vibrates. If it's between nine and ten p.m., it has to be Jimmy. The man has been so habitually punctual with his calls and texts that I would actually bet my gram's life that this is him. I peek at my phone.

JIMMY: I'm heading to bed. Hope you had a great day, doll.

I swear, Jimmy has a sensor that beeps every time I'm thinking about what Weston might sound like when he orgasms. But really, he's been texting and calling nonstop. And now, he has a new nickname for me in addition to "beautiful." At the rate this is going, by the time I leave Aruba, we're going to be engaged without my consent. How did billiards buddies turn into a long-distance relationship?

I frown. I'm not going to respond, because I have something more important to do—get back to speculating about Weston's intimate sounds. Is he a grunter? Maybe a groaner. Wild hog variety, or more of a hilarious sex talker who says outrageous things in the heat of the moment?

If I ever find out, it'll be because I overhear him hooking up with someone. Which hasn't happened. That I know of. *Yet.*

I lie back on my bed, stretching, ready for a cozy night of rubbing one out. I usually use my tried-and-true vibrator, but since I have an irrational fear of my vibrator turning itself on inside my luggage and being discovered by the security luggage checkers, I never fly with one. And yes, I know I can take the battery out—but then it would still be *discovered*, surely. And that sort of uncertainty—*did some stranger fondle my inert vibrator in the name of border control or no?*—is not what I want to live with. Some things are better left tucked behind stacks of unused underwear in the third drawer of your late great-grandmother's rickety lingerie chest.

Before I slip my hand down my panties, an idea occurs to me. The camera! What an evil genius I am. I lunge for the camera bag, hurrying to scroll through photos to a picture I captured of Weston the day before that has honestly not stopped cycling through my subconscious. It was on the sailboat. He was looking out at the horizon, mouth parted, brows drawn in concentration. I'm clicking the left arrow so fast I'm going to get a blister on my thumb.

And then—wait a minute. I screech to a halt. There are pictures here I don't remember taking from earlier this morning.

Orangey-pink streaks place the photos at the six-thirty sunrise, but the figure in the photo is not someone I remember being at the beach.

I zoom in, and with a flash of realization that feels more like a fatal lightning strike, I place the person: *me.*

Weston took pictures of my sunrise dance session and said nothing.

My heart is in my throat as I scroll through the pictures, every inch of my body stiff and horrified and curious. The first thing I notice: *holy shit, Weston knows how to take pictures.* And the second thing I notice: *holy shit, these pictures he took of me are excellent.*

I sit in the uncomfortable realization that I am looking at gorgeous photos of my own body. It's not something I ever thought might happen, I'm sad to say. But it *has* happened. And Weston caught it. Like a quiet, selfless gift to me. One that means more to me than I can actually let him know.

I abandon my quest to find Weston's hot picture, jarred by the discovery. Instead, I set down the camera and lie on my bed, staring at the ceiling, for so long that I lose track of time. It could be ten p.m. or two a.m. I honestly have no idea.

But eventually, the horniness returns. Oh lord, doesn't it always? Except this time, I don't need his picture, and I don't even want to be on my bed. I want running water and the memory of Weston as I saw him this morning, belly crinkled and cheek dimpled as he smiled up at me. These are dangerous thoughts for a girl like me. Because what turns me on the most is not the idea of some erotic hookup with any old hot guy.

No, what turns me on the most is the image of Weston as I've come to know him over the past few days. Annoying bits and all. With his cocky heartbreaker smiles and his endless abs and that way he can get under my skin with just a scoff or rolling his eyes.

The shower is spraying warm water, and I've shucked my bra and panties. I step into the stream, and my head lolls back. I press up against the cool tile of the shower wall, my hand venturing between my legs as the water washes down my chest and legs. My pussy is wet, and not from the shower. I've been in a permanent state of arousal since discovering Weston here, and it's a miracle I haven't knocked on his door in the middle of the night, demanding we violate a noise ordinance together.

I bite at my bottom lip as my middle finger slips back and forth over the tight nub of my clit. My entire body jolts, sending my back arching. I start to moan but I swallow it. It already feels too good, too necessary. I spread my legs, rubbing my fingers in long, looping swirls around my clit. I buck my hips, loving the teasing, even if it's coming from me. My nipples have turned into tight points, and just imagining Weston's pouty lips on one sends a moan tumbling past my lips.

Oops, I couldn't hold that one back. But it's okay. The ocean is so loud, and nobody is here anyway. I could probably stomp my way through an aerobics workout without any of my hut neighbors realizing. I slip a finger inside myself, fantasizing about Weston's cock. How thick. How long. What his favorite position is.

The mere thought of Weston's fully naked body on top of me sends my head thumping against the wall. In my head, I'm moaning *Oh, Weston. Oh, Weston.* Imagining his rough hands cupping my breasts. My core tightens—I'm fucking close, and I haven't even fantasized about having sex yet. That's how hot the man is.

Another thump comes, registering distantly. My head lolls to the side as my fingers slip in and out of my pussy easily.

And then I hear a tentative bass say, "Nova?"

Everything screeches to a halt, like someone pressed pause on the movie. Finger buried inside myself, I stare at the showerhead. Maybe I imagined the voice. Like how I imagined Weston's nakedness and hot kisses on my nipples. My eyes flutter shut again. *There's nobody outside. You totally heard that in your head.*

"Nova, did you call me?"

My eyes shoot open again. *Fuck fuck fuck.* There is most definitely someone out there, and there's a 100% chance that it's Weston.

"Uh…" I push to standing, the water hitting my shoulders as I look around, trying to figure out where to go from here. I turn off the water, stepping carefully out of the tub. "Who is it?"

"Weston."

I stand in the middle of the bathroom, hands covering face as my embarrassment drips down and pools beneath my feet with the water. There's no way this is happening. What did he mean by "call me"? This has to be one of his little jokes.

He thumps on the door again. "Nova."

I clear my throat, finally reaching for my towel. "I'm sorry, do you need something?"

"I just wanted to make sure you're okay in there. You called my name."

Oh god. I'm living in the worst-case scenario. That *Oh, Weston* was *not* only in my head as I intended. It leaked out of my goddamn lips.

"Uh…" Every cell of my body is doubling over with humiliation. I would just melt onto the floor and drip into the sand beneath this hut if I could. I press my hand over my eyes, struggling to remember how to think. What breathing feels like. If there's any protocol for being interrupted during a masturbation session by the subject of the masturbation fantasies.

If there are guidelines for this included in the handbook of womanhood, I certainly never got the updated version. Or even the damn handbook itself.

"I heard some noises." Jesus, this sexy man just *will not take a hint.* I need him to leave, so that I can complete my transformation into a mortified beet without any witnesses.

But no. He insists on adding more. And this time, when he speaks, my stomach dislodges from my body and shatters into pieces on the ground.

"Actually," he adds, "It sounded like you were masturbating."

CHAPTER TWELVE

WESTON

If Nova were anyone else—and I literally mean *anybody else on the face of the planet*—I would have just kept walking.

I would not have lingered around her hut, listening intently to the sexy whimpers and occasional moans escaping through the high vent window of her bathroom.

Hey, we all need private time in the bathroom. I'm no exception. I've jacked off four times in three days, each time with Nova's creamy legs in mind and imagining burying my face in her lush cleavage. But up until now, I wasn't convinced that Nova saw me as anything other than an irritating addition to the wedding party whom she was forced to tolerate.

And hell, maybe she still believes the annoying part. But there's a very important new dimension of her little game here that has been scientifically verified by the power of observation and measurement.

She fucking wants me.

She wasn't calling out for her boyfriend, who I'm not even convinced she has. She wasn't moaning any other guy's name. No. She fucking said "Weston."

Checkmate, Nova. You lost.

Now it's time for both of us to win.

When Nova doesn't say anything, I repeat myself. "Did you hear me? I said it sounded like you were masturbating." I'm being brash. So unforgivably bold. But I'm sick of her cowering. Not when we both want it and there's a measly two inches of palm-frond tiki hut separating us.

"God, Weston! Go away!"

A grin stretches across my lips. The exasperation in her voice is amusing. Yeah, I'd be pretty exasperated if someone interrupted me before orgasm. She just doesn't understand how much I want to be there when she reaches it.

"I wanted to talk—"

"About what? Jesus, this is mortifying."

"What's mortifying?"

"You're really going to make me say it?" she wails. Footsteps stomp through the hut. I can just imagine how flustered she is. The pink creeping across those cheeks. The wild tousle of her hair—or maybe those red locks would be hanging damp down her back. My cock is swelling the more I think about it.

"If I had to choose a word," I say, my heart pounding as I assess the ridge showing in my swim shorts. "It wouldn't be mortifying."

"Oh, I'm sure you could come up with a hundred other words for it, all synonyms for 'hilarious,'" she spits.

I drag my thumb across my bottom lip. "No, I would call it pretty fucking sexy, overhearing that. Which, by the way, was an accident."

There's an unnerving silence from inside the hut. She's probably disappeared into the shower to wash away the humiliation.

"You should come out here," I say, firmer this time. My ears are ringing, I'm listening to the silence so intently. But nothing comes. No stomping. No sighing. No quiet trek to the door, which she will eventually open to invite me inside.

I can't be imagining this attraction. I've seen the heat in her gaze. I know she can feel how bad I want her. How hard it is for me to keep this attraction under wraps. I'm at her door, practically begging for it. Will it be enough? Or does she need me to lay it balls out and obvious for her?

I look behind me, maybe searching for some backup. Some moral support. Someone to say, *No, no, keep going Weston, this is totally a great and sane idea.*

"I'm actually going to stay inside my hut until the earth reclaims my body," she says. "So if you could just leave now, that'd be great."

I laugh. "Promise me you won't deprive the earth of your amazing body."

More silence thuds between us. And then she says, "You must be high."

"Not high. Not even drunk. Just a red-blooded male with a pair of eyes."

There's more silence, and now the reality of the situation is setting in. Does this qualify as harassment? Knowing somebody wants you, but the only obstacle is actually herself? Maybe this is as far as Nova and I will go. Being horny for each other from opposite sides of a palm-frond wall. Forever wondering just how well we might get along, underneath the bedsheets and beyond.

"Listen. I get the sense that you have no idea how fucking hot you are. Which is hard to believe, but I don't know, I guess it's possible." My heart is thumping, and I press my forehead against her door. "But more than that, I think this is my chance to lay all my cards on the table, Nova. So yeah. You're hot. Big deal. But you're weird and funny and a really fucking great photographer, and I like you." All the breath whooshes out of me with that line. I take a moment to recoup. "So if you change your mind...you can find me at the pool. I'm serious. And wear the green bikini. I'll be waiting."

I wet my bottom lip, wondering if she can hear from in there how hard my heart is pounding. I listen for some sign that I got to her. Some sign that she has any interest at all in exploring the sexual and emotional connection that has always sizzled between us, even when we didn't realize it.

"You'll be waiting a long time, because I have some decomposing to do now," she says, her voice fainter.

"Decomposition is sexy too," I say, then tear myself away from her door. Everything is dizzy and wild. I would spend the next twelve hours at her door, trading quips and conversation until I couldn't stand on my own two legs anymore. But I need to go. I have enough sense to know that if Nova doesn't want it, then I need to leave her be.

I left the metaphorical door open for her. All I can do is hope that she runs through it.

I stop at my hut, flick on the light, and rummage through my big backpack for my notebook. I'd been in the middle of readying to go to the pool for a late-night, low-people swim when I overheard her in her hut. But then *all that* happened, so I need to focus my energy on something or I'm going to snap.

So sketching it is. Tried and true method of handling intense energy. Like when the woman you've been fantasizing about non-stop for the past three days is fantasizing about you too but won't do anything about it.

I don't expect her to show up, not even a little bit, even though every cell of my body is vibrating with hope. So that means I bring everything with me. Including a condom, because I'm trying to be positive. My phone, my sketchbook, all my pencils, my camera, a second notebook. I shove it all into a little hippie tote bag I picked up in Morocco years ago, sling it over my shoulder, and head for the pool closest to our neck of the resort.

Each footstep away from the huts is a reminder of what I'm walking away from: Nova, possibly naked, definitely turned on, probably with her hand between her legs thinking about me. I falter in my quest, ready to turn around and make a second attempt at convincing her to replace her hand with my mouth, but no. I force myself to keep walking to the pool.

The small kidney-bean pool set off in an alcove of gardenias and palm tree cover is one of the less-used pools here, probably because it doesn't have a bar attached to it, or a diving board. I drop my bag on one of the cushioned lounge chairs and start pacing. Who am I fucking kidding? I'm not going to be able to sketch. I need to burn off this sexual energy. I tear off my clothes down to my swim trunks and slip into the pool.

This warm water at the end of long, great day—it should be exactly what I've been waiting for. But when the water fails to soothe me in any discernible way, it's because the truth that has been simmering below the surface has now kicked up to a dangerous boil.

I want Nova.

Which means it's time for laps.

And lots of them.

CHAPTER THIRTEEN

NOVA

I'm taking stock of my life in the pulsating and painful eternities that follow Weston calling me out. Thinking back on all the failures and quiet victories I've amassed in the three days on this special-though-possibly-cursed island.

Negatives: I've failed at being someone's intimacy partner. Basically farted in Weston's mouth. Tripped and needed his help saving my life and my most precious camera equipment. Got caught masturbating and moaning his name.

Pluses: Are there any? Oh wait, yes, there's one major one. Enormous one, actually. He called me hot and funny and weird.

My heart is thumping so fast that I feel dizzy. I'm balanced on a particular type of tight rope, the one that precedes making life-changing decisions. Which way I fall off the rope—because I'm going to—determines if I fall into the future or into the past.

And for once in my fucking life, I want to fall into the future.

If I've farted and failed *and* flailed, and somehow Weston still wants me?

Then by God, the man deserves this hot mess.

I fumble through finding my bikini, because I'm so jazzed and nervous that I can barely see straight. First I can only find the bottoms, then after I find the string bikini top, I've lost the bottoms all over again. I ram my knee into the bedpost, rediscover the bikini bottoms, and then put them on backward. Finally, I stand in the middle of my room, bikini ass backwards, and expel a fortifying breath of air.

Get your shit together. I can't go meet Weston for my very first illicit island encounter and just unravel on the spot. At this rate, I'll probably orgasm before he even touches me. He has the upper hand, and he probably knows it. I need to arrive cool and collected.

Yes. Nova, cool, calm, and collected, before hooking up with the world's hottest playboy.

One hundred percent not happening.

I barely remember to grab my beach towel before I bolt out of the hut. Of course, doubts lurk in the back of my mind. *Will he really be there? Is he actually serious about this? Is this the adult version of the cool kids playing a trick on me?*

But something warm and inviting about Weston makes me willing to throw caution to the wind for this wild one-off. Call it my Aruban insanity. But however hard it is to accept that Weston actually *wants this bodacious bod,* it's even harder for me to accept a reality in which I wake up tomorrow and didn't at least try.

I don't even take sandals with me; I just speed walk down the boardwalk, breathless and focused on whatever might come next. Palm trees blur past me. I trip twice on the wood planks. I might have a splinter, but I *do not even care.*

Then I arrive. Oh lord, I arrive to the kidney-bean pool, lit up in in varying neon colors, the cerulean water lapping gently at the edges. The pool nook is empty, except for what I assume to be Weston's ridiculous hippie bag stashed on an abandoned lounge chair. A dark figure moves beneath the water, and my heart starts racing again. As if it ever stopped. Now I'm approaching bona fide *I might need a doctor* territory. I drop my towel next to his bag and climb down the ladder into the warm pool while he's swimming underwater.

Weston surfaces after a moment, sputtering water. He's facing away from me as I silently ease into the now-neon-pink water. My toes reach the bottom of the pool, but just barely. He's breathing heavily, staring out at the boardwalk.

Excitement shivers through me. He has no idea I'm here. I feel so powerful, drunk on possibility and potential. Should I sexily swim up to him and lick his shoulder? Wait, that's not sexy. Or just wait until he spots me and let him come to me? This is like every single adolescent fantasy come to life at once—being lusted after, being chased, being wrong about a man, being eyed by the hottest man on the planet. I'm so close to meltdown, and we haven't even kissed.

Weston sighs and runs a hand through his damp hair. The broad muscles of his back are dripping with water, biceps bulging as he sinks down into the water again. And then he turns.

The air cinches tight between us, every millisecond of time stretching long and bloated and charged. I can feel his gaze shivering over me, the pinpricks of awareness and delight as he beholds me. And fuck, yeah, maybe I'm imagining all of this? But maybe I'm allowed to get swept up in the fantasy for one night. If he's willing to go there, then I should be too.

The most deliciously evil smile curls at his lips, his blue eyes flashing. Water sloshes around him as he launches toward me, arms stretching out as he makes powerful strides through the water.

I've never felt so simultaneously ready and on edge. As he nears, my impulse is to back up, to float away from his overwhelming masculine energy. I've never been approached like this, even though I've been waiting my whole life to receive it. I barely breathe as I watch him swim toward me. And then suddenly his gorgeous face is in front of me, closer than it's ever been. I'm getting lost in the infinite swirl of his ice-blue eyes, tripping over the tiny smile lines at his eyes and the fullness of his lips when the masculine warmth of him hits me.

"You came," he says, his voice a guttural scrape as he floats inches away from me. He's treading water in front of me, our heads level, lips so close that it hurts. My gaze ping-pongs back and forth across his intense face. His strong collarbone. The watery transition into the rest of him, which I'm dying to get to know for myself.

"No, I actually thought I'd stay in tonight," I say, because I am unable to control my mouth. His mouth slants in an amused smirk.

"Real funny," he says, swimming perilously closer, so close that I can feel his hot breath. My eyes flutter shut, reminding me of the seriousness of what is about to happen. "Open your eyes."

I snap them open, forcing myself to meet his intense gaze. "Why?"

"Because we need to get on the level." The currents of water from his moving arms send shivers up my spine. The spicy tang of him is mind-numbing. Beguiling. Something I might never want to live without.

"What level is that?" My gaze wanders along the strong lines of his collarbone, over his tanned shoulder. I might be drooling.

"Your boyfriend back home."

My brows draw together, the brakes pumping on the lust train. "And who is that?"

"You tell me." He comes to standing now, rising out of the water, reminding me of how much taller he is than me. Water drops run down his chest, partially erasing the protests on my tongue. Sorry, say what? This flat, broad, tanned chest has completely derailed me.

"I don't—" The rest of my sentence dissolves. We are *so close* to touching, the planes of his chest making my fingers curl with the urge to dance across his perfect body.

"I don't want to start trouble," he says, wetting his bottom lip as his gaze washes over me. "But you need to tell me now because I'm about ten seconds away from starting trouble anyway."

My eyes flutter shut again as the sexiness of his words wash over me. I made the right decision in coming here. That sentence alone makes everything worth it.

"I don't have a boyfriend back home," I manage to say, glancing down at where his belly meets the water. Wondering what else is happening down there. "Or anywhere. I am chronically single. I'm a born-again virgin, basically."

The words barely escape my lips before Weston surges forward and cups my face and smashes his lips to mine. He is heat and crushed velvet against my lips. Every inch of my body screams with relief as he kisses me once, then again. Then his tongue presses past my lips and oh! Oh my heavens, my core is aching, and everything I thought I knew about good kisses prior to this moment dissolves in a puff.

He's backing me up as our kisses grow deeper and longer. My chest touches his as he floats me backwards, one of his hands dropping to my leg. He urges it up to his hip, and in one fluid motion both of my legs are around him, ankles crossed behind his butt. He grunts through a kiss, his palms pushing up the wide expanse of my thighs until he's got my ass cheeks overflowing in his hands. My kneejerk reaction is to apologize for my size, to remind him that I don't look like half the girls on this island, to explain that I already *understand* that I'm big.

But I'm too distracted. By the kissing. The sensations. The body buzz that is so desperately close to an orgasm. Finally, my back touches the cool tile side of the pool, and then his chest presses against mine. He has a solidity I never knew I needed. I melt against him, finally remembering through the haze of the mind-numbing kisses that I have hands and can use them.

I tentatively touch his chest. His skin is firm and warm beneath my fingertips. I palm the expanse of his chest, finally daring to drag my fingers lower until I find the ridges of those washboard abs. I whimper though another kiss.

Weston pulls back, chest heaving. He searches my eyes, and the look of kiss-bitten lips on him reaches an unknown level of sexiness. My kisses gave him this drugged-out look. *Mine.*

"Jesus Christ, Nova," he breathes, pressing his forehead to mine. He squeezes my butt, sending lust racing through my veins. And then I feel it. The hard ridge of his cock trapped against my hip. If there was any proof out there that this wasn't just a cruel trick by the cool kid, well, this is it. He wants me. He fucking wants me. I tighten my legs around him, wanting to abolish any inch of space that remains between us.

"I can't believe this is happening," I whisper, nuzzling his cheek with my face. Part of me is terrified that I'll wake up and find myself alone in my hut, hand buried in my underwear. Maybe this is a hallucination prompted by the beach air.

But when Weston presses his lips to mine in another kiss, truth sears through me. This is no hallucination. Hell, this isn't even a trick. This is unabashed sexy time.

I squeeze my legs around him even tighter as our kisses pick up, more intense than the first round. I moan through a kiss, pushing my hand lower, lower, lower, until my fingers brush the soft, velvety tip of...his penis? I gasp, pulling away. Weston expels a low breath, his hips jerking.

"You know I have a dick, right?" he jokes.

"Yes, I just wasn't expecting to touch it already." My mind catches up with my words, and I hurry to clarify. "I mean, don't get me wrong. I want to touch it. Today. And put it other places like...my mouth." As I talk, his smile slowly grows wider. "And, you know...other places. I just..." My fingers drift back down to caress his exposed cockhead. "I just didn't realize it would be escaping from your pants already."

His grin grows evil, and he dips down for another kiss. "It's kind of big. Your fault, though."

I tip my head back and smile as he kisses me again. This is heaven, right here. I'm not sure I've ever felt this sexy, this turned on. My pussy is throbbing as he adjusts himself, allowing the ridge of his cock to press up against the crotch of my bikini.

"Ohhhhh," I begin, my vowels bleeding into a moan. He thrusts ever so slightly, that steel heat nudging my clit in just the right way. My thighs go tighter around him, and heat zips through my veins. My breath wheezes out of me—just narrowly missed that orgasm.

"Be careful," I say, though I'm not sure the words actually leave my mouth.

His lips find the curve of my neck, tracing a damp path down to the hollow. His teeth scrape against my collarbone, and I arch into him, squeezing my arms around his neck.

"Mmm. Fuck, Nova." He jiggles my butt cheeks, reaffirming his healthy handful. His eyes are shrouded with lust. "Do you know how many times I've imagined this?"

His simple question leaves me sputtering. He's actually imagined *doing this* with *me*? It seems impossible, like some sort of theoretically null math equation just designed to fuck with scientists' heads.

Of *course* Weston's penis does not equal Nova's vagina. It's baked into the fabric of reality.

Unless my whole concept of life on Earth is wrong.

"You mean like, before right now?" I clarify.

His hoists me higher, nearly out of the water. His biceps bulge, but he doesn't falter. His lips drift lower, perilously near to my cleavage. My breath catches as he takes a soft bite of the top part of my breast. How is it possible that ten minutes in, he's already the best lover I've ever had?

"Mm hmm." His tongue finds the ravine of my cleavage, and my hands go to the back of his head, tugging gently on his hair. I flex against him. I love having my tits played with, and the sight of his head buried there is nearly fatal to my composure.

"I...I can't..." My head lolls to the side as he bites at my hard nipple through the bikini.

"Three times today alone," he says, rocking his hips so that his cock rides up against my clit again. "Five times yesterday."

"F...Five?"

His tongue flattens over my nipple, and even through the fabric of my bikini, it feels amazing. He straightens again, his cock finding the crease of my pussy. The molten heat of him slips up against my clit, just as he tweaks my aching nipple. I gasp, everything going taut and explosive inside me.

NO NO NO. I cannot orgasm yet. A sound like choking escapes me as I fight against the sensation. Orgasming with Weston *is* the goal, just not in the first ten minutes of chaste pool floating. Well, okay. This is far from chaste. But it's far from penetration, too.

"Noooova," he growls, tweaking my nipple once more in time with another thrust of his powerful hips. And then that's it—I'm a goner. I squeak out a feeble protest as the pleasure washes through me in sticky, surprising waves. I bury my face in his shoulder as my body jerks once, twice. When I peer up at Weston, he has a satisfied grin waiting for me.

"That easy, huh?"

"Stop it. I've just been really horny lately."

His gaze grows clouded. "Oh yeah?"

"Some super-hot guy wandering around the resort constantly," I wheeze as he begins nuzzling my cleavage again. "Picking fights. Being shirtless. It's a turn on."

He grunts, gathering me closer to him. "Your hut or mine?"

My heart starts racing again. "Mine."

"Let's go." He pauses to snag another kiss, this one sloppy yet somehow more intimate. "Except you need to go first."

I frown. "You don't want to be seen with me or something?"

A humorless laugh escapes him. "Trust me—it's not that." He rocks his hips in a slow circle again, leveling me with his gaze, as if to say, *Do you get it now?*

"Ah, yes. Well, I can lead the way, if you want."

He takes a soft bite at my neck. "I'll follow you wherever you go."

His sexy, oddly romantic words sizzle through me, prompting one of those silly grins that it's so easy to make fun of friends for. "Even if I go straight back to the bar?"

He snags my lips in another kiss. "Don't do that. I don't want to scare the families with what I plan to do to you."

Excitement shivers up my spine, every inch of my body tingling and ready. "Okay. I'm ready to get this show on the road." When I try to push off, he holds me tighter.

"Wait." Grinning, he coaxes another kiss from my lips. And then another.

"Now?" I ask, once round three of kissing is completed.

He grunts, brushing his lips against mine. "You're hard to let go of."

The compliment sinks all the way to my bones, where I hope it lives forever. There's no hiding it—Weston is a fantasy come true for me. I might geek out about this for the next three years.

We kiss sloppily, noisily, for another few minutes, until both our chests are heaving and his cock is absolutely throbbing against my aching pussy. I'm five seconds away from telling him to just stick it in now and end the torture.

But finally he steps away, resting his palms on the top of his head. He lets out a low exhale, gaze stuck on my cleavage.

"Okay. Hurry," he says.

I do as he says, pulling myself out of the pool by the ladder. When I look back at him, he's biting his lower lip, intently watching me walk back to where our things are stored. He pulls himself out of the pool then. A laugh bursts out of me when I catch the insane tenting going on between his legs.

"Oh my god," I say, reaching for it. He stays a safe distance away though.

"Nova, if you touch me right now—" He fists the front of his hair, looking down at his pants then at me. "We're not making it back to the hut."

I wrap my towel around my waist. "But what if I just touch it a *little*?"

His eyes narrow to slits. "Not helpful." He snatches up his bag, slinging it over his chest, his gaze drifting back to me. "But once we get back to your hut, you can touch it all you want."

I drift back toward him, but he pinches the bridge of his nose, squeezing his eyes shut. "Nova, you have to leave. I can't touch you or look at you or I'm never gonna make it back."

This is the most gratifying compromise I've ever had to make. Leave the hottie alone so he can *recuperate* from being turned on by me. I make a big display of blowing him a kiss, and then I saunter away, as outrageously sexy as possible. I wink over my shoulder at him, and the sight I'm leaving behind is something I wish I could photograph and frame for all of eternity: Weston, dragging his thumb along his jawline, his heated gaze stuck on me.

In those blue eyes I see everything. Desire. Passion. Amusement.

But more than that, I see a deep appreciation. The type of glimmer in his eye that makes me think we've been poking and prodding and playing around for years instead of hours.

It's the type of look I want to dive into.

And tonight, I plan to drown in it.

CHAPTER FOURTEEN

WESTON

I pace the side of the pool for approximately thirty seconds before I say, *Fuck it.*

I will risk looking like a fool with a banana in his pants because each second spent without touching or kissing or inhaling that luscious woman is a second wasted.

I arrange my crossbody bag so that it *sort of* obscures my hardon, even though it doesn't at all. At the boardwalk, I look up and down the path—coast is clear—before booking it toward the beach. I race toward the pot of gold at the end of the rainbow—Nova's hut—and I'm knocking and anxious like I'm escaping a zombie attack.

She flings open the door, eyes wild and hair plastered to her shoulders. I grip the wood of the doorframe, drinking her in, still unable to believe that we made it here. Somehow. *Finally.*

I cup her heart-shaped face as I step inside, kicking the door shut behind me with my foot. She giggles, her glittery green gaze bouncing across my face. I back her up toward the bed.

"You're mine now, Nova."

Her breath catches as the backs of her knees hit the bed. My crossbody bag is trapped between us as I dip down for another mind-numbing kiss. The woman's lips are the lovechild of fairies and porn stars. She inspires mischief as much as screeching lust, and I could spend a year kissing her and still want just one more pass at that mouth. Her hands go to the strap of my bag, and when the kiss breaks, she's lifting it up gently.

"What the hell is in here?"

"Nothing." I gather the focus to take the bag off. I set it carefully on a nearby chair.

"That's awfully delicate handling for nothing."

I smirk, returning to my post between her legs. I guide her back to sitting, hoisting her by the hips so that her thighs splay open. "It's my sketchbook. And my camera."

Something unreadable passes over her face. "You sketch?"

"Yeah."

She groans, flopping back onto the bed. "Why'd you have to go and get hotter?"

Desire thrums through me, pulsing and urgent, as I assess her splayed out on the bed. My cock is trapped beneath the waistband of my swim shorts, the head bulging out. I drop my head down to her creamy belly, smoothing my lips over the smooth skin. She shivers beneath me, goosepimples flaring over her skin.

"Weston—"

"What?" My kisses venture lower. I honestly don't know where to start. I want to eat her pussy as much as I want to tease her nipples until that look of languid shock creases her face again. I push my palms up the sides of her cool thighs, tugging at the top of her bikini bottoms with my teeth.

"You aren't—"

"What?" I grin as my plan becomes clear. Pussy-eating is definitely first on the agenda.

"Don't feel obligated. You don't have to."

"Have to what?" I tug at the knots holding her bottoms together at the sides. She gasps, wriggling beneath me.

She lets out a little grunt. "You know what I'm talking about."

"I don't. You can't possibly be asking me not to eat your gorgeous pussy." The knot on the left side dissolves. I press my mouth to the damp crotch of her bikini, taking a few measured breaths there as I look up at her. Her legs have splayed open even farther.

"You don't know it's gorgeous."

I yank hard at the bikini, revealing her swollen pussy. Tightly trimmed, dark red hair adorns her mons, and she is juicy, dripping with arousal. I wet my bottom lip, my cock twitching.

"I actually do know it's gorgeous."

She squirms, so I press soft kisses up the inside of her thigh. A long sigh escapes her.

"You understand that I *want* to do this, right?" I kiss higher up her thigh, enjoying how much she's wriggling in anticipation. I'm so close I can taste it—and smell her. Another kiss up her thigh. She whimpers.

"I just...can't take it."

"Hm." I nuzzle the seam of her thigh where it meets her groin. "You're gonna have to."

She bucks, as if urging me along. "Westonnn."

"What is it, Nova?" I bring my mouth up toward the swollen lips of her pussy, but I don't touch them. Yet. I just breathe.

She groans. "Are you trying to torture me? Like some sort of payback for the yoga class?"

I pull back, genuinely ticked by the suggestion. "You think I'm not taking my pussy-eating duties seriously."

She snorts, going limp on the bed. "I swear to God."

"You didn't even want me to do it, and now you're criticizing my performance." It's too easy to spar with her. It's too fucking *fun*.

A helpless laugh escapes her as she stares up at the ceiling like she's pleading with God himself.

"Maybe I won't even now," I tease, nuzzling her thigh so she knows I'm full of shit. As if I could stay away from this. From her.

She wriggles again, sighing. "You are trying to kill me, aren't you?"

"No," I say simply, finally bringing my lips to her swollen folds. "I'm trying to make you feel better than you ever have before."

I flatten my tongue against the tight bud of her clit. She goes limp, a low moan escaping her, as I flick my tongue back and forth. I watch her reactions as I fuck her with my tongue. This is the type of shit I like to do with the right women, but they don't come around often. I don't know why Nova feels like the right one, except that she does.

"Ohhhh my GOD."

I press my lips to her clit, easing a finger into her pussy. And lord, she's tight. Tighter than I imagined. My cock twitches again, reminding me of the urgency here. How my fantasies are minutes away from becoming reality. Scratch that. Actively becoming a reality.

I scrape my teeth against her clit. Her ass comes off the bed, accompanied by a whimper. I pin her down at the hips with my palms, burying my face between her legs.

And this time, I don't tease. I don't let up. I want her juicy and unraveled and losing it. I need her that way if I'm ever going to fit inside her. Nova squirms and whines and calls my name over and over and over. She's fighting an uphill battle, trying to escape this orgasm that I am hellbent on giving her. She's bucking and moving against me at the same time, and I just hold her down and lavish her clit with attention.

Soon she's quaking, her tummy going tense and her thighs rigid. She moans and covers her face with her hands. The bedspread beneath her is soaked. I like to see evidence like that. It means I'm doing a damn fine job. She's breathless and heaving while I push to standing and head for my bag.

Her nipples are tight points beneath her bikini, rising and falling as she recuperates, hair tousled and wild around her on the bed. I rummage for the condom, unable to see straight from how much my cock is taking over all my available brain function. I have to remove every single fucking thing from my bag before I find the foil packet at the bottom.

"You thought ahead." Her voice is husky and sated. She's propped up onto her elbows, blinking lazily with a little smile on her face. I like that I put that look on her face. I consider myself a generous lover in general, but something about Nova makes me want to go above and beyond.

"I was being optimistic," I confess, holding the condom packet between my teeth as I step out of my swim trunks. My cock bobs heavily, hard as a fucking rock. Her mouth form an O as she beholds it.

"That's just a prosthesis, right?" she asks. "Something you can take off, and your normal-sized, smaller dick is hiding inside?"

I crawl onto the bed, grinning like a fool with the condom between my teeth. Yeah, they're XL. I might be the softest Daly brother, the true bona fide last place of the family...but swear to God, I've got the biggest dick. And maybe that balances the scales.

"Bad news, Nova," I tell her letting the condom fall onto her chest. "This *is* the small dick."

She wriggles again, her pink lips quirking into a teasing smile. "I don't know if this one is gonna work. It's too big for the job."

I tut, shaking my head. "I think your own equipment is perfectly prepared. Why else do you think I got you all juicy and lubed up?"

She snorts. "You make me sound like something a mechanic works on."

"Just consider me the pussy mechanic." I lower myself, coaxing a long, sloppy kiss from her. She hums at the tail end of it, a smile covering her face as I pull away.

"You're goofy," she says, but the warmth in her tone tells me she means it as a high compliment. Because that's how I feel about her. She's goofy, in the best way possible. I've never wanted to be a pussy mechanic for anyone else, much less on the first night of sex. But Nova is a confusing blend of familiar and erotic. Splayed out here on the bed like this, she looks and feels like a lover I've been coming to—and with—for years. Even though we only ended the cold war earlier today.

I dip down for another kiss, and then another. I'm so ready to feel her deepest, most intimate part, I could come if thought too hard about it.

When we break apart, I tear open the condom packet, and my hand trembles as I roll it down over my cock. Her breath catches when I ease back on top of her.

"I'll go slow," I promise when I catch her nibbling on her bottom lip.

"Don't split me in two," she whispers, smoothing her hands over the tops of my shoulders.

"Can't promise that," I whisper before planting another kiss against her velvety lips. "But only the good splitting, I swear."

I reach down between our bodies to help guide myself inside her. My cockhead slips in after a few glorious moments of pressure and sighs. Once it's in, warmth floods me and she's moaning.

"Jesus, Weston."

"I know." I catch the tremble in my voice; I wonder if she does too. I sink into her slowly. Deliberately. Watching her for any sign that it's too much or too fast.

But she takes it all, her eyes alive and wild, locked with mine as I sink deeper and deeper. Her chest heaves, that green bikini covering her full tits and rock-hard nipples. I pause, tugging the scraps of fabric down until her breasts spill out. Beautiful, pebbled pink nipples greet me, and I scoop up each one in my mouth in turn.

"Ohhh, Weston." Her voice is breathier now. Farther away. I snag a nipple between my teeth as I push into her a little more. And then a little more.

"Tell me if it's too much."

She whimpers, stilling me with her palms pressed to my shoulders. "Oh, my God. Your dick is literally coming out of my back."

I laugh into her shoulder. "You said you wanted to be impaled, right?"

Her laughter is low, guttural. A little crazy. "Yes. Now give it all to me."

I sink deeper inside of her, burying myself to the hilt. Her pussy has swallowed every last inch of me. Sweat beads at my temples. I haven't even moved against her, and beating back this orgasm is a herculean effort.

"Oh, my lord," she whispers, her eyes fluttering shut.

"Open your eyes, Nova." I press soft kisses along her collarbone. "Look at me."

She does as I say, her green gaze snapping to find mine. I rock against her, loving the wash of emotions that cross her face. A strangled noise escapes her, equal parts feminine and animalistic. *Yes.* That's what I want to hear. Exactly that level of pleasure.

"You are so...fucking..."

"Hard? Close to coming?" I rock against her again, enjoying the jiggle of her breasts as I do. "Both are true."

"You forgot sexy." She digs her fingernails into my biceps. "And sweet. And sooo fucking sexy."

I smirk. "You said sexy twice. Be more creative."

A sharp laugh erupts from her. "Shit. Did I? I meant snarky. Sexy, sweet, and snarky as fuck."

I begin easing myself out of her, gritting my teeth against the heat stalking my insides. If I give in, it threatens to spill over and drown me. "Well that's nothing compared to you."

"Oh, please," she slaps at my arm.

"You are the sexiest and the snarkiest of all," I tell her, sitting back to grab my cock and rub it all over her juicy folds. She inhales sharply, closing her legs around my sides as I rub my cockhead back and forth over her clit.

"Ohhhhmyfuckinggod," she says, and then I plunge myself back inside her. There's less resistance this time, but she's still tight as hell. My shoulders prickle as she lifts her hips, pussy clamping around me. I scoop her up into my arms, burying my face in her cleavage. Happiness—and a whole lot more—buzzes through me.

I never counted on this. On it feeling like this. On her meshing with me like this. I push into her again, and then I guide her legs up, so that she can hook her ankles behind my back. A groan rips out of me as I sink even deeper this time. She claws at my chest, cheeks flushed.

"It feels too good," she moans. I pull out of her again, my belly going taut. I'm at the end of my rope here. Sweat starts to trickle down my temple. I push into her, more forcefully, grinding up against her so that she can feel every last inch of my desire. I rock my hips in a slow circle, burying my face in her neck.

She clamps down around me again, consuming the last ounce of my control. I sink my teeth into the soft part of her neck as my belly jerks. A moan rips out of me, my cock spasming as the orgasm pummels through me.

Once I can hear and see again, Nova's chest is heaving. She's clutching my arm as if it's a life raft, and for a minute I think that maybe I left her hanging.

"Nova," I say, pushing onto my elbows. "I didn't…You came, right?"

"Like, a hundred times," she says, a lazy smile overtaking her face.

I nuzzle her nose. My heart is still pounding, and I'm drawing deep, labored breaths. Finally I roll off of her and sit up, gently freeing my cock from the sticky condom.

If this were a normal travel hookup, I'd have tossed the condom and be out the door by now. Hell, I wouldn't have spent so much time between her legs. Wouldn't have given half as many kisses.

But I don't want to leave. Not right now. Sure, my hut is ten feet away. But I'd rather stay less than ten inches away. And no, that's not a dick reference.

I toss the condom in the bathroom wastebasket, stumbling over my own swim trunks on my way back to the bed. Nova has her hands tucked under her cheek, watching me with a blissed out smile that says it all.

This was fucking great.

I'm not ready to let it end quite yet.

CHAPTER FIFTEEN

NOVA

Attentive. Sensual. Forceful but sensitive.

These are just a few of the words I'd use if I had to write a Yelp review of Weston's sexual performance. But since our society hasn't yet reached the point where we evaluate our bedromp proficiency on social media—THANK GOD—then I'll just have to giggle into my palm for the foreseeable future while I relieve every last dirty, hot, sexy thing that man and I did in my tiki hut.

The next morning, I rise naturally just a few minutes after six. Odd, considering Weston and I continued having sex until after two. But as I sit up, yawn, and catch sight of the gorgeous man lying next to me, his head resting on his big bicep, arm still draped over my hips as if making sure I'm not going anywhere, the adrenaline returns.

Did last night really freaking happen?

The perma-grin is back as I hobble toward the bathroom. I'm not sure I've ever felt so sexually satisfied, or so *sore*. Not even in my best fantasies have I ever felt so looked after. And I certainly never thought to fantasize about how sore my pelvis could be the following day.

But the aches don't matter. Not even a little bit. It's all worth living through the biggest surprise of my life, when the jerk-face ended up being the sweetest lover.

I tinkle and then pause by the front window to peek at the night. Dawn is on its way, the cobalt warning signals streaking across the horizon. I look back at Weston, wondering if he might want to catch this sunrise. But maybe he needs his sleep. I decide to venture out alone, and I hunt for my bikini in the darkness of the room. Once I've replaced the still-damp emerald green bikini that I will never get rid of simply because Weston is a fan of it, Weston is stirring in bed.

He cracks one eye open. The sight of him there—tousled, bleary, sculpted—makes me want to melt back onto the bed and never leave his side.

"You going swimming?" he asks, pushing up onto his elbow. The rough scrape of his just-woken-up voice makes something wrench in my chest. The same creeping realization began to unfold like a lotus last night.

"I wanna catch the sunrise."

He comes to sitting, blinking blearily as he looks around the room. "Can I come with?"

"Of course. I wanted you to, but I thought maybe you'd rather sleep."

"Nah." He heaves a sigh, rubbing at his face. "Sunrise wins every time."

He rolls out of bed, stumbling briefly as he searches for his swim trunks. I grab my camera bag and a towel, and once he's tugged his shorts on, he follows me out the door.

"You cold?" He slips an arm around my shoulders as we head toward the beach.

"No. But you can keep me warm anyway."

He smiles down at me, but I can't make out the best parts of his face in the darkness. Luckily, I absorbed enough details about last night that I could sketch his face for a detective if he were wanted in a murder.

Once we're close to the water, I drop my bag. Weston arranges the towel for us to sit on. He sits down, cross-legged, and caresses my ankle as I fiddle with my camera.

I know it's only been a few hours since our sex-a-thon ended, but part of me likes that he's keeping up the dream. This fantasy of *being together*.

I know I shouldn't be thinking like this, but it's hard not to. Because of who I am. Because of what Weston represents to me. Because how can I deny it? Weston is the guy of my fantasies. And not just because of what he did with his tongue last night.

"The show is starting," Weston says. I settle onto the towel next to him, nuzzling into his side when he slings his arm over my shoulder. The sky at the horizon is transitioning to indigo. As the sunrise pushes out the darkness, my gaze drifts to what's around me. Notably Weston at my side. The way our knees are touching. The warm security of his arm around me. He yawns, and then tips his head against mine.

And then the color show begins. Coral streaks the sky, illuminating some cloud wisps that had been lurking in the darkness. Weston says, "Mm hmm," as the sunrise stretches into infinity. I bring the camera up to my face and snap the nascent day. This is bliss. Pure and simple.

"Damn, day. You're looking pretty good," Weston says.

"Are you hitting on the sunrise?"

"Just stating facts."

I grin, twisting so that I can snap a picture of him. His heartbreaker smile fills my viewfinder. That wrench in my chest returns.

"Speaking of facts…" Weston says, wetting his bottom lip. "Damn, Nova. You're looking pretty good too."

I snicker, resting my head on his shoulder. "Don't toy with me. I know it's the sunrise you're after."

"Sunrise, and a little extra. You still down to do the dancing in the waves thing?"

"Oh, my God." I slap my forehead. "I can't believe you got pictures of that."

"So you found my secret."

"Yeah, I did!" I expel a sigh, but as the strawberry streaks turn into a brighter, clearer sky, I soften. "And you know what? Those were really lovely pictures."

"Thought you might think so. And if you didn't think so, I was ready to plead my case."

This attention doesn't just feel nice, it sizzles through me. Some part of me wants to curl up in his arms and never leave. Is this what all his other vacay-lays experience? The magical charms of Weston Daly have conquered probably too many women to count. Way more than I care to know about.

I didn't want to be just one more notch for him. But I couldn't resist. He's too thoughtful, too much of a snarky softie, for me to care right now.

"I guess we can dance in the waves, if it's so important to you," I say, snapping another picture.

"Look at those colors." Weston shakes his head. "Looks like a damn ice cream sundae."

"Does it?"

"Strawberry right there." He points at the sky. "Peaches there. And a dollop of whipped cream."

I grin so hard my cheeks hurt as I follow his vision. He's not wrong. "I bet it would be the best-tasting ice cream sundae of all time."

He looks down at me, laugh lines appearing around his eyes. For a moment, I get lost in his gaze. It's almost full daylight now, so I have no trouble drinking in all the details of his face. His nose is just this side of crooked, which makes his lopsided smile even cuter.

"Why did we never hook up before?" he asks, voice softer.

I shrug, looking back at the water. "You were always interested in other girls."

He scoffs. "Yeah right. I tried with you the first time we ever traveled together."

My jaw clatters to the towel. This information is so outrageous that I barely know how to process it. Weston actually liked me *since the beginning?* "You are crazy. You *never* tried."

"I did. And I was Rejected with a capital R."

I shake my head. "I don't believe you."

"You were so bristly, I never tried again."

Now my eyes pop wider. "Bristly? *You* were always the bristly one!"

"I've never been anything but an accommodating gentleman," he says, with a shit-eating grin on his face.

"Right. Like in the yoga class on Monday night?"

His eyes narrow. "I still want to redo that class."

"From what I remember, when we were in Amsterdam four years ago, on the *very first night*, you chose some Valley girl backpacker to bring back to the hostel."

His lips curve downward. "I don't remember any Valley girl."

"I do. And you chose her. Trust me—when I first met you, I would have done anything you asked of me."

"Is that why you've been full of bristles? Like a hairbrush," he says.

I snort, even though he's spot-on with his assessment. It feels wrong to admit that it was something so trivial that turned me off him. But he didn't do much to combat his playboy image over the years. And maybe he's truly no different now. I don't know—and for now, I just want to sit here and enjoy this.

"Calling me a hairbrush is the best insult you've got?"

His smile goes smooth. "Trust me. I wasn't trying to insult you." This time, when he looks down at me, the air goes taut between us. My breath evaporates, and then our lips are getting closer, ever closer, until we kiss in the strawberry swirl of the morning.

Whatever I thought prior to this moment about happiness was wrong. *This,* right here. This is true happiness. An exhaustion-tinged sunrise with a body buzz. The warmth of a man—no, *this* man—improving upon the already perfect air. Equal parts barbs and tenderness floating between us.

And I wonder, has it felt like this for him with anyone else?

My heart is throbbing, so I break the kiss and look back at the morning. This got too intense, way too quickly, but this peach cobbler dawn isn't helping things. Weston shifts at my side, resting his head against mine.

"I think this is the best sunrise I've ever seen," he says.

"Really? Of all the places you've been?"

"Yeah. Look at those clouds." He points. "You don't see those too often."

I snicker. But I agree with him. Not because of the clouds, though. It's the best sunrise because for the first time in a long time, things make sense.

"You don't see this too often, either," he says, his hand slipping down to squeeze my hip.

"Now you're referring to my enormous ass."

"No. I'm referring to this." He looks over at me. "Look at us. We're not fighting, for once."

"Give it time," I warn him with a grin. "If you aren't careful, I'll sign us up for another partner yoga class."

He leans in and kisses me again. "Go for it. We can only go up from here. Failing at yoga one day." The smile on his face grows slick, almost mischievous. "Farting in my face the next."

My eyes nearly pop out of my head as all sorts of conflicting responses clamor for airtime. Shock. Humiliation. Maniacal laughter. He must be able to read the shellshock on my face, because he just laughs and leans in again.

"Don't give me that face. It was cute."

I cover my face with my hands. "Weston! You can't say that me farting in your face was cute!"

"Pretty sure I just said it."

I laugh despite the embarrassment. Where else to go but up, like he said? "Couldn't you have just done the sweet thing and pretended it never happened and continued acting as though I don't have a butthole?"

This time, his laugh is a guffaw. "Sorry, but no. Your ass is one of the best things to happen to humanity."

For how uncomfortable this all is, he's sure making it right. "Fine. I disagree, but fine."

Weston releases me, pushes to standing, and then offers his hand. The breeze is moving his longish chestnut tresses, and the wild sparkle in his blue eyes is something I could get lost in for the rest of my life.

I understand why Weston has throngs of women in his wake. He's too easy to fall for. He's sexiness layered with middle school teasing and something undefinably magical and laidback. He's irresistible. And I, for one, cannot resist him.

I take his hand, allowing him to help me to my feet. When he pulls me into a hug and brushes his lips over my ear, I already know that I'm going to acquiesce to whatever it is that he wants of me.

"Let's go dance in the water together."

And with this cotton candy sunrise, how could I say no?

I just need to remember to protect my heart. Because with Weston, I can already tell he's going to make it too damn easy to fall headfirst. And if there's any souvenir I don't want from Aruba, it's a broken heart.

CHAPTER SIXTEEN

WESTON

Despite only four hours of sleep, Nova and I do not rest. Not even for a minute. There are too many important things to do, like flirting and taking pictures and readying ourselves for another amazing day of paradise.

After we dance and laugh our way through the waves of the Caribbean Sea, we tumble back into her hut, where we shower together and have sex one more time under the warm rush of water. I hoist her onto the built-in ledge of the ocean pebble-themed shower. We don't break the seal of our kisses even once as I ease into the glorious hot silk of her pussy, over and over. When I ask her if this is better than what she imagined yesterday, she moans and comes so hard that her head hits the wall.

There's some serious chemistry here, and it's got me reeling. But our day is too busy to think much about it. Once we're dressed for breakfast—her in a green and white sundress that I helped pick out, me in chinos and a light button-up that I snagged in the thirty seconds I left her side—it's hard not to walk around with a silly smile that says it all. I might as well have a sign on my forehead that says, "I got laid sooo fucking much last night."

A knock sounds on her door at eight forty-five. We share a guilty glance. "Who is it?" she asks.

"Hey, babe, it's me." Amelia's super-chill voice wafts through. "Heading to breakfast now, just wanted you to know!"

"All right, girl, I'm almost ready." She grimaces at me, the question in her eyes: *Do we out this now?*

"We were up all night with my uncle. He got really drunk and started fighting with the receptionist," Amelia says. "I am sooo tired."

"I can't even imagine," Nova says, though she absolutely can.

"All right. I'll see you at the table!" Amelia's footsteps scuff away, and Nova casts me a curious look.

"Okay, so, I don't know how to handle this."

"Handle what?"

She waves her hand dismissively. "These...beach affairs, or whatever."

I snort. "I don't know. We can say whatever we want. Though I'll warn you, if your suggestion is to continue acting like there's nothing between us, that plan is going to fail almost immediately."

"Why's that?"

"Because there's no hiding the way you look at me now," I tell her, easing my hands over her hips. My own silly grin is back in full force because it's impossible to hide.

"I just won't look at you then." She slides her palms over my chest. "Lies."

She snorts. "I know. But would you be able to not do this?" She gestures to the way I've gathered her against me. "I mean, hell, after what happened in the bathroom this morning, who's to say you wouldn't do the same thing in the buffet line?"

"If you want me to fuck you on top of the scrambled eggs and pineapple, just tell me," I whisper seductively into her ear. She dissolves into laughter, and my cheeks hurt from how hard I'm grinning. She kisses me, cupping the sides of my face as if she's afraid I might drift away.

"I don't know how to do this. I don't actually...*do* things like this."

"Have sex on salmon?" I ask.

"You know what I mean." She nibbles on her lip, looking down at the ground. "Hooking up. I'm not really into one-night stands or—"

"Trust me, this won't be just for one night." I've been doing the mental math since I caught her masturbating. We've got ninety hours left until my flight departs. We can fit an eternity of nights into that span of time. At least, I plan to.

"I know. I just don't want to...make things weird. I don't want Amelia to have a ton of questions, or for her to be all, *Oh my god, what's happening between you two.*"

"So I need to kiss you in secret," I say slowly.

"Yes."

I grunt. "Okay. If that's what you want."

She leaves the hut first, checking both ways to see if the coast is clear. When she waves me out, we walk side-by-side up the boardwalk for a while. She's got her camera around her neck already, her red hair pulled up into a loose topknot. I keep my distance as we walk, though every inch of me wants to sling my arm over her shoulders.

Once we get to breakfast, the energy of the wedding group is buzzing and distracting. Nova immediately slips into stealth picture-taking mode, and Rhys waves me over so that I can place my drink order while the server is there. For all the drunken antics and lack of sleep from the night before, everyone is in good spirits.

Conversation swells along the massive table, and I get pulled toward one end, Nova to the other. Breakfast melts away in a happy, delicious blur. Still, I find myself looking her way too many times to count. Our gazes snag a few times across the long table, each time prompting a little smile and a blush from her.

It's shit like that that makes it impossible to stay away from her. But she wants me to play it cool, so I'll try. I'll honestly try. It's just not gonna work.

Our group heads to the first activity, which we pile into two huge vans for. First stop is a dock, where we get onto a boat and head to a private island. Nova is in her element, snapping photos, chatting with Amelia and Laney and Rhys's sisters. The white sand beach of the private island is honestly jaw-dropping. Our group wanders around the crystalline shoreline, dipping our toes into the water, posing with the vibrant pink flamingoes who wander around completely unamused by us until food is involved.

While Nova is paused in the ankle-deep water, engrossed by images on her camera, a flamingo wanders her way. The elegant pink bird starts nipping at the frill of her bathing suit. Right at her butt cheeks.

Nova squeals, splashing away from the bird, who continues to pursue her. I grab for my phone to record the attack for posterity.

"They really don't get engaged unless food is involved…" our tour guide is saying.

The flamingo is just highlighting what I already know: nobody can resist Nova's ass. Not even a pink bird. Least of all me. I'm doubled over with laughter once Nova finally races to safety, crouching behind a lounge chair underneath one of the various sun umbrellas dotting the beach. Amelia squeals, and Laney races to provide moral support.

Once her girlfriends have wandered back toward the water, and Nova is resting on the lounge chair, I go to the empty seat at her side.

My shit-eating grin must say it all, because she immediately says, "I don't want to hear one word about being attacked by the flamingo."

A laugh snorts out of me. "But it was *so* fucking epic."

She's smiling and shaking her head.

"That bird just wanted a piece of your ass." I look around for curious ears who might be too near. "Don't worry, I won't tell him what he missed last night."

She's shaking with silent laughter, gaze stuck on the ocean. Is she pretending we're not connecting as hard as we are, or not wanting me to know how funny I truly am?

"Your ass cheeks are *that* delicious. I never thought part of my achievements in Aruba would be to make a bird jealous, but here we are."

This time, a sharp laugh rockets out of her. Victory.

"You are ridiculous," she says, covering her face with her hands.

"No, I'm just factual." I glance around again, locating the bulk of our group of friends at the shoreline. "I want to kiss you."

She jerks her hands down to her side, scoping out our surroundings as if we're going to pull off a heist. "Here?"

"Nobody's looking."

"But the flamingo will get pissed." Her lips quirk into a smile, and I take that as my cue.

I dip forward, smiling like a fool, and snag a sloppy, passionate kiss from her. The electric jolt that courses through me feels like we've been denying ourselves this for years, not hours. I go for a second kiss, and then a third, but she pushes on my chest, eyes cloudy with lust.

"Weston."

"Nova."

"Are you trying to be publicly indecent? Because we're going to be arrested or evicted if we keep following that train of thought."

She's not wrong. My cock is already making the slow trek toward iron-weapon status, and we're just three kisses deep. I grunt, pushing back onto my own lounge chair.

"Fine. You're right."

She makes a big display of checking a watch she's not wearing. "Well, that lasted a whole two hours."

"What?"

"You keeping yourself off me."

I smirk, stretching out on the chair. "I knew it wouldn't last long, but I didn't want to dash your hopes."

Nova and I linger around each other for the rest of the day, always ready to snag a moment alone when the friends aren't looking, as we move from lunch on private flamingo island to shipwreck snorkel expedition. Nova initially offers to stay behind and take photos, and she catches an epic bro shot of me, Rhys, Elliot, and Keko. Amelia, Laney, and I finally convince her that she deserves a shot at experiencing a real, live shipwreck for herself, too. Once Nova gears up and is paddling through the crystalline waters, the shipwreck barely visible through the lapping waves, I document her experience as best I can. It just seems right.

Nobody ever takes pictures of the photographer, and if I can give her anything, I want it to be some pictures of herself to look back on. I would have done it for her even without our tiki hut hanky-panky in the mix. I caught my older brother Dom's marriage proposal to his girlfriend London last month on video, and let me tell you—that was a rush. I kind of love documenting moments for people, which only throws a bigger wrench into the whole question, *Where does Instagram-influencer Weston go from here?*

Because the truth is, even though I've chosen Thailand, I can go anywhere. I can do anything. And no matter how many skillsets I have—at this point, my resume is looking more like a scroll than a neatly tailored professional document—nothing seems right.

Nothing except keeping moving.

Catch the next flight.

See what comes next.

Maybe what you're looking for is at the next destination.

It's late afternoon by the time our group hits the island again. Everyone is readying to head back to the resort, lining up for the two shuttle vans coming to pick us up. There's a fun dinner tonight with live dancers, so most of the older family members want to go back and take naps before then.

Nova's got something else on her mind, even though she hasn't said anything. She keeps glancing up and down the street, where locals amble by and cars make slow passes on the gravel-edged road. Spiky bushes edge the asphalt, looking both desert and tropical. Her thumb rubs back and forth over the shutter button of her camera.

"You don't want to go back."

I mean it as a question, but I have enough of a hunch to assert my dominance over my observation. She nibbles on her bottom lip, hesitating before she speaks.

"You think it would be far to walk back?"

Her secret intent blossoms inside me, in the same way a secret handshake can speak volumes. I step closer, glancing around like we're about to do another naughty thing and I'm checking for witnesses.

But instead of kissing her, I say, "You wanna go walk around a little?"

She can't hide the eagerness in her glittering green eyes as she nods. In a hushed voice, she says, "I've been dying to get out of the resort."

"Me too. Fuck it. Let's ditch." I jerk my head over my shoulder, down the open road. Truth is, if this were my own trip, I would have been wandering the streets for days now. Resorts aren't my style, though they are a fun departure. I appreciate all types of travel, all types of people—but when left to my own devices, I gravitate toward the backpackers, the hippies, the free spirits. And maybe that's why Nova and I ultimately came together. Out of this whole damn group, she's the only one itching to really *know* Aruba.

She nods determinedly, eyes stuck on the tourist vans that have clustered at the pick-up point. "I'll let Amelia know that I plan to stay here for a little longer."

I watch as she walks off to where Amelia and Amelia's parents are crowded near our resort's van, counting heads and trying to figure out who goes where. While she and Amelia chat, I head for Keko and Elliot.

"I'm gonna take a walk. A solo walk," I clarify, before either of them can offer to join.

"Hurry back. Don't want to miss the grub," Elliot says, patting his stomach. The man loves to eat, and I swear he's gained five pounds since we've been here.

I promise them I won't, even though I'm not sure I can keep my word.

Truth is, there's something much more important on my schedule today.

Wandering a remote island with a fiery redhead seems like the absolute best thing I could ever choose to do.

CHAPTER SEVENTEEN

NOVA

Once the shuttles disappear, Weston and I exchange grins as if we're about to embark on a *Ferris Bueller's Day Off* adventure. Except instead of Chicago, we're wandering the back roads of Aruba, pausing at fruit stands, inspecting any and all patches of flowers and shrubbery that catch our eye.

The air is heady with humidity and the wafting scents of a fire nearby. Yet my skin is fresh from my unexpected dip in the ocean. Weston has offered to carry all my belongings in addition to his own backpack, which is both unnecessary and extremely sexy. Why is it sexy? Because everything he does is sexy. He could fall and scrape his knee and I'd still probably have to change my underwear afterward.

Weird, but it is what it is.

My phone vibrates just as we set out. I'd ignore it if I weren't irrationally worried about something happening to Gram. But of course it's Jimmy, responding to a picture of the resort I sent him that morning.

JIMMY: God, that place looks incredible. I wish I could visit.

NOVA: You should! It's literally the most gorgeous place I've ever been.

JIMMY: You really think I should?

NOVA: Why not? Life is meant to be lived.

It's a timely platitude that I also happen to believe in. But Jimmy's version of *lived* involves drunken nights at the same watering hole for the rest of his life.

Weston and I chat about everything and nothing as we wander along a road we have no familiarity with, in a direction we can only guess is east. It's a natural decision between us, and neither of us doubt it for a second. And for how natural it is, it still strikes me as outrageous. Because if this were anyone else—perhaps most of all *Jimmy*—I'd have to reassure them plenty of times not to freak out. Hell, I doubt even Amelia would want to do something like this—wander into the unknown without a map. We cross paths with plenty of locals, and even stop to have an interesting conversation about the necessity of trying an authentic *bitterballen* recipe with a man who punctuates every sentence with the sound "yanoo."

The late afternoon sunlight beats down on us. Weston helps me reapply sunscreen approximately a hundred times in our hour-long wander through cactus-spiked paradise. Finally we come upon a little village outpost where attractive apartment buildings sit next to cactus-infused parks, and the clear blue of the sky makes everything inside me ache with something powerful and unknown.

"God," I sigh as we scuff down the road between street vendors selling clearly not-name-brand sunglasses and other accessories. Christian Dior does *not* write his name in Ariel font on the front of the glasses, just so we're clear. "I wish I could move here."

"You could, couldn't you?"

Weston's simple question forces my mouth shut. It's not as easy as doing it or not doing it. The question never even comes up. It's simply *not on the drawing board.* "Are you kidding me? That's about as likely as me moving to the moon."

"Why?"

I fumble for a way to convey the past twenty-five years of bone-deep understanding centered around my family's obsession with finances. Namely: we never have enough money, and there will always be more debts to pay.

"I need to have a stable job before I move anywhere. I've got a lot of bills." I shrug. "It just seems a little unlikely that I'll find something somewhere else that will pay all my bills back home *and* let me lead a decent life."

"What are all these bills about?" He nudges me, a joking tone in his voice. "Gambling problem?"

I laugh, but its humorless. "Actually, yeah. Not me, my grandpa. He kind of ruined the family with it."

Weston is quiet for a moment, so long that I start to think he didn't hear me. Then he slings his arm over my shoulders and squeezes me against him.

"Sorry, Nova."

"You didn't know. And there's nothing to be sorry about. I've accepted my fate."

"You could still live someplace like here," he says, almost like he's trying to be helpful.

"In an alternate reality, probably," I say with a laugh. "Trust me, I used up all my Get Out of Small Town Free cards when I went to college. I worked my ass off to attend that school and got so many scholarships that I graduated with just a couple loans. And even that didn't put me ahead."

"But *you're* not in debt—"

"No, but my family is, and that's what I'm part of, so I need to contribute." I sniff, feeling a strange swell of emotion clamping my throat. I thought this was supposed to be a relaxed late afternoon walk, not a psychological nosedive.

Weston and I continue walking, admiring the sights in silence. Palm trees spring up, stuck in the sidewalks, in front of storefronts that grow progressively more colorful: teal, coral, lime green. Even though he hasn't said anything, hasn't even hinted at judgment, I feel compelled to defend my position.

"I live with my grandma," I blurt, looking up at him to see if he'll look disgusted or amused or maybe something worse. "She and I live on my parents' property, in a little shack in the backyard."

His brows lift, and he nods. "That's cool."

"No, it's not. I'll probably die there, Weston."

"It doesn't matter where you die. As long as your entire life up until that point was lived as you wanted."

His words start a heavy cyclone through me. The meaning is so intense I can barely think about it.

"If I moved here, I'd have to bring Gram," I say as we pass a bright red building. I jerk my thumb at it. "Hell, we could live here. She'd probably be thrilled."

He laughs, but it only reminds me of the fact that I've opened up to him. A lot. Like, way more than I planned. I don't like people knowing how brutally poor my family truly is. That we're so poor it might take us three lifetimes to shovel ourselves out of debt, and if this were olden times, all of us would be in debtors' prison by now. Instead, we're in modern times, so I have to live in my own internal debtor's prison, where my family secretly hates me for anything I spend my money on that isn't *helping them.*

"What about you? Why don't you move to Aruba?" I ask.

He shrugs. "I could move to Aruba. But I could move to Ibiza. Or I could move to Morocco. Why choose?"

"If only I had the luxury of money, I *wouldn't* choose. Or rather, I'd choose all of them."

"So do it," he insists. "Life is too short to spend it wishing you could do something."

"Only if I have a job waiting for me."

He shrugs. "You could make your own job."

My heart sinks. This is the exact conversation I have with myself weekly as I grow more dissatisfied with my life and prospects. But it's not that simple. If I don't have a weekly paycheck coming in, guaranteed, then my Gram doesn't eat. She never had life savings, and anything she'd thought she could count on, my grandpa spent gambling. My parents aren't much better off, having inherited a metric shit ton of medical debts from my mom's side once her parents passed. There's no end in sight.

"I can't just up and do that," I say in a low voice, feeling the familiar claws of conflict.

"You can do anything you want to."

I sigh, rolling my eyes. "Yeah, I know that. Thanks. You're starting to sound like some out-of-touch Instagram influencer, though."

"Is that out of touch?" He fingers the fronds of a stout palm tree as we walk past a tiny flower patch surrounded by a wrought iron fence. "Maybe I just want to be the one voice in your life telling you to go for it."

That's equal parts heavy and beautiful. "How do you know you're the only one?"

"I don't. But am I wrong?"

I choose to say nothing. We're coming up on a gated boutique hotel with fascinating balconies and about a million ferns lining the entryway. But my chest feels like it's nearing implosion, so I need to change the subject.

"All right. So what are *you* going after, Mr. Inspirational?"

"Freedom."

I sigh. "That is such a cop-out answer."

He laughs bitterly. "Fine. Then what's the right answer? Tell me what *you're* after."

I struggle to think of anything that isn't "freedom." But dammit, he's right. It *is* what I'm after. I need my slice of freedom, within the bounds of my financial restrictions. And as far as I can see, there is no mathematical equation that provides me with a solution. Living the life of my dreams can never happen if I'm duty bound to New York State.

"Fine, I want freedom too," I grumble. "But it's more than that. I want to be able to provide for my family *and* not have my soul shrunk into the shape of a senior portrait."

"Lofty." He nods approvingly. "I like it."

We walk along the palm-lined boulevard a little longer, silence settling comfortably but tinged with question marks. Finally, curiosity kills my cat. "What about you? What do you even do?"

Weston hesitates, sending me a sidelong glance that makes my gut shrink. "I'm an influencer."

"Shut up."

"I'm serious." He laughs, reaching up to caress the wide, flat leaves of another tree as we pass by. "A few of my posts went viral throughout my travels, and I've just been building it up. Now I get marketing offers and publicity and all this stuff."

It's *really* hard to compute this information. "Wow. So do you have like...a lot of followers?"

He shrugs. "Almost three hundred thousand."

My eyes nearly pop right out of my head. He said it so casually, in the same way he might mention he planned on ordering steak for dinner. "That's...closer to half a million than anything else."

"I try not to think about that."

"So have you been posting about this trip?"

"Not yet. My posts lag behind my actual travels. So I can figure out my angle and message and everything."

I can't tell whether I should laugh at its outrageousness or cry with envy. I've never met a real influencer, much less hooked up with one.

"This is how you make a living?"

He laughs softly. "One of the ways."

"And you've always been doing this?"

"No, it's...more recent." He shrugs, raking a hand through his hair. "And kind of accidental. I needed to find something new a couple years ago. I had to pivot. This is where I ended up."

"Hm. What did you pivot away from?"

He shrugs again, and his silence tells me I should leave the topic be. But I don't listen to social cues with Weston anymore. If he could blatantly interrupt my masturbation session, then he deserves some unappreciated probing into his personal life.

"Come on, now," I goad him.

"What?"

"Tell me what you pivoted from. Was it a heartbreak? A secret baby? Maybe Mafia involvement."

He smirks, scratching at the back of his head. I've never seen him this nervous before. This hesitant to dive headfirst. It's shocking, really.

"I told you about my gambling grandpa. Don't I deserve to know about your pivot?"

A sigh leaps out of him. Finally, he says, "I got fired from my job."

Wow. This information *really* does not compute. He seems like he breezes through life and excels at everything, minus yoga. "Say what?"

"Two years ago." He shoves his hands into his pockets, his energy drawing tight.

"Did you like the job?"

He nods. "Yeah. It paid really well. Was a good career job. My first out of college. But then..." He shrugs.

"Then what? I can't imagine them firing you for anything other than being too good looking."

He snaps a dead leaf off a bush we pass by, crumbling it in his hand. "Let's just say, corporate life and Weston didn't jive too well."

"Okay. So what does that mean?"

"Not performing the job for which he was hired." He accentuates the words with air quotes. "Missed deadlines. Poor performance. Total fucking failure."

Something heavy settles over him, and he spends the next few steps squinting out at some unknown point on the horizon. I don't know how to grapple with his performance review. I can't even fathom those assessments of him. Then he looks over at me and says, "Don't tell Amelia. Okay?"

"Why would I tell her that?" I've never seen him like this—skittish, like I hold all the cards and he doesn't trust me to put them away safely.

"You're her best friend."

"True. So Rhys doesn't know?"

"I shouldn't have said anything."

"Hey." I grab his shoulder, making him stop and turn toward me. His face is a gorgeous mask of indifference. Something practiced and hard. I push onto my tiptoes so that our noses touch. "If it's that important to you, I will protect this information with all my might."

The corner of his lip twitches upward. "All your might?"

"With sword and stone, and...oh, shit. I dunno. I'm trying to make this majestic. Honorable. Am I failing?"

"You're failing," he confirms.

We resume walking, and I grab his hand. I bring his knuckles up to my lips, watching him closely to see if I can coax another smile out of him.

"Let's see what your half-million followers think about it, then."

And just as my lips brush over his knobby knuckles, I see it. The curl of the heartbreaker grin. The smile that will forever stain my heart and remind me of the epic week on Aruba where we hated each other and then fell into each other.

Weston loosens his hand from mine and slips his arm back around my shoulders. He buries his lips in my hair and murmurs, "Three hundred thousand. Don't inflate my numbers. And I'll trust you on this one. You better not let me down, *Nover.*"

A giggle bursts out of me at the unexpected use of the British pronunciation of my name. Warmth spreads through me, sticky sweet and alluring. Is it so wrong to be delighted by the fact that he shared a deep dark secret with me?

He has no idea, but I'm as loyal as they come.

First, I was loyal in my hatred.

But now?

I'll be head over heels for him until the end of my days.

CHAPTER EIGHTEEN

WESTON

We make it back to the resort just in time for dinner, thanks to some guy in a battered Jeep who offered us a ride. We hurry to the huts. There's only five minutes until dinner, but I'm not worried.

"Go on without me," I tell her once our teal and fuchsia homes are in view.

"Aren't you coming?"

"Yeah, I just gotta make a phone call first," I tell her. It's not true. There's nobody to call. But I need a timeout. Nova presses a fast kiss to my lips before she goes to change her clothes. I slip into my own hut, back pressed against the thatched surface of the door, listening to the muddied silence. The waves crashing in the distance. The murmur of conversation from further down the boardwalk. A distinct "Fuck" from Nova's hut.

I grin, and when I hear her footsteps thumping down the board-walk again, I whoosh out of my hut and snag her for one last kiss.

Her sweetness and prickliness is too much to resist, even in the throes of an anxiety attack.

The distraction doesn't last long. She races off, and I slip back into my hut. This time, I press my palms to the door and let the silence sweep over and drown me.

Because here's the fucking truth: I don't know what I'm doing, and that's the secret I don't want anyone finding out, not even Nova.

My phone vibrates in my pocket, and I fish it out, bracing myself for the worst. Nova is in financial debt, but I am in career debt. I am in lifestyle debt. I am living on borrowed time and question marks, struggling to stay afloat without knowing if I'm in water or quicksand.

It's a new email alert. The subject line reads: "RE: YOUR AP-PLICATION FOR PROMO TOUR."

When I told Nova my posts lag behind the trip, I wasn't being entirely truthful. Really, I've lost my spark. Cliffhangers Gear is the biggest name I've pitched to, but beyond them, I've sent out roughly ten pitches for smaller promo tours for different businesses around the world, trying to leverage my *Weston Wanders* brand and my follower count in exchange for continuing my travels.

I swipe open the email, a knot forming in my gut. Snagging Cliffhangers would signal my shift from aspiring amateur to resident influencer expert. The gig would take me through Thailand, Morocco, and Ireland in an all-expenses-paid promo blitz tour. But more than that, it would finally prove to that I know what I'm fucking doing with my life.

The email is swift and direct:

Thank you for your interest in our brand! We are taking all the necessary steps to make sure your package jives with ours, so please allow us additional time to crunch the stats.

I frown. It's not a rejection, but it's not acceptance either. It seems a lot like the formality that precedes an prolonged letdown. They already know they don't want me. Which just forces my mind back to the sordid truth.

I lost my job two years ago because I'm a failure, and I've spent every minute since then trying to hide this secret from the world.

I haven't told anyone that I was fired. Why would I? I left that place behind and closed that chapter of my life. But there's something about Nova that prompts me to open up. Not just because I've been so deep inside her that my dick came out her back—her words. Despite the prickles, she's got a buttery soft center. She won't look down on me. My secret can be safe with her.

But I don't want her knowing all of it. That my influencing gig isn't half as profitable as I make it out to be. That if I'm not careful, I could botch everything I've been working towards. That I've doubly inflated my success so that my family doesn't find out I'm in last place.

It's a balancing act, and Nova came sniffing too close. Nobody else gets the details, because I don't get close enough to anyone for the details to leak out. But somehow, Nova is slicing me open after so little time. Sawing at the tethers of my guard, like she's been studying exactly where the weak spots are.

There's an ache inside me. That much I know. It's an acid ache, something simmering, but I can't find the source. Every part of me wants to spill it out, like a modern-day leeching ceremony where I can bleed out the sickness and scourge. But doing that violates the cardinal rule of not catching feelings. I shouldn't get that deep with Nova. Even though I get the sense that she's not only in the same boat as me, but she might have a map that shows me where to turn. It's still too dangerous to go there. Map be damned.

And I can fucking think clearly again, now that she's not around me, being gorgeous and provocative and witty. Her sparkling wit glints so bright it blinds. Being at her side feels *too* good.

I need to keep an eye on this, because the last thing I need is anyone getting heartbroken. And yeah, I'm talking about her. She's sweet, and I don't want to hurt her.

Because I will. That much is certain. If she gets too close—if I let her get as close as I know she wants to—then she'll be one more Daly casualty for the history books. I don't want that to happen. So I need to make sure we both keep our heads on straight. We have to remember this thing between us has a deadline of Monday, when our flights leave.

I take a shower and dress slowly, letting my thoughts churn heavily. This sort of thing has never been a problem before, so I don't know why it's cropping up now. Nova is great. Amazing, actually. Well, stunning. I'll definitely miss her when we have to part ways, which means that I should do my best to enjoy every last second that we have left together.

But not too much, because then it might be hard to actually board my flight. So I'll have to keep the emotional investment right in the middle zone on the spectrum between emotionally petrified and ready-to-propose.

Easy enough. I'm a pro at this, after all.

But even though I've had too many international lovers to shake a hippie backpack at, Nova feels different. I don't know why. Especially since we spent the first four years of our mutual existence disliking each other.

The doubts follow me all the way to dinner, where everyone is chatting and digging into appetizers. Since I'm last, my seat was chosen for me—Rhys must have nabbed it on my behalf, since I'm sitting next to him and Amelia. Nova is right across the table from me, and that gemstone sparkle is in her eye as our gazes lock over the bottles of wine between us.

And just like that, the silly grin comes back. The butterflies are whispering through my insides, prompting me to forget everything I just settled on back in my hut.

But when I'm looking at this spunky redhead's smile, every inch of my body is anticipating what she might say. What level of absurd and prickly we might reach.

"Welcome, mate. You look refreshed," Rhys says as he claps my shoulder.

"I showered," I tell him. "And jerked off too."

Elliot snorts at my side. Keko starts a slow clap. Nova's eyebrow arches into the heavens.

A moment later, a text arrives on my phone.

NOVA: Did I not satisfy you, Mr. Horny Pants?

The grin on my face is too wide to contain. It's going to break my face in two if I'm not careful. But at this point, I can't stop myself from grinning right at her. Who cares if our friends find out? It feels more than obvious at this point. We've been disappearing together. Smiling like buffoons at each other. Watching each other far too much for two people who supposedly don't get along.

And no, it's never been like this with anyone else. Which means that even though I know exactly how straight I need to keep my head, and exactly how little I need to be diving headfirst into anything with her...

Tonight, I say fuck it.

I'll be smart tomorrow.

CHAPTER NINETEEN

NOVA

Thursday night ends with enough heated, drunken looks between Weston and me that we could possibly start a forest fire. Except there are no forests on Aruba—it's desert (I remember my Wikipedia research)—which means that we could ignite fifty acres of sprawling cacti in a *second* if we aren't careful.

The more martinis I drink, the drunker I get (surprise!), and when I stumble back to the hut in a desperate bid to pass out before I faceplant in the sand, Weston is at my side in no time. He guides my giggling, stumbling butt back to my fuchsia paradise, and that last thing I remember is him trying to tug my dress over my head—and failing.

Elegant, I know.

But then Friday morning, he's gone early, because Friday is one of the biggest days we have other than the wedding day itself. Weston and all the men in both families are heading out on a massive fishing expedition, while the women get to go shopping in Oranjestad. Gender-role predictability aside, it's a fun day. I find approximately eighty-five dresses I like but could never fit into. Nothing new.

All I can think about that day is Weston, and the occasional anxiety that I might trip over something on Amelia's wedding day and ruin it for her. No—I can't think like that. *Her wedding day will unfold without a hitch.* That's what I need to tell myself until it becomes a mantra.

After shopping, we all head back to the resort to freshen up for the rehearsal dinner. By the time we start trickling into the gorgeous outdoor patio—outfitted with gemstone mosaic backdrops, waterfalls, and plenty of moody sconce lighting—I spot Weston immediately. Because he's the only signal my radar detector is configured to receive, apparently. Dressed in a short-sleeve button up with chinos, he's sun kissed and casual and oh-so-handsome.

I remind myself to keep things friendly in public. Don't want to tip off the family and friends. So we share a private smile—one that speaks volumes, in a way I can't even comprehend—and every nerve ending inside my body lights up with anticipation for *more.*

By the end of the rehearsal dinner—where nothing at all was rehearsed—we're all tipsy and shouting with laughter. My photographer duties are officially over for the day, so my camera bag is left on a table as we migrate toward the moodily-lit lounge space on the expansive outdoor patio. A fountain burbles next to me as all the friends and family members mix and mingle.

I grin over my chilled Sauvignon Blanc. There's something so cinematic about being wrapped up in the hustle and bustle of a gathering. Being part of the crowd. My brother and I grew up on the outside looking in, but I don't think he ever truly cared to enter the "inside world." Of the Hendersons, I'm the only one infected with this virus known as *longing.* I met a very serious graffiti artist in Portugal who explained to me the concept of *saudade*, which is stronger than simply missing someone. It is longing and melancholy all wrapped up in one. I have *saudade* for experiences I have not lived, and it's something that my family might never truly understand.

I am so incredibly thirsty for life. Thirsty for nostalgia. Memories. Experiences. And you know who else is too?

Weston.

It's not a surprise; it's not even news. It's simply *stunning*. And being around him awakens some serious saudade in me. I *long* for more than just new experiences. I long for someone to share them with. Someone who is on that level with me.

This is why I feel like an outcast. Because my family would rather stay home than encounter the serious graffiti artist in Portugal. Because Jimmy would have encouraged me to go back to the safety of the resort instead of explore an unknown place.

But Weston is there with me, every step of the way. I've been bumping into him all around the world. At sunrise. In the quiet fringes of the group activities. Weston and I, we're more alike than I ever realized. And for some reason, this is just as scary as it is thrilling.

I see him across the lounge, chatting with Rhys as his gaze slides my way. He can't keep his eyes off me. Just like I can't keep my eyes off him. This whole scene is ripe for a pop ballad music video, Ariana Grande style, but since there's no camera crew on hand, I'll just make the tune up in my head. We've been winking and smirking at each other all night.

Yes, it was my idea to play it cool, keep things under wraps. But each hour spent at this man's side feels like celebrating another year of friendship. I know more about him after our trek through uncharted Aruba than I do my own damn brother. I could start a list of our inside jokes already. He's given me more orgasms than my ex ever did, that's for damn sure. If we keep this up, we'll be celebrating our first anniversary by the time the wedding wraps up.

And that's the throbbing vein of it. Right there. These thoughts are swirling inside of me, urging me into insanity, propelled by Weston's easygoing smiles and his ice-blue attentiveness. Every inch of my body is on pins and needles, waiting for him. Waiting for another smile. Waiting for the next opportunity to trade sweet barbs.

We've been drifting toward each other all night, the stretch of dusk clawing at my attention just as much as the occasional laugh I overhear from him. And then finally, blessedly, he's coming at me from across the patio, one hand stuffed into chino pants, an intolerable smirk resting on those juicy lips I have kissed enough times to fucking paint from memory.

He corners me in the alcove I've been enjoying, tucked under draped silks that are backlit and gently billowing. I feel exactly like a princess.

"Princess Nova."

His rough bass makes my thighs tense. I'm leaning into him without even deciding to move nearer. Space shrinks between us on instinct, because he is *that* hard to resist.

"Sir Weston."

He looks down at me, tenderness written across his face. I feel like I've been looking up into his icy blues for years, not hours. Nobody says anything, and then he dips down to capture my lips in a kiss. The first one is slow, thorough, the kiss you give someone when you've been falling in love with them for an entire evening.

But the next one is pure fire and need. The kiss you give—and get—because you're burning alive on the inside with lust for the same person.

His rough palm finds the dip in my neck. A whimper escapes me, and when we break apart, he's got question marks in his eyes.

"Should I say sorry for breaking the rules? You kissed me like you were fucking hungry for it."

"Don't say sorry. Just keep doing it."

He grins as he dips down again, onlookers be damned. I couldn't care less anymore, not when this need is so throbbing and serious. We kiss messily. He dips me backwards. I giggle and cling to him. I wish someone were there to capture *this* moment. The moment when he made me feel like a breathy, feminine goddess. Halfway between Marilyn Monroe and Aphrodite.

His hands find the dip in my waist. He pulls away, drawing a deep breath.

"I just came over here to say hi, not get roped into a live-action porn."

"Aww. You think our kissing is good enough to be in a porno?"

He cocks a grin. "At least a soft core."

"I'm flattered. We really kiss that good?"

His eyes narrow to slits. "Babe, if you're not aware of how seriously fucking good you kiss..." His eyes flutter shut. "Then consider this your memo."

I'm not sure what to be more turned on by. The fact that he called me *babe*, or the fact that he called me a good kisser. Both will haunt me for the rest of my days.

"Okay. So, what do you wanna do about it?" I brush my lips against his again, just to tease.

He cinches his arm around my waist. "Get out of here?"

"Sounds good to me."

When we break apart to leave, I catch Amelia's stunned expression from across the patio. A smile tugs at her lips, and she brings a hand to her mouth as she watches Weston and I scuttle away. I pause, opening my mouth like I might attempt to explain from twenty feet away, over the din of a party, what's really going on. But Amelia shoos me away, and I blow her a kiss.

Tomorrow. At our sunrise bridal session. I'll tell her everything. Well, everything except the caught-in-the-middle-of-masturbation part.

My heart races as I collect my bag and follow Weston away from the party. My hand is swallowed in his firm, rough grip. Maybe he's afraid I'll change my mind, even though there's no risk of that. Not now, not ever. I've gotten a taste of Weston, and my palate has been forever changed. I don't even want to think about that right now. He might have ruined me for the rest of my life. I need to just enjoy him while I can.

But what about after Aruba?

The question has been stalking my subconscious like the killer in *Scream*—not very stealthy, wielding a large knife, inevitable in its arrival. Weston scoops me against him once we hit the boardwalk, pressing a kiss to my head. He doesn't need to be sweet with me. He doesn't need to make this feel so good. So complete. So *fulfilling*. But he does. And that's precisely why he's dangerous.

Because I can see myself with him long-term.

"Here's the plan," he says, his voice a rough rasp. "We're going to go back to the huts...drop off your camera bag...and grab a big towel."

"A big towel?"

"Maybe a few of them."

"Are we going to try to sop up the ocean?"

He tuts. "I think we'll be a few towels short."

"A few billion, you mean."

"Possibly trillion. Or some other number far larger that I don't know about yet."

I nuzzle into the crook of his neck, finding my favorite spicy, sandalwood-infused scent there. "Okay. So a few big towels. Then what?"

His grin turns wicked. "Sex on the beach."

Excitement prickles through me. "Ahhh. Won't we need more than just a few big towels?"

His gaze drops to my cleavage, and he tugs on the fabric of my skirt. "Nope. We've got everything we need right here."

I'm slightly confused, but I trust that Weston knows the way forward when it comes to public indecency. I drop off my camera bag in record time while he goes to his hut to grab an extra blanket. We traipse through the sand, holding hands, a geometric orange and black blanket draped over his shoulder. We walk along the shoreline for a while, watching the final streaks of the rusted Aruban sunset on the clouds overhead, while the water licks at our feet and then recedes.

The air is sultry and salty, guiding us toward a destination that only we know. When Weston slows, I scan the dark coast for the right spot. Not knowing what I'm even looking for, I lead him toward a thicket of trees, but he pauses in the middle of the beach.

"Here," he says.

"Here?"

"Yes." He pulls me into him, wrapping his arms around my waist. The heat of him is beguiling. He could tell me to purchase mangoes while naked in a busy international market, and I'd agree to it, if only he asked me with this embrace, with this seductive gaze.

So when he kisses me—slowly, thoroughly, like every romantic movie in the history of time is taking notes—I acquiesce. It's all I *can* do with Weston. He breaks apart only to shake out the blanket, which splays out over the sand. Then he kisses me once and sits right in the middle of it.

"Shouldn't I lie down first?"

He shakes his head, the ice blue of his eyes glinting in the moonlight. Everything is shadows and crashing waves out here, and the lights of the resort simply cast a golden glow above the palm line. He takes my hand, gently tugs me in his direction.

"Sit down."

"On top of you?"

"No, a mile away." He snorts. "Yes, on top of me."

"I'll crush you." Anxiety is breathing down my neck, but as his fingertips find the inside of my ankle, my breath catches. Maybe doing what he wants isn't so bad. Naked mango markets, after all.

"I promise you, you won't."

I hike the skirt of my dress up a little before I stand with my feet on either side of him, and then I fall to my knees. He captures my lips in a kiss and then eases me down to sit on top of him. I settle nicely into his lap. The ridge of his cock is waiting for me.

"Oh, hello," I whisper.

"Spying on you all night got me horny," he mumbles against my lips. He tugs at my bottom lip with his teeth. I draw in a sharp breath, rocking my hips against the thick ridge in his pants. "Mmhmm." He bucks beneath me. "See, this is the hack to sex on the beach. Huge towel. And cowgirl."

"Of course you would know," I tease, but all my conviction is gone, now that the steel of his arousal is pressed against my clit. I just want him inside me. I want to erase the barriers of clothing and have him *penetrate me*. "And are you calling yourself a horse?"

"You can call me whatever you want." I can hear the smile through his words. "Just as long as you get on top of me."

He's pushing up the fabric of my dress until it bunches at my hips. The humid ocean air tickles the tops of my thighs. Every deep inhale is freedom. Risk. Unfettered lust. And I only want more.

"Fine. My sexy horse." I buck my hips against that rock-hard ridge, and he grunts, palming my breasts, fingers seeking the tight points of my nipples beneath my bra. I suck in a breath. I never imagined being on top. Not with him. Much less on this beach, where hundreds of people roam freely each day. But hey. *When in Aruba.*

"That's right." His lips find my collarbone, leaving a damp trail to my cleavage. Every inch of my skin lights up with goosepimples. Between him and the moonlight and the humid sea air, I'm halfway to climax.

"Okay. I need you to stick it in already," I moan, flattening my palms against his sturdy chest. He doesn't respond, not verbally at least, but he kicks into action all the same. He's fumbling with his pocket, and then I hear the soft *rrrrip* of the condom wrapper. He guides me backward for a moment, and I watch the shifting shadows beneath me as he unzips his pants, frees his cock and rolls the condom on.

"You ready, Princess Nova?" His voice already sounds strained. He guides me back on top of him, the fleshy heat of his dick finding the damp crotch of my panties. He tugs away the scrap of fabric with his thumb, exposing my intimate, throbbing parts. He rolls my clit between thumb and forefinger, his breath coming out hot on my chin.

"So fucking ready," I whisper. He grips my hips, which feels like he's taking the reins. And that's fine. I want him controlling this as much as me. He guides me into the right spot, cockhead nudging at the slickness between my legs, easing into the tightness. And then the slow, mind-numbing creep of warmth as he pulls me back down on top of him.

I let him control the pace, because oh my god, there's never been anything that feels better than this. My eyes flutter shut. Everything in my brain goes deathly quiet. All I can think, hear, see, or feel is Weston pushing himself into me. Even though we did this roughly twenty hours ago, it feels all new, because this *is* all new. We've never done it on the beach before, under an almost-full moon, with the waves lapping at my heels while the anxiety of being *discovered* streaks like a comet at the back of my mind.

It all adds up to a powerful equation. One that threatens to push me over the edge before Weston's even pushed himself fully inside me.

"Holy shit," I whimper, gripping the ridge of his shoulder.

"I know." He grunts, finding the last inch of depth inside me. He fills me so completely that it seems like explosion is the only option from here. He cinches one arm around my waist, erasing all the remaining space between us. His other hand is pressed onto the towel behind him, the arc of his bicep lighting up silver in the moonlight. "You feel so fucking amazing, Nova."

The gritty honesty in his voice makes me limp, vulnerable. I don't know why, but this is the most romantic thing I've ever experienced in my life. He's not *trying* to woo me, yet he is. This is special in a way I can't even articulate, and I'm not sure I'll ever be able to move past this.

How could I? He's so warm and perfect, moving beneath me like we've been practicing for centuries. His breath comes out in husky grunts as he drills up into me in slow, thorough thrusts. I rock back and forth in time with his movements, the friction sparking like electricity.

I love you. The thought is ludicrous. I bury my face in his neck, embarrassed I even thought it. But the embarrassment fades quickly under the steady waves of pleasure. He reaches a part of me that's never been touched before. And I don't just mean his dick.

"Why does it feel this good?" The question is rhetorical. There is no answer. It's an anomaly even God himself can't account for.

He grunts again, his lips skating along my jawline. "You know why."

He thrusts deep into my core, both stunning and eviscerating me. The meaning sears through me. I don't know why it feels this good...but somewhere deep inside, actually, I do.

"Look up, Nova." His gritty command makes lust streak through me, giddy honey through my veins. I tip my head back, just as he takes a big handful of my breast through my dress. His thumb draws a lazy path back and forth over my rock-hard nipple as I drink in the inky black sky. The yawning expanse of the galaxy greets me just as Weston drills *deep*.

A choking noise slips out of me. I'm gurgling at the sky. He moans and buries his face in my chest.

"Fuuuck," I moan, not bothering to moderate my volume. It doesn't matter anymore. Let anyone and everyone hear us.

"Did you see?" His voice is breathy now. Like he's close to the brink.

"See what?"

"The fucking universe."

Silent laughter overtakes me. If I laugh any harder, I'll dissolve into tears. This man has me bumped up against three different precipices at once. "Yeah. Yeah I saw it."

"I want you to come while you look at the universe."

More laughter. Tears prick the corners of my eyes. Have I just fallen in love? Like right here, on the spot? Only Weston would encourage me to leverage the galaxy for an orgasm.

"Only if you do it too," I say, rocking against him again. The tightness in my belly is a warning sign. I'm one hard thrust away from spilling over the edge, stargazing be damned.

"All I need to do is look at you," he whispers, tugging at my earlobe with his teeth. "Because every time I do, I see stars."

My laughter cuts through the roar of the ocean. "You don't need the pick-up lines, Weston. You done picked me up."

He sucks at his teeth as he buries himself inside me, as deep as he can. "A guy can never be too sure, with a babe like you."

That's cute—funny, even—that he thinks *I'm* the hot one. He's so wrong. But I don't have much time to laugh internally about it because he sinks his teeth into my neck. The pressure, combined with the clit action and his enormous cock buried balls-deep and his plea for me to *come with the universe* has got me twisted all sorts of ways. My head tips back, because he has commanded it, and the sticky, slow tendrils of pleasure begin to unfurl, like the close rumble of thunder on a sultry summer night.

And this orgasm, oh, it's the rainfall, the blessed rainfall after the humid, expectant dance preceding the storm. Just as the thunder gives way to clear skies, this orgasm is a relief. It blasts me open, resets something unseen and partially obscured inside of me. My thighs jerk and the shout gets caught in my throat as I come, come, come, drinking in the galactic black expanse just as Sir Weston has asked of me.

Yes, I get lost there. Yes, I am so consumed by the passion and the perfection that I cry. Except I'm not aware that I'm crying, until Weston has scooped me into his arms, heaving chest and all, drawing labored breaths as he comes down from his own climax and rubs my back.

"Those are good tears, right?" he asks.

Of course they are. He's the only man who'd ask me to share my orgasm not just with him, but with infinity.

"Yes. That was just...amazing."

"It was." He laughs softly, nuzzling my nose with his. "Holy shit."

And I melt into him, pressing my sweat-and-tear stained cheek against his.

I'd say that I don't know what happened here tonight between us, why it felt like this...but I do.

I actually do.

It's because of those three little words I don't even want to think about.

CHAPTER TWENTY

NOVA

Dawn comes early. Way too early, for how late Weston and I stayed on the beach, rolling around on that blanket, kicking sand everywhere and giggling up into the heavens.

But it's not just a new day—it's THE day. The wedding day.

The sheer amount of orgasmic tranquility that Weston gave me last night would have assured I'd sleep until noon today. But Amelia and I, we have another sunrise photo shoot scheduled. So I'm up by six thirty and packing my camera bags when Weston rouses from his angelic and handsome sleep.

"Beach?" he asks.

"For me," I clarify, fighting the silly grin that threatens to reverse all my forward motion. If he so much as blinks at me wrong, I'll tumble back into bed with him, *so help me God.* "Amelia and I are doing one last sunrise shoot."

He grunts, sinking back onto the bed. "Can I come?"

"Unfortunately not. She's probably gonna be partially naked at some point."

He nuzzles into the pillow, his voice sounding farther and farther away. "I won't look. It's just that you need my help. I should be there."

I grin. It's sweet that he wants to help. Even sweeter that I'm considering making him my second shooter for no reason at all. Wouldn't that just be perfect? Nova and Weston—photographers at large. Hell, we could even set up a business in some far-off corner of the world. My heart twists at the thought of it. Better not get too wild with my fantasies. After all, there's a pretty serious end date to all of this, and it sits just two days away.

I need to make the most of the following forty-eight hours, and pretend that end date is never going to arrive.

My chest is tight as I bend down to kiss him before I go. "I'll stop back after the sunrise shoot. We can get ready together."

"You better," he mumbles, and then a moment later he is asleep again. I grin, watching him for a few moments. It's too easy to get lost in Weston. But I tear myself away—the longer I watch him, the more tempted I am to crawl back into bed with him—and quietly let myself out of the hut.

The morning air is damp and roaring. Dawn has started the cobalt creep across the horizon. Footsteps scuff down the boardwalk, and I see Amelia just coming down the steps toward the huts.

"Good morning, *bride*!" I gush, sweeping her into a hug. She wraps her arms around me, and we stand there for a few moments.

"Good morning, *bestie and photographer.*" She sighs. "I'm so worried everything is going to fall apart."

"Normal jitters. Let's start the day off right with some epic pictures."

She expels a cleansing breath, and we hurry off toward the other side of the resort, where the more picture-perfect, wedding-ready beach is. This is where we'll have her shoot—and where she'll get married in roughly eight hours. A flimsy white robe billows behind her as we glide down the steps toward the white sand. She already looks epic and gorgeous, and she hasn't even done hair and makeup. She gathers her blonde tresses to one side, nervously flicking the ends of her hair, as we assess the best spot to take pictures.

"Over here," I tell her, where the sand is mostly undisturbed and dry. She stands against the backdrop of the brightening sky, and I take a few test shots while she arranges her hair and robe.

"So are you going to tell me what the hell is going on between you and Weston?" she asks, mischief curling at her lips.

Thank God I have this camera in front of my face so she can't see my blush. "Oh, right. About that."

She snorts. "Yeah, *that*! Spill it, girl. You made me wait all night to hear the story."

I fight a dopey grin as I check out my test shots, but apparently I didn't fight it hard enough. "Ah-ha!" she shouts. "Look at that smile. How long have you two been hooking up?"

"Just a couple nights," I tell her. "And trust me—this was very unplanned."

"No shit! On Monday, you two were at each other's throats."

"And now, we're at each other's...well..."

"Genitals?" she cracks.

A laugh bursts out of me. "Yes. Precisely."

The shutter snaps a few times as I leap into photography mode without telling her. The way she's looking at me, so candid and earnest, is precious. The money shots are close, and I can feel it in the way my skin is vibrating. There's something intuitive about photography, as much as mechanics. And the best shots lay just around the conversational corner.

"Is it wrong to say I'm glad you two hooked up?" she asks. "I always thought you would make a cute couple."

"You did?" *Snap, snap.* "Even though we've been clashing for the past four years?"

"Yeah. There was just always something about you two that seemed to mesh."

She's not wrong. I feel this meshing now, harder than ever. I clear my throat, pretending to examine the screen. But really, I'm just trying to see past the emotion welling up inside me.

"I just never could figure out why you two didn't click before," Amelia murmurs.

"I think it wasn't our time," I say, moving to capture a new wash of light. "And I'm not gonna lie. I'm falling for him."

Amelia squeals, bringing her knuckles to her mouth. I capture the sweet gesture, wink at her, and then keep the shoot moving along. "Enough about me and this budding romance. Let's talk about *your* romance."

I guide her into new postures—toward the sunrise and away from the sunrise. With the robe, without the robe. And so on. I keep her talking about all things love and romance, because the dreamy look she gets in her eyes is too perfect not to capture. She's going to love approximately all of these pictures, and if there's anything I want to give my friend, it's that feeling of *forever* contentment. She'll get that with her actual wedding pictures too, but this shoot exists just for her. Her last moments as a bachelorette. The morning before she wed her love.

This is the type of thing I love doing.

This is the type of thing I'd love to make a *living* doing.

Senior portraits are great and all, but let's be real, the sparks it ignites in my chest are hardly a fire hazard. But this, right here? I could do this for fourteen hours a day, seven days a week, and still want more. Especially in some place like *Aruba*.

I remember Weston's words—*You can do anything you want*—and imagine some far-off life where I'm able to blend both beaches and making a living from photography. It would have to involve Gram, too, somehow, and I just can't see a solution. If she wasn't in the picture, maybe—but leaving her out of the picture is a non-option.

She's my gram. She's my ride or die.

"How did you know Rhys was the one?" I ask Amelia as we're winding down. She scratches her head, contemplating the pink and red hue in the sky.

"There was a sign," she finally says, giving me a mysterious little grin. "And that's how I knew."

"A sign?"

"Yes. I'd already been thinking that I loved him and wanted to be with him long term. But it was when I went to visit him in London two years ago that I got the sign."

For how close we are, I somehow missed the story about *the sign*. "And it was...?"

"His tie. It sounds silly, which is why I never talk about it. But when I went to meet his parents, he was wearing a tie that looked exactly like the one my dad used to wear."

Her father passed away when she was fifteen, so this is a big deal. My face softens, the gravity of her meaning settling between us.

"In fact, I'd never seen Rhys in a tie before then, and I haven't since," she says, laughing a little. Her eyes are shining as she looks out at the water. "It just felt like a sign from Dad that Rhys was the one. Giving me the green light."

"That's beautiful," I say, squeezing her wrist as I come to her side.

"I think we get signs," she says, looking over at me. "Before big decisions or big moments. Maybe they're just little nudges. But they're there if you look for them."

I don't know what to think about this idea. Because part of me *does* rely on signs. Even though they all point toward returning to my shitty job and meager bank account. My innards are equal parts rational and dreamy, which makes things even more confusing.

The sun has shed its light over all of creation by the time we wrap up. She has to hurry back to her room for hair and makeup, which means that I need to be ready as well. We part ways, and on the way back to my room, only one thought cycles through my head.

What sign will I get about Weston?

CHAPTER TWENTY-ONE

WESTON

Wedding days are always a blur. But when you're fucking—no, dating...well, *having fun with*—the official photographer, things turn into a special type of Tilt-A-Whirl.

For starters, she is zipping around with both photographer *and* bridesmaid duties so I can't cross paths with her for even a second. And I'm dying over here. It's been four hours since I last glimpsed her, and I'm officially jonesing. I want to see her dress. Her hair. What sort of lipstick she's got on. Whether or not I can sneak a kiss or ten or more behind the altar before everything gets even crazier.

I'm fully decked out and ready. All I'm missing is Nova.

The groomsmen are all wearing taupe seersucker suits with pressed white linen shirts, and we look *sharp*. The altar and seats are arranged on a semi-circular wooden patio jutting out over the northern beach. White fabrics drape behind the altar, moving gently in the breeze. Romance is in the air...at least, it's getting there.

There's a lot missing; that much is certain as I scan the area. I'm with Rhys and the rest of the guys, reporting for official wedding duty. But nobody else is here.

Not caterers. Not florists. Not even the wedding planner.

"*Weston!*"

I spot Nova on the third story balcony. She's leaning over the Roman column-inspired balustrade, waving her arm to get my attention. Her hair falls in gorgeous, soft waves around her face, her lips shining pink and plump. My heart races as I drift toward her across the patio and through the elaborate paths leading up to the side of the building.

"Hey!" she calls down. "You busy?"

"Waiting for you to tell me what you need, My Juliet."

She cocks her head and grins. "What a Romeo."

"Let me clarify. Anything except mutual death, okay?"

"Not today, at least," she cracks. "Meet me in the lobby?"

I give her a two-finger salute and hurry through the big double doors into the hotel. The *clip-clip-clip* of her heels sounds on the winding marble staircase a moment later, and she rushes up to me, wild eyed.

"I need your help."

I blink a few times, taking her in. She's got on a floor-length maxi dress in tropical green, which just makes every single other thing about her beauty stand out even more. I think I actually hear my jaw clatter to the floor as she grabs my forearms.

"Weston?"

"Sorry, I was too busy ogling you." I force my gaze to meet hers, where a wry little smile awaits me. "You doing anything later?"

"Only you," she says in a sweet purr. When I lean in for a kiss, she dodges me. "I can't fuck up my lipstick. But I promise you—we will make out so hard later."

I grunt, taking a soft bite of her neck instead. "Fine."

"Right now, though, we have a problem."

I straighten, setting my face to serious mode. "What is it?"

"I'm an hour behind because hair and makeup didn't get started on time." She grimaces. "Can you use my other camera and be my second shooter so I can get all the pre-ceremony pictures done?"

Something warm and soft begins to flutter in my chest. It's like butterflies, but bigger. Maybe the mutant offspring of the butterflies one gets when utterly falling for someone. Which means I might be in way over my head with Nova. But it's impossible not to give her what she wants right now. Maybe ever.

"Babe, are you kidding me? Of course I'll be your second shooter."

She expels a huge breath of relief. "You just saved my day."

"Did you actually think I'd say no to you?"

"I don't know what Rhys had planned for you guys."

"Absolutely nothing. The guys are out there twiddling their thumbs. I'm sure they'll start drinking soon."

She smirks. "Good. Let me go grab my cameras, and we can get started. I'll meet you down here." She blows me a kiss and then scoots up the stairs, the sway of her hips leaving me mesmerized. Once she's out of sight, I whistle and stroll around the lobby. Being a last-minute second shooter doesn't sound like such a bad gig. A hell of a lot better than my actual gig, which is influencer-on-hold. I remember to check my email again, which I haven't done since yesterday. Nova is a consuming distraction, and while I'm thankful for how easy it is to get lost in her, I also can't forget to stay on top of my shit.

The truth is, I'm desperate to know what Thailand is going to look like. Will it just be wandering aimlessly, or totally directed by a hard-won sponsorship that will inject meaning back into my life?

A lot of this shit depends on the unpredictable magic of travel, sure—but the rest of it comes from meticulous planning, sponsorships, and having your fucking ducks in a row.

And my ducks are not in a row. They are not even in the same area. One of my ducks swam out to go live with those flamingoes, and the rest of the ducks are drunk at the bar.

Three hundred thousand followers means nothing if you can't leverage them for some goddamn income.

My chest gets tight again when I realize no new word has come from Cliffhangers Gear. Nova sweeping back down the staircase reminds me that this is not the time to fret. Today is meant for holy matrimony. Celebrating it, that is. Not participating in it directly.

Catching sight of Nova coming down that staircase for the second time in ten minutes does that weird thing with the butterflies in my chest again. I seriously doubt I'll ever get married, but if I had to? I'd do it with someone like Nova. I could see us eloping somewhere weird. But it's a thought that needs to stay a fantasy, because come Monday, we're both flying our separate ways.

I just can't figure out why those words sound more like a desperate reminder than the simple truth they've always been.

"Madam," I say, offering my arm. A sigh escapes her.

"Are you trying to make me melt into a puddle?"

"No, I just wanted to accompany you like a gentleman." I clear my throat, effortlessly lifting the camera bags from her shoulder before she tucks her arm through mine. "The melting business will come later."

She sighs again. "I can't handle you looking this good today. I'm not fully re-formed after last night on the beach."

"That was pretty good, wasn't it?"

She narrows her eyes at me. "*Pretty good* is an understatement. I still see the Milky Way when I blink."

My smile is straining my cheeks now. That's the type of feedback I like to hear. And yeah, *pretty good is* an understatement. But I'm hesitant to let her know just how galaxy-shatteringly good it was for me. That points back to the whole parting-ways-Monday thing, and I think we should avoid that reality for as long as possible.

And according to the *Weston Wanders* handbook, that will be until Monday morning itself.

"Better keep those stars out of your eyes today," I warn her as we head toward the beachfront area reserved for the ceremony. "Wouldn't want it to mess up your pictures."

"That's why I have a second shooter," she says, knocking me with her hip. The sun hits us full blast as we come out from under the shaded veranda of the resort patio. Elliot and Keko are still milling around, but Rhys is off to the side, conversing with some of his family members.

"Where are all the flowers and stuff?" I ask as we come up on the altar. "I thought it was going to look, you know, done up."

Nova doesn't answer immediately, but she scans the area, looks back at the balcony she'd called me from, and then back to the altar. Finally, she mutters, "Fuck. You're right. I don't think the florist is even here yet."

"Do you have the number? Maybe we should tell the wedding planner."

"I'll call her." She fumbles with her camera bag to extract her phone, makes the call, and then hangs up with a cluck of her tongue. "Straight to voicemail. Let's go take pictures of the reception area for now. At least so we can get *something* done."

I follow her down a path leading closer to the resort. It's lined with archways, dripping with hydrangea and hibiscus. The reception area is an enormous patio with a bar tucked off to the side.

Except that there's nothing here.

Not even a table.

"Shit." When Nova looks at me this time, there's real worry creasing her face.

"Are they supposed to be set up by now?"

"That's what the wedding planner laid out for me. She said that the ceremony area would be done by noon"—she checks her phone and shakes her head—"and it's one. Wedding is at three. Do you think everything is behind?"

"It's possible. Try the wedding planner again."

Nova gets out her phone, but before she can swipe it on, there's a call from Amelia. Nova answers, putting it onto speakerphone.

"Nova! We have a crisis." Amelia's stress is evident through the phone. "Where are you right now?"

"Down in the reception area," she says, nibbling on her bottom lip as she watches me. "What's going on?"

"My wedding planner isn't answering her phone, and I keep getting calls from my mom asking where she is because something about the caterer! I'm stuck in makeup, and I can't do a damn thing from up here."

"Shit. Okay. Let me figure it out."

"How does the reception area look?" Amelia asks.

Nova bites at her top lip, her gaze swinging over to the totally empty patio. "It's very fragrant. Surprisingly fragrant."

"But what about—"

"Hey, I'm getting another call. Let me look into this, and I'll call you back," Nova rushes to say. I admire her handling of the situation. It's hard to fib to a best friend. She hangs up and looks over at me, clutching the sides of her face.

"Weston, I feel like shit is exploding. Is shit exploding?"

"There may be a rumble, yes."

She snorts, swatting my chest. "I love how you can confirm my worst fears but still make it not seem bad."

The use of the L-word stops me up for a second. She's allowed to love something about me. Hell, I'm in love with her sparkling wit and that bodacious ass. But hearing it out loud? It goes against the ingrained truth of the traveler spirit. And maybe even worse, it goes against the player instinct of the Daly family. I can hear Maverick's cocky laugh in my head. Even though he's the youngest of us, he's the true player among us. Even more so now that my three older brothers are all happily engaged and ready to tie themselves off for the rest of their lives.

I'd join their ranks if feelings didn't automatically equal cramping my style.

"It's the wedding day. Things are destined to completely unravel," I tell her. "Let's call the wedding planner again."

Nova nods and swipes through her phone. It rings once, and then clicks over to voicemail. Not a good sign.

"Shit," she says.

"Yeah. We need to start problem solving. Keep your phone on you—I'm going to hunt down the caterer myself while you track down the wedding planner."

Nova nods firmly. "And once we figure something out, I'll let Amelia's mom know."

"Deal." I grab her hand between both of mine and give her an encouraging squeeze. "I'll be counting the seconds until I see you again."

She giggles, pushing at my chest. "You really *are* Romeo."

"Only in Aruba." I wink and press a soft kiss to her perfect cheek. "Parting is such sweet sorrow."

It's really that hard to rip myself away from her, but we've got some shit to figure out. She heads back toward the resort and I turn back to where I last saw Elliot, Keko and Rhys. Except when I near the boardwalk again, Elliot and Keko are the only ones to be seen, hands stuffed into their pockets with anxiety drawn tight around them.

"What's up, buddies?" I ask, squeezing both of their shoulders.

"Rhys is acting funny," Elliot says, squinting out at the water. "He's a little bit *too* laid back this morning." He jerks his chin toward the beach, where I can just make out the dim outline of a man sprawled out on the sand.

I grimace. "What is he doing out there?"

"Meditating, I think," Keko offers. "Or waiting for the water to consume him. He might have said that."

"Wedding day jitters?" I ask. It's hard to imagine Rhys doubting his decision this late in the game, but nobody can truly predict what a wedding day will bring.

"Or something," Keko says.

"Hey, I gotta go figure something out with the caterer. Will you guys keep an eye on him?"

"Of course," Elliot says. "We're on Rhys watch. Unsure if he's going to fling himself to the sharks or into the arms of his beloved."

"It's a question as old as time itself," I say, grabbing one last look at Rhys flung out on the sand before I head toward the resort's central reception area. Things are not looking promising, but I'm nothing if not a problem-solver. The sun beats down on me as I hurry toward the official central command of the resort, demanding to speak with anyone involved with the weddings. I'm passed off to various employees, until finally a harried-looking man approaches me with a smear of flour on his cheek.

"Are you the groom? Apologies. Apologies. We are setting up."

"I'm not the groom, I'm just trying to—"

"For the Noordvak reception, right?" he sighs, running a forearm along his glistening forehead.

"No." My heart sinks lower. "Not Noordvak. This is for the Bradford/Baker reception."

"Right, right. That's what I said." He tuts and starts to walk away again. "Listen, we'll be setting up shortly. No worries. No worries."

I'm gaping after him, unable to judge just how few worries I should have, when footsteps rush up behind me.

"Weston!" It's Nova, and she looks wild-eyed. "I found the wedding planner. She was having a blowup with the florist. They double booked events today and don't have flowers for Amelia's wedding!"

She's clutching my forearms, everything drawn tight between us. The news keeps getting worse, but there's got to be a silver lining somewhere. "Okay. That's bad, but I at least found the caterer. He says they're going to set up shortly." I opt not to add that it might be for someone else's wedding altogether.

"The planner is up with Amelia and her mom. Her mom is in tears over this. It's a total clusterfuck up there."

"We'll figure something out." My gaze drifts around the lobby, landing on plenty of exotic blossoms tucked into various arrangements. "How many flowers would we need? Bouquet...altar decoration...?"

"Table centerpieces," she adds.

"Let's downsize a little bit. What if we could get enough for a bouquet and decorations for the pictures? Hell, we could steal a few flowers here and there, and nobody would even fucking notice."

She blinks. "That's not a bad idea."

"Let's see how many we can get."

She grins like we're the bad guys hatching a plan to rob a bank, and we make a beeline for for an ornate flower arrangement in the middle of the lobby. We pause, looking around like there might be spies.

"Put your camera around your neck," I tell her.

"Why?"

"We can use the camera bag for the flowers."

"You never stop thinking, do you?"

I help her remove the camera and unzip the bag. Then, like a magician practicing sleight of hand, I snag three big white roses from the centerpiece. I look around, trying not to act suspicious.

"That was easier than I thought," I admit. "Let's go outside and see what's out there."

We hurry toward the front doors. Guests are milling all around, but still, it's hard not to feel like we could be outed at any moment by workers or security cameras. Outside, the pickings are plentiful. Huge hibiscus plants line the front landscaping, with the occasional swaths of bougainvillea and wild orchids. Nova gasps.

"This is fucking perfect." She goes up to the bougainvillea. "Look. These vines would be so beautiful on top of the altar."

"There's so much of it too, they won't even notice it missing," I say.

She reaches into the burst of color and gasps. "Okay. This motherfucker's got thorns."

"Hang on." I reach into my back pocket, where I keep a swiss army knife on me *most* days—unless I'm swimming. "I got this."

The impressed look on her face satisfies me more deeply than I can explain as I gently saw off a few gorgeous vines of the plant. What we're doing is wrong, but desperate times call for desperate measures. I'm not going to let my best friend's soon-to-be mother-in-law weep in a hotel room because the florist forgot to put her daughter's wedding on the schedule. Not on my watch.

"Uh, Weston?" Nova places a hand on my arm as I go for the third bougainvillea victim. "This stuff isn't gonna fit in my camera bag. We either need to leave immediately or conjure a trash bag in the next ten seconds."

"Why the next ten seconds?"

"Because there is a very stern security guard heading our way."

I don't need to hear another word. I guide her by the small of her back toward the lobby doors, stuffing the contraband beneath my arm. I'm using the oldest trick in the book—don't make eye contact and they won't formally come after you.

"Definitely will have to come back later," I murmur. "But I think we've got a good start."

We speed walk through the lobby once more, but not so fast that I can't pluck a lily from a different floral arrangement by the guest bathrooms. My phone vibrates just as we cross paths with the wedding planner. Nova updates her on our flora robbery while I answer Keko's call.

"We figured out what's wrong with Rhys." He doesn't sound happy.

"Does it entail a hospital visit?" I'm joking, but terrified at the same time.

"Uh...*possibly*." Keko clears his throat. "Rhys ate a bunch of magic mushrooms this morning."

I blink about a hundred times, my steps slowing as I process this information. But then I hear a shout behind me—that security guard is still eyeing us. I hurry toward the wedding planner.

"But Rhys doesn't do shit like that," I insist in a low voice. "Are you *sure* he ate shrooms?"

"We are, like, one thousand percent positive," Keko says, a little laugh escaping him. "He's tripping his face off right now." In the background, I can hear Elliot snorting and saying, "No man, you gotta leave the pants *on*."

"How did Rhys find fucking shrooms?" I demand, much louder than is necessary. But this does not compute. Rhys is not the type of guy to just go on a psychedelic bender mere hours before his wedding.

"That's what we're trying to find out. I just hope this shit wears off before he says 'I do.'"

By the time I hang up, Nova is watching me with concern creasing her face.

"Things got worse," she says ruefully. "I can tell. I have no idea what happened, but I can already tell."

"Much worse," I confirm, keeping up my brisk walk through the resort and out into the bright sun of the patio. "But let's look on the bright side. It can only go up from here, right?"

Nova's eyes narrow to slits. "I wouldn't be so sure about that."

CHAPTER TWENTY-TWO

NOVA

The guests start arriving while Weston and I are finishing tying off our last-minute jury-rigged floral design, and more bad news continues to trickle through the pipeline.

Amelia found out about the catering situation and started crying in full makeup, as reported by Rhys's sisters. Rhys's father got into an argument with the security guard who was chasing us and almost went to real live Aruban jail. Amelia's uncle is already drunk. And perhaps biggest of all, Rhys is still under the influence of drugs on the beach.

At this point, all of us could easily go to real live Aruban jail. It's just a matter of which one of us will go first.

Elliot and Keko have at least convinced Rhys to keep his pants on by the time three o'clock rolls around, but he's drifted further down the beach and has been sitting next to an Armenian couple for the past half hour, dragging his fingers through the sand while they sing folk songs from their home country. Weston doesn't seem confident that he can convince Rhys to move. Which is surprising, because Weston has been confident about damn near everything since the shit started hitting the fan.

"You know, we had too good of a week," I blurt as Weston and I put the finishing touches on Amelia's bouquet. All things considered, this thing is gorgeous. Even if it was made piecemeal out of blooms stolen from around the resort.

His brow lifts. "Say what?"

"The wedding week. It's been too perfect. No issues, just pure fun and sun." I tut, shaking my head. "If we could have spaced out some of the disasters through the week, then maybe her wedding day would have been spared."

He snorts. "You act like you didn't get attacked by a flamingo the other day."

"That's not a disaster. That's just inevitable."

"I don't follow, but that's okay, because it still makes sense somehow." He uses his Swiss army knife to cut off a piece of hemp that he procured somehow, twisting it around the base of the flower stems to create a makeshift wrap. And yes, it's sexy somehow. Because everything he does is sexy. Especially in the seersucker. "All set. What's next?"

Marry me? I roll my lips inward, making doubly sure the words aren't accidentally spoken. But oh lord, I've fallen completely in love with this man over the past three hours. As if the previous three days weren't enough, he had to go and thieve some flowers in the name of true love. I suddenly understand how the contestants on *Love is Blind* might have kinda-sorta fallen in love with their partners during that week in the pods. Spending every waking second with someone, talking and connecting and now problem-solving, fast-tracks the feelings.

And I am one hundred percent *all about* Weston Daly.

"Nova?" He's prompting me, because I've spent too much time counseling myself not to admit I'm in love with him. Which is not something I'd actually say, because yes, I'm aware of how insane it sounds. Go from hate to love within four days? Absurd. Even by Romeo and Juliet standards.

"I think it's time for some pictures. And let's check in with someone about formally postponing the start for at least a half hour." I jerk my chin toward the taupe seer-sucker out on the northern edge of the coast. "Unless Keko and Elliot can convince him to come back to Earth a little sooner."

"A half hour is probably on the low end." Weston's hand settles at the small of my back as he guides me toward the reception area. I've been relishing his small touches all day. Part of me wants to read it as possessiveness. But of course, these are conversations a sane woman does *not* have with her island lover.

Even though every inch of me wishes he could become my year-round boyfriend.

Weston presses a small kiss to my temple—he's been avoiding my lips as instructed, even though I'm willing to smear every bit of makeup on my face for one good, juicy kiss from him.

"Are you going to give a speech today?" I ask him as we reenter the reception patio. Our floral adornments have helped slightly. The caterers are just beginning to set up, which is a small relief, at least.

"Maybe. Once he's done tripping on drugs and can remember who he is."

I laugh. "Don't want to waste a good speech on a guy who's drifting in a different dimension."

"Exactly. But really, I don't have much to say that's PG. All the stories I could share would make his parents faint."

"Some of the backpacker stories are best left on the open road," I muse as we walk past some of the catering staff setting up steam tables. "But really, you don't have anything to say? What about something about true love and soul mates?"

He shrugs. "I don't know anything about true love or soul mates. What could I possibly add that they don't already know?"

"I find that hard to believe." I pause at a stone ledge to set down my camera bag so we can start taking pictures. "You've never, like, been in love before?"

Weston's gaze slides away from me, and the sight of his immaculate, effortless profile steals my breath yet again. There's something about the seersucker style combined with his dark, slicked back hair and the ice blue of his eyes. I need to call *Vogue-Aruba* right now and report Weston as too gorgeous. I will *not* be surprised when half of my photos tonight are of him and him alone.

"I don't stay in one place for too long," he begins.

"You've never had a girlfriend? Even a long-term fuck buddy?"

He shrugs. "I've been with plenty of women. Just never found anyone that stuck."

"Always the groomsman, never the groom?" I crack.

"I'll *never* be the groom."

"Ah." Something deep inside me tightens and begins a long, slow sink to my feet. It's not like I was already imagining Weston's and my wedding on a different beach in Aruba or anything. "Well, in that case, if you have no experience to draw on, maybe you could just tone down one of your wild stories from traveling with Rhys so that his great-aunt doesn't have a hernia along with her salmon."

He smirks as I hand him my second camera. "Not a bad idea."

"Amelia told me this morning about how she knew Rhys was the one." I sniff as I uncap the lens and begin setting up a test shot. "She said there was a sign."

"Like, Ace of Base-style?"

I'm unable to resist belting out the chorus. *"I saw the sign, and it opened up my eyes..."* He joins me, and we sing together, finally dissolving into laughter. It's somehow cathartic—and draws looks from the catering employees.

"I don't know. She said she received a sign that let her know Rhys was truly the one. And I guess I kind of look for stuff like that, too."

He's quiet as I unload camera lenses and get things set up. Finally, I hazard a glance at him.

"You do see yourself settling down with someone someday, right?"

The clouds in his eyes blow back in as he glances at me. "I don't like the idea of settling down."

"Spoken like a true backpacker." I force a smile, but on the inside, his words are slashing through me. It's the quiet confirmation of what I know to be true: that Weston and I can never be. Not with how we live our lives. Not with how my only *goal* in life is to settle down and scrape together a beautiful life. Weston and I could exist together nowhere except in my fantasies, where he will continue to rule for the rest of my life.

Awesome.

But now's not the time to think about it. Even though I'd love to receive a flash-bang sign from Zeus himself about Weston's and my inevitability as a happily long-term couple, that is *not* going to happen. And I don't want to be sad quite yet. I zip up my case once I've gotten everything we need ready, and I put my camera around my neck.

"Ready, second shooter?"

"Ready, player one."

I smirk. "The only Easter egg we're looking for in this simulation is a smooth wedding. Let's get cracking."

By now the tables are at least covered in white linens and some of the centerpieces are set up. I direct Weston to take the wider shots while I go for the close-ups. We migrate this way to all the different areas related to the wedding—the ceremony patio, the boardwalk, the beach itself. I've already taken Amelia's photos in all her stages of preparation, which came out amazingly well and thankfully happened before the florist-and-caterer meltdown. But even though we're catching up, there's a knot in my chest that I can't get rid of.

Is it the fact that my best friend is probably beside herself with anxiety and stress right now, in her resort tower, awaiting the wedding? Or maybe because the groom is now pensive and shirtless a half-mile down the beach? The family members gathering at the folding chairs look happy enough, but there's tension lining the paradise breeze. On the edge of the boardwalk, Amelia's uncle is talking aggressively with a resort worker, and I'm terrified to find out what about. Weston must notice at the same time I do, because he gives me a look and jerks his head in that direction.

"I'm going to defuse whatever the fuck is about to blow up here," he says, then presses a kiss to my forehead. A tiny, contented sigh escapes me, and I watch him walk away, because I'm a thirteen-year-old teenybopper on the inside, and Weston is the closest approximation to Harry Styles.

My phone vibrates a moment later, and I struggle with my camera bag to extract the damn thing from its pouch. Amelia is calling. My insides go tight as I answer with a tentative, "Hello?"

"Nova? Are you downstairs?"

"Yeah, I'm...here." I look toward the resort, trying to spot her out on a balcony somewhere. "Can you see me?"

"No. I'm in the lobby." She sounds calmer, at least. "Getting ready to walk down the aisle. But the wedding planner told me Rhys isn't ready."

My tight insides turn into a clenched fist. "He's...not."

There's a disconcerting pause. "Nova...is Rhys about to leave me at the altar?"

A breath of air whooshes out of me as I process all the worry and heartbreak my best friend must be living through, *on her wedding day.* "Oh, my god, *no.* No, it's not that at all! I promise. He just, uh..." I twist to look down at the far end of the beach. "He took a pre-ceremony walk, and he's not quite back yet." I won't add that the walk was to the other side of the universe, in his head.

She tuts, and when she speaks again, I can hear the emotion trembling in her voice. "Are you sure?"

"Amelia, I have never been more certain of anything in my life." I can see Rhys starting to walk this way with Keko and Elliot on either side of him, so I'm at least 99% sure at this point. He's not in handcuffs and isn't struggling to flee with the Armenian couple, so it seems like he's ready to get married now. "How are you feeling? Ready to fucking tie the knot?"

"This has been the afternoon from hell," she tells me in a low voice. "And I am ready for a goddamn steak and thirteen glasses of wine with my new husband at my side."

A sharp laugh bursts out of me, and I cover my mouth. "See that, right there? That just made everything good again. You've officially reversed whatever Aruban curse was placed on you, I'm pretty sure."

She lets out an exaggerated sigh. "I hope so. What do you think got me cursed? Was it when the flamingo bit you?"

"That flamingo might have been an undercover witch," I tell her.

"They always are," Amelia murmurs. "Babe, I'm nervous. How is everything looking out there?"

My gaze sweeps over the scene—Weston now involved in the angry conversation between uncle and resort employee, the milling family members, the mostly-not-ready caterers that somehow have to feed fifty mouths in an hour, the half-assed stolen flower arrangement created by Weston and me. But more importantly, the brilliant sun, the achingly beautiful surroundings, and the reassuring rhythmic rush of the ocean.

All Amelia and Rhys want today is to get married. None of the rest of it matters even half as much as all their friends and family sharing in the important moment. And if that's the only requirement, well, they've already got it. Besides, the wedding days that go wrong make for the best stories. And at this point, Rhys and Amelia will have all sorts of stories to tell their eventual kids and grandkids.

"It's looking like you're about to have the most memorable wedding of your life," I tell her, and we snicker together.

Rhys has finally rejoined the boardwalk, looking oddly triumphant. I hang up with Amelia just as Rhys raises his fist, causing his unbuttoned linen shirt to hang open, exposing his tanned chest.

"The skies opened. The marital union is a go."

Elliot and Keko exchange a look behind his back. Elliot is carrying Rhys's shoes, and Rhys pads barefoot up the white aisle to the grand, bougainvillea-adorned arch where the officiant is waiting.

"I'm ready to get married," Rhys says, clamping a hand onto the man's shoulder.

"You're not marrying him, mate," Elliot begins, but Rhys waves him off.

"I know. I know. He just needs to hear my conviction," Rhys says.

And all the while, I'm snapping pictures. Because I can hear his conviction. And oh, my god, there's a lot more than conviction here.

There's love and weirdness and frustration and everything wild about a wedding day.

I look to my side and find the ice-blue cool of Weston sauntering my way, my heart goes into knots all over again. If it weren't for Weston at my side, I wouldn't have handled my shit half as well.

And even though I know it's ridiculous, I need to tell him how I feel.

How much I disliked him at first. How different he is from what my parents want for me. How my friend Jimmy back home is literally his opposite, and how close I was to just settling down and sucking it up.

But more than that?

I need to tell him how in five short days, I fell so hard for him that he might be the only man I ever think about again.

CHAPTER TWENTY-THREE

WESTON

The wedding starts forty minutes behind schedule, which is great, all things considered.

Rhys refused to wear shoes or button his shirt, which mortified his parents.

And there was the beach hog incident. Two grunting, feral hogs that were either flirting or actively mating stumbled onto the patio, one of them actually knocking over the officiant and shattering a vase. But I was there to help the officiant back to his feet, so they could get to the whole *kissing the bride* part and seal the deal on this wild wedding while the hogs grunted weirdly from the beach.

And the whole time, Nova flitted around in the background like the photographer extraordinaire that she is. The wedding should have taken precedence, but I could hardly stop admiring Nova at work. It's a thing of beauty to see someone excel at what they love doing. It's how I used to feel about my job, before I was fired.

The way I hope to feel about something again, someday. And somewhere between wrangling Rhys from the far reaches of his mushroom trip and weaving a flower adornment that my best friend would stand under, I realized that influencing isn't it.

So when Rhys and Amelia are kissing while the thunder of applause surrounds us, I'm grinning like an idiot. Happier for them than I could have fathomed. And wondering when I'll be able to kiss Nova and get her back into my arms for the evening.

But Nova is all business. Once the wedding wraps, it's off to pictures. She herds the bridal party down to the beach, where the wedding planner is still dabbing her eyes and going on about the beautiful ceremony. Nova gently but firmly guides us into photos while the wind flattens her dress against all those beautiful curves. Once it becomes clear she plans to photograph all of us without even one picture including her, I jog toward her, gesturing toward the camera.

"What are you doing?"

"Second shooter override. Get in the fucking picture."

She laughs a little, glancing toward the group. "You don't have to..."

"Nova. This is a big day for you, too," I say gently, guiding her toward the group by the hips. "At least humor me with one picture, okay? Now go get with your friends."

She sends me a grateful look and scoots off to join Rhys, Amelia, and the rest. I capture a few amazing pictures, and then Nova is back in go-mode. While she's calling out for Amelia's family, I go to her camera bag and remove the second camera. I want to make this as easy as possible, and besides, I forgot how fun it was to be a part of big productions like this.

The adrenaline. The laughter. The moving parts that lead to an unexpected equation. I see why she loves doing this, and it's something that I have always loved as well. Though I'm less about the photos and more about graphic design, there's still something in the art of the event wrangling that appeals to me. And even though this was the last thing I expected to end up doing in Aruba, it's somehow been the most meaningful.

All thanks to Nova.

Once photos are done and everyone is beginning the slow trek to the reception area, Nova pulls me aside and plants a juicy kiss on my lips. One that steals my breath and absolutely, most definitely ruins her lipstick.

"Thank you," she breathes when we break apart. "For everything."

"What did I do?" I ask, all coy-like, as I wrap my arms around her waist. Here it is. The moment I've been waiting for. This woman is a drug, and I do not even fucking care that I'm addicted. Just give me more.

"All the second shooter shenanigans." She smirks. "Do you know how much time you saved me? Shit. A girl could get used to that."

"You trying to ask me to come back to New York with you?"

I mean it as a joke, but when something serious slides over her face, I realize I need to back track. I don't even know where those words came from, only that they slipped out, unbidden, and that more are liable to follow in their wake.

"I doubt you need much help with senior pictures," I add. "Unless you've got someone *really shitty* working with you."

She laughs weakly, but it seems forced. She looks over my shoulder toward the resort. "They're not even hiring. But I don't want to go back there."

I squeeze her hips, ready to change the subject. I shouldn't have gone there. Couldn't even say why I did. "Ready to head to the reception? More mayhem awaits us."

"Please, God—no more accidental mushroom doses or feral hog interruptions."

"There's still time for someone to get arrested," I whisper against her lips, "or all the food to come out burnt. Just be optimistic, okay?"

She dissolves into laughter against me, and we laugh like this, lips touching but not truly kissing, moving with the echoes of our amusement. She's the only type of girl I've done this type of thing with. The only one I've dared to open up to. And for as scary as it is...it's been going okay.

Still doesn't mean I should do it anymore.

In fact, the night ahead of us reminds me that it's time to start distancing myself. We've got two more nights together before we both fly far away. Two nights is nothing, but it's also *everything*. At the rate we've been diving into each other, two nights is the same as six months. If I want to make it off the island unscathed—and I *always* make it out unscathed—then I need to begin my detachment plan.

It's just that Nova makes it so damn hard.

We walk hand-in-hand back to her camera bag, where we pack up the lenses. Nova fishes out her phone and frowns down at the screen, swiping tentatively.

"What's wrong?" I ask.

"Nothing," she says. But after a few more moments of silent staring at her phone, I poke again.

"You look like you're reading very bad news."

She lets out a sigh. "I just got some weird texts from my friend Jimmy."

My insides do that accordion thing where they crumple up all tight like my organs are about to eject themselves. Jimmy is the guy who I thought Nova was with. And even though she assured me that she's not, I still don't exactly love that he's texting her right now.

And I love even less that I fucking care.

"And?"

She glances up at me, confusion in her gaze. "He asked for the resort address."

I go ahead and ask the obvious question. "Why does he need the address?"

"He's probably looking it up on Google Maps or something."

"Why would he be looking it up on Google Maps?"

"To live vicariously, I guess? Haven't you ever spied on a random bed and breakfast in Romania on Google Maps?"

"No, but...I'll add that to my to-do list," I tell her. "If you ask me, sounds like ol' Jimmy is on the island."

She laughs so long and sarcastically that it makes her point without saying. Still, she adds, "That's one thousand percent not possible."

"Why, was he banned from travelling to Aruba?"

"No, he's just...not a traveler. I doubt he even has his passport."

"Did you give him the address?"

"Of course I did," she says. "I'm not going to keep him from checking out the resort on Google Maps."

Part of me can't believe it, but she seems so convinced of his intentions, that I have to go with the flow. After all, what do I know? And why do I care *this* much? As we walk back to the boardwalk, I realize my fists are balled, as if Nova just told me she'd been approached by a creep at night. And given the fact that I'm supposed to be detaching as of *immediately*, this is not good news.

On the boardwalk, a man approaches us, a hotel employee I've seen lingering near the edges all day. It seemed like he'd been watching us, and maybe I was right. He offers a hand as he comes up.

"The incredible photography duo," he says in a smooth baritone. "Pleasure to meet you. My name is Edward. I work for the resort event planning office, and I've been keeping an eye on the wedding today."

"Nice to meet you," Nova says with a little smile.

"Would the two of you be able to swing by my office tomorrow? I don't want to keep you from the celebration tonight. There's something I want to chat about before you leave."

Nova swings her gaze to me, question marks and exclamation points there. "Uh, sure?"

"Yeah, that sounds great," I finish for her.

"Awesome. You two have a great night. And just ask for me in the lobby. They'll show you right where to find me." He passes Nova a business card before he walks away, whistling. She looks at the card incredulously.

"I wonder what that was about?"

"He probably wants copies of these pictures," I say. "Or maybe to feature the wedding in promotional material?"

"Either of those would be fantastic," she says as we drift toward the reception. As soon as we step onto the patio, the festivities sweep us away. Stringed globe lights crisscross the space, but they're not lit up yet since the evening is still blazing orange and red all around us. The caterers finally got their shit together, unless they just overlooked the Noordvak wedding altogether, and servers bring around appetizers on small trays while everyone chats and laughs and poses for selfies against a nearby backdrop. A small band is playing reggae-style tropical music, and it's hard not to immediately start moving with the beat.

Nova and I set our things down at the table reserved for the bridal party, and she's immediately swept away by Amelia for a heart-to-heart that looks like it involves lots of happy tears. I head for the bar to grab myself a beer and a Sauvignon Blanc for Nova. I've seen her drinking it enough times, it seems like a safe bet. I wonder what her favorite beer is. Whether she's into IPAs. And I already know at least three solid breweries and wineries I'd love to show her, if we're ever back in the US on the West Coast together.

Stop that, Weston. This ends Monday. Remember?

As soon as I get my beer, I've downed half of it. I smile and nod my way through the people who have come to feel so familiar after so few days together.

"Jimmy?"

Nova's sharp squeak makes me stop in my tracks. I turn, following the sound of her voice. She's across the patio, near the table where we left our things, one palm pressed to her chest.

And there he is. The guy who very clearly was not just using Google Maps. The illustrious *Jimmy*.

He's got the look of a brute who's dressing up on his own for the first time. His button-up is untucked, his hairstyle is overgrown, and from the way he's watching Nova, I can tell he's in fucking love with her.

My stomach turns to an acid knot, and I'm walking that way without even deciding to. I need to keep an eye on this train wreck, or I need to intervene. One of the two will happen. A million questions create a logjam in my throat as I storm across the patio. First and foremost being confusion: *Which one of us is Nova playing here?*

But the answer is apparent as soon as I set my beer down on the table. Jimmy's holding his arms out because he wants a hug, and Nova is grimacing every step of the way.

I'm at her side as soon she pulls away from him. I sling my arm over her shoulder to make my point.

"Who's the new arrival?" I ask, looking down at her.

Her eyes turn into green saucers, and when she opens her mouth, nothing comes out.

Jimmy doesn't look enthused.

"Weston! This is my friend Jimmy, from back home." She sweeps her arm in his direction, as though there was any doubt which one he was. "We play pool together a few nights a week. Jimmy, meet my friend Weston."

I stick out my hand, eager for Jimmy to even fucking try to assert dominance. What would Nova have done if I wasn't here? I'm getting the sensation that she played the nice card a little bit too often with this guy. And whatever signals she's sending out, he's not reading them.

"Pleased to meet you." His handshake is limp, which annoys me. To Nova, I say, "Aren't you going to give me a lead-in?"

Part of her spell breaks. "What?"

"Like, 'Weston—he excels at partner yoga and knows how to find the best sunsets.'"

When Nova sends me a tight little grin, I know she gets what I'm saying. I jerk my chin toward Jimmy. "What brings you to Aruba?"

His brows draw together. "I came to surprise Nova."

Again, the doubt flashes through me. Nova could have been lying to me, but somehow, I just don't think this is the case. Call me head over heels, but I'm pretty sure I haven't misread her this entire time. Jimmy? Jimmy looks like a guy to misread things.

"At a wedding you weren't invited to?" I ask, my tone much sharper than I intended. *Oops.*

Jimmy throws his arms out to his sides. "It's a resort. Who cares?"

"I'm...shocked, Jimmy," Nova says carefully. "Why would you make a trip like this without saying something first?"

"I told you. I wanted to surprise you." Jimmy's gaze drags over my arm, where my hand is dangling perilously close to Nova's cleavage. Exactly the plan. "Can we talk somewhere else?"

Nova's confused—I can feel it in every inch of her body. She doesn't know how to handle this situation, because it went from weird to sticky in about five seconds flat.

"Do you want me to come with you?" I ask in a low voice. I'm not trying to flex in front of Jimmy. Well, not entirely. But I want Nova to feel safe. I don't know this guy. She says he's a friend, but to me, my Dude Senses are telling me it only takes him about two Busch Lights before he starts pushing his chest out.

"It's fine," Nova says, looking up at me with a tight smile. She's all strained edges and bewilderment; I can see it flashing in her eyes, feel it pouring off of her. Does this guy feel it? Does he even fucking know Nova?

She squeezes my hand before she heads off, Jimmy on her trail, leaving me with my tense thoughts. Jimmy glances over his shoulder at me as they walk away, something dark and threatening there. And of course I respond. Of course I start following him, because the longer I stare at him, the more things are making sense.

This guy is trying to pick up Nova, but little does he know, Nova is mine.

CHAPTER TWENTY-FOUR

NOVA

My legs have turned into butter as I lead Jimmy off the patio and down the sidewalk lined with sculpted bushes. This will afford us some privacy, at least, as I figure out *what in the actual fuck he's doing in Aruba.*

As I sink onto a bench and try to find the words to clarify this clusterfuck, I can't help but think that I was right. We had too good of a week. All the mishaps coalesced into one giant shit volcano. And just when I thought I'd dodged all the ash and lava from the explosion and we'd all made it to the other side with amazing memories and plenty of disasters averted, well...here's Jimmy.

Acting like he's about to get down on one knee.

"Did you reserve a room here? How did you even get here? Do you like...have a passport?" These are only the first questions I have for him. Jimmy sinks down onto the bench beside me, that same defeated sigh he always uses that sounds exactly like my father escaping him.

Like he's fifty-five instead of twenty-five.

"I'd been planning this for a while. And I've actually had my passport for a few years. I went to Canada with the boys for a hunting trip."

I'm not sure what to be bewildered by first. The fact that Jimmy has been to Canada and I haven't, or the fact that he's been *planning to surprise me in Aruba.*

"I don't understand," I sputter. "I...I thought we were just friends."

He lets out an exasperated sigh. "Isn't it obvious I've been wanting to take things further?"

The sound of approaching voices makes me sit upright. Elliot and Keko have stepped out of the reception area, just barely visible at the end of the sidewalk. They're chatting lightheartedly, though I can't hear what they're talking about. The edge of Weston's body comes into view, making everything inside me warm and fuzzy all at once.

"Jesus. That guy again," Jimmy spits. He leans forward, calling down the pathway to Weston. "She didn't want you to tag along, buddy."

"Jimmy," I say, pressing a hand to his forearm. "He's just talking to his friends."

"He's fucking watching you. I don't know what right he thinks he has. Are you with him?"

The question knocks me off center. I don't know how to answer it other than *yes*, but it feels so wrong to say that when Weston might vehemently disagree. But God, all I want to say is *yes*.

Yes, he's with me. Yes, we're planning on moving back to New York state together. Yes, he and I will be opening our own photography studio someday.

"I don't know," I finally say.

"How can you not know?"

"I don't understand why it's anybody's business." My cheeks are heating up, and the onslaught of emotions is suddenly too much to bear. I'm equal parts mortified and bewildered. This feels like a joke, one that nobody is in on.

"I don't know why your parents thought this was a good idea," Jimmy mutters, running his thumb back and forth over his cracked knuckles.

"My parents?"

He scoffs, crossing his arms over his chest. "They said I should show you I like to travel. Well here I am. Overpriced hotel, shitty roads, and weird bathrooms."

I want to cover my face with my hands and groan until the cows come home, but I don't think Jimmy would take that very well. And really, he shouldn't. Because this has been one of the more illuminating moments of my entire life, the lightning crack realization that going for the safe guy just because he seems fine and stable enough is unequivocally a bad idea.

I cannot believe my parents encouraged Jimmy to come here. But maybe they did me a favor. Maybe seeing Jimmy outside of his natural habitat is the final nail in the coffin.

I can't settle. Not for Jimmy. Not for anyone who doesn't share this pulsing *need* to move and see things. Not when I've got these longings bursting in my chest. Not with all the pictures I have yet to take. Not when there is a path for me alone to carve, even if I'm not sure where the next fork in the road is.

"You shouldn't have come, Jimmy," I say softly, even though it hurts to say. I'm used to making things pleasant around him. Letting him think he's funny. Meeting him in his comfort zone—the pool hall, the bar, his backyard for bonfires with friends. "I didn't think you were serious when you said you wanted to visit. I mean, just last month you told me you hated flying."

"Yeah, well, I flew for you." He shakes his head, looking at the ground. "This was all for you."

Well, hello, guilt! This is my most well-known companion on this little journey known as life. And with these words, Jimmy reminds me just how often he lobs it at me. The words he used here remind me of the words he used the night I didn't want to go to the drive-in theater. The words he used when I told him I was even planning this trip to Aruba, when he said my money would be better spent in the state of New York.

It just ties into a long thread of ways that I'm wrong in life. Who's guilty for wanting more than what her parents expected for her? This girl right here. Anyone feeling guilty for not liking a perfectly fine man who just doesn't spark with her? Also this girl. What about someone who feels guilty simply for thinking about spending money when she and all her relatives are buried in debt?

Surprise! Also me.

But if there's one thing Weston was right about—I *can* carve out the life of my dreams. Even if it just starts with not stepping into a relationship with a guy I only sorta like, simply because he's available and makes good money.

I might be ready for a relationship, but I'm not desperate. And dammit, that might be the only upper hand I have right now.

An awkward silence settles between us. I need to pull myself out of this, and fast. Because if guilt serves any purpose, it's eroding logic and rationality. If I sit here stewing much longer, I'm liable to tell Jimmy we'll see where things go once I get back, just because I feel like I owe him somehow for the trip down here. Since, you know, being a woman is not complicated or confusing at all.

"I'm not sure what you want me to say." The words barely make it past my dry lips. "I didn't ask you to come. We aren't on the same page, apparently."

I stand, ready to end this conversation. Because his being here is not my responsibility. I am here to celebrate my best friend getting married, and to get drunk. That is *it*.

And I plan to continue that ASAP.

Weston begins making his way down the sidewalk, clearly taking my movement as a sign that he can approach. I watch him come, all my insides going melty and fangirl-ish. His arm slides around my waist once he's back at my side, and Jimmy just scoffs.

"What are you, her guard dog?"

"I don't know, is there something I need to guard her from?" Weston shoots back.

The air draws tight between them. Jimmy drags his unamused gaze back to me.

"You really had to pick a douche like this? You're better than this loser." He jerks his chin toward Weston. "What do you even do? Live off Mommy and Daddy's money? Maybe you sell drugs on the beach. Just kind of drift along until you panhandle enough money to eat?"

Weston's arm drops from my side, and he scrubs the side of his jaw, gaze stuck on Jimmy. "Nova, I'm gonna punch this guy. I'm trying really hard not to, but I'm pretty sure it's gonna happen."

I sputter, looking between the two of them. "Guys, you don't need to—"

"What, you need her blessing or something?" Jimmy sneers.

"Just trying not to ruin my best friend's wedding is all," Weston barks back, taking a step closer. "Not like you fucking care. You don't know anyone here. Not even Nova."

Jimmy steps up to him, but now they're too close for me to intervene. This is going to end with fists, and I'm too shocked to do anything.

"Hey, Weston, buddy, what's going on?" Elliot comes up from behind, Keko trailing.

"Just having a chat," Weston says. His face is edged with something hard. Like he's truly fighting a battle inside himself...and losing. I've never seen it before. I just want this all to stop.

"I can't believe you think you know a damn thing about Nova," Jimmy says. "What, you met her twelve hours ago and suddenly she's the love of your life? Fucking childish bullshit right there."

"What's worse? Falling for someone over the course of a week or chasing them for months and not even fucking realizing they're not into you?"

Jimmy swings, but Weston dodges. All hell breaks loose. Weston lunges and socks him in the face, while Keko and Elliot shout from behind, trying break up to the fight. Elliot tries to intervene while Keko goes to Jimmy's side, but Jimmy pushes him off. Keko goes tumbling into the bushes. My jaw lives permanently on the ground. I will need a broom to scoop it up from the sidewalk. I cannot even comprehend what I'm witnessing.

Are they fighting for my honor? It seems so ridiculous, but then again, this whole day has been. What's a little scuffle in the name of love to wrap things up?

Jimmy lands a punch or two, but Weston has him pinned to the sidewalk before long. Jimmy's lip is bleeding. By now hotel staff are rushing to the scene, and unknown men are pulling Weston off Jimmy and restraining Jimmy as he tries to lunge for Weston again.

Weston's hair is mussed but he still looks *Vogue* ready, which seems impossible after a fistfight. Weston is cornered by Elliot and Keko, while the hotel employees try to calm the scene.

"Jimmy, just go," I tell him, my voice cracking.

"Wow. You'd think that traveling eight hundred miles might mean I'd get laid at the end of it," Jimmy mutters, and then spits on the ground. Weston breaks through the Elliot-and-Keko barrier and rushes Jimmy again, pushing him backward into the sculpted bush. The perfectly trimmed foliage bends and gives way under their weight, ruining the clean lines of the bush. The employees haul Weston off again, shouting, "Don't play in the bushes!"

And this time, Weston grabs my hand.

"Life's too fucking short for bullshit like this," Weston spits, and I let him lead me away.

Because he's right.

CHAPTER TWENTY-FIVE

NOVA

We drink. Like, *a lot.*

Because not only did we help save Amelia and Rhys's wedding, we lived through a lot of shit that should not have happened in one day. I still can't believe those hogs sniffed Amelia's dress. More than that, I can't believe that was the *least* outrageous thing that happened.

The reception flies by in a blissed-out blur. I do not worry about Jimmy one bit, because he is not my burden to bear. He is his own damn man, and I am having my own damn fun.

And even though it seems like there is so much left to talk about and figure out between Weston and me...tonight is simply not the night. We are blowing off all the steam and stress of the wedding day like the jubilant revelers we are. All around us, face are smiling, glasses lifted, shouts ringing through the night air.

Weston and I finally leave the party around one a.m. We stumble back to my hut, where the rush-hum of the waves feels like a warm embrace.

But not as warm as Weston's. That embrace feels like coming home. He backs me up against the door of my hut as soon as we're inside, kissing me deeply. Thoroughly. So passionately that my panties are soaked before we've taken a step toward the bed.

"You kiss too gooooood," I groan once we break apart.

"No, you," he says, bending down to gather the fabric of my dress. He pushes it up to my hips, and then makes quick work of his fly. "All I need to fucking do is look at your lips and I'm hard. You think that makes life easy for me?"

I dissolve into laughter, but it turns into a gasp when the hard ridge of his cock pushes against the damp crotch of my panties.

"I've had a fantasy of fucking you in this dress all night." His teeth scrape at the hollow of my neck. "Please say I can make it come true."

"*Puh-leeeze* make it come true."

He fumbles for a condom, somehow rolling it over his cock while I'm still pinned to the door. Then he's kissing me again, and nudging himself into me so gingerly, so lovingly, that tears are pressing at my eyes before he's even fully inside.

"Why are you so great?" I wail, banging my head against the door.

He grunts, burying his face in my cleavage. Exactly where I wish his head would be *all* the time.

"Don't even fucking start, Nova," he warns me, flexing his hips as he claims more of the space inside me. "You're the great one here."

"You stole flowers to save Amelia's wedding," I remind him, my voice growing wispy as he buries himself inside of me. The stretching sensation is too good, too primal, for me to focus much longer on words.

"You took pictures *and* problem-solved like a boss," he says.

"You protected my honor when Jimmy showed up," I say, sinking my nails into his shoulder as he claims even more depth.

He grunts, hoisting me a little. "You protected your own honor."

His words hit me like a gut punch and a sweet kiss at the same time. Because he's right. And that's just one more thing I love—yes, love—about Weston. He challenges me *and* appreciates me. He protects me and pushes me. He will stand up *to* me and stand up *for* me.

Now the tears are coming for real. Brought to you by the *it was a good idea at the time* mixture of cosmopolitans and red wine.

I bury my face in his neck. I want to drown on the scent there so that I never forget it. So that it becomes part of my own DNA. Because Weston is the type of man I never want to live without, and I'm pretty sure I'm not just being drunk about it.

"Oh, Weston," I breathe as he claims the final inch of space inside me. He rocks himself in a slow circle, grinding up against my clit. All my emotions turn into a cyclone, and with the incredible wind speed of what's happening inside my chest, I'm no longer able to hear the quiet whisper of rationality.

"I just love you," I blurt, precisely as he's pulled himself out and drilled back inside me.

My confession turns into a moan, which turns into breathy pants as he fucks me senseless. He doesn't say *I love you* back, because he is either, A.) not as drunk as me, or B.) a sane adult who doesn't fall in love after four days. Luckily, the force of his passion distracts me from my embarrassing gaffe.

He fucks me too good to care right now. I squeal and clench and ride the waves of pleasure as the door goes *thud-thud-thud* into the night. I can't care. He clearly doesn't care. This is just too fucking raw and right.

I come twice—first when he grinds up against my clit for the umpteenth time, and then again when he takes big handfuls of my breasts, tweaks my nipples, and drills into me so hard that I see stars. Weston can play me like a goddamn fiddle, and he knows it.

Yet another thing I love about him.

By the time my toes touch the floor, I am pure liquid. I somehow stumble and flop over to the bed, where I immediately splay out and prepare to fall asleep. Weston just chuckles as he undresses.

"So I take it you came," he says unnecessarily.

I groan something and raise my hand, and then it flops back to the bed. Because I have no energy left.

And I pass out. Hard.

When I finally come to, I feel like Sleeping Beauty waking up after her eternal sleep. The sun is shining. I hear birds. I look around, and I am somehow magically in PJ shorts and a tank top after a one-hundred-year rest.

And Weston is there, head propped on his arm, looking over at me with so much tenderness in his gaze that I feel the tears coming back. Which means they *weren't* entirely drunk tears the night before.

Not a good sign.

"Good morning," he says, dragging his fingertips over my forearm.

I stretch and yawn, relishing the early moments of this day. Relishing all the different ways *perfection* has manifested inside this hut over the week. "How long have you been up?"

"A couple hours?"

I jolt, reaching for my phone. It's almost eleven. "Oh my god. How did I sleep this long?"

"You needed it." He grins, twisting to reach for something on his nightstand. Then he tosses his sketchbook onto the bed between us. "I needed it too."

My gaze washes over the page, where he's drawn...*me*. Or at least the coolest representation of me I've ever seen. Something part comic book hero and part live figure study. Think the music video for "Take On Me" combined with anime. And it's *good*.

"Did you just do this?"

"Yeah. It's an idea I had knocking around. And sketching it out gave me more ideas. So...thanks."

"How long did this take you?"

"A half hour."

I blink rapidly. "This is phenomenal."

"I kind of see a comic book set up. There would be different frames on your adventures battling the wedding gremlins. Jimmy would show up, possibly with tentacles."

I grin, envisioning it right alongside him. "You'd be in it too."

"Sure."

"Princess Nova and Sir Weston." I hand the notebook back to him.

"Are those our comic book hero names?"

"Why not?"

He looks pleased by this. I scoot closer to him, and he stores the notebook again so he can welcome me into his arms. I nuzzle into his warm embrace. Even in the light of day, sober as a bird, it still feels like home.

Which reminds me of my embarrassing admission the night before.

I could leave it lying there and never address it until the end of time. But much like when Weston caught me masturbating while imagining him, I'm not sure I'd be able to live without facing it head on.

I sigh, running my thumb back and forth over the ridge of his abs. "So...about last night."

"Oh, you mean how you totally passed out after I fucked you against the door?"

"Yeah." I clear my throat. "Actually, a little before that."

"What was it?"

I can't tell if he's playing coy or really didn't hear me say the words, which makes this even more awkward. But today marks our last full day on the island, so it's now or never.

"What I...said to you."

He's quiet.

"Are you going to make me repeat it?"

"I don't know what you're talking about."

"I said that I loved you!"

I can hear the smile in his voice as he responds. "Actually, you said you *just* love me."

"Ugghh, so you *do* remember!" I bury my face in his side and sigh exasperatedly. "Well, whatever. Just don't hold it against me, okay?"

"Why would I hold that against you?"

"Because...I don't know." I'm at a loss for words suddenly, and the tears have returned, making my throat clamp shut. Weston is my island lover, but he is also so much more. And he could be so much more, still. But suddenly, the truth finds its way to my lips, and it all comes tumbling out. "I don't know how to do stuff like this. I'm not well-versed in *lovers*. And the truth is, I don't want you to be my lover."

"Ouch."

I sit up, looking down at him through tear-blurred eyes. This was a lot more heaviness than I planned on, especially before brushing my teeth. "That's not what I mean. I'm saying..." I pause, trying to find some other way to say the truth without baring my soul. There is none. "I don't want this to end."

His face softens, and he looks up at me, lazily swiping his thumb back and forth over my wrist. "I don't either."

"So…what should we do?" I tuck some hair behind my ear, feeling out the words in my head before I say them. "Let's…keep seeing each other."

His brows draw together. "But there's no way we can do that."

My throat closes off again. "Why not?"

"Because you're flying to New York tomorrow, and I'm going to Ohio."

"They're not that far away."

"No, but in two weeks, I'm flying to Thailand. And *that* is pretty far away."

My gaze drops to the bed as his meaning settles like uncomfortable boulders around me. Whatever excitement and perfection we were able to find here, it was never destined to last. It was only meant for Aruba.

Tears are welling up again, so I turn and scoot off the bed.

"Where are you going?" he asks.

"Just brushing my teeth." I need a minute to regroup, and staring at myself while I excise my sadness via tooth cleaning seems like just the ticket. Weston leans against the bathroom doorframe while I'm angrily applying toothpaste.

"What?" I ask, careful not to look at him in the mirror, lest I break into tears.

"You should come with me."

I falter, my gaze sliding to meet his in the mirror. "To Ohio?"

"Sure. But also to Thailand." He shrugs. "Let's make the trip together."

The toothbrush tumbles out of my hands and hits the floor, sending a white spray against the wall. I curse, hurrying to rinse it off. Once I've got my toothbrush back in hand with a new squirt of paste, I find his gaze waiting for mine in the mirror.

"You want me to go to Thailand with you?"

"It makes the most sense."

I laugh, but its humorless. I hadn't heard an ounce of sense in that suggestion, but part of me is still warmed by it. *Because he wants to go on adventure with me.* "I don't have a job waiting for me in Thailand."

"You'll find something."

"Says who?"

He expels a terse sigh, uncrossing his arms. "I don't know. The fucking universe? You've gotta take the leap to find out."

"Yeah, but if I take the leap and fall into the ravine? There are real life consequences."

He doesn't say anything as he heads back into the main bedroom. I finish my brushing my teeth, finger comb my hair, and take a hard look at myself.

I feel both on top of the world and like everything is in shambles. How can two extremes be true at once?

Weston is looking at his phone as I come back into the bedroom. "Rhys just messaged me. Brunch is almost over and he's asking where we are."

I frown. "Shit. I forgot. We should go to that."

Weston sits down, his broad, sculpted back facing me as he types out a message on his phone. I hunt for my clothes, unsure where I fall on the scale between heartbreak and frustration.

"What if we tried long distance?" I blurt. The idea has been knocking around in the back of my head as a last, desperate resort. And here I am. Using it already.

The silence that settles between us is consuming. It's deafening. It's telling me everything that he isn't saying: *That's a ridiculous idea, and it will never work.*

"Nova," he finally begins, twisting to look at me. "Let's enjoy our last day together."

"I fully plan on it." I tug my tank top off before rummaging for a bra and sundress, trying not to let the subtext of his response completely derail me before I even make it out of my hut. "I just wish we had more days to enjoy together after this."

I try not to let the sadness get me down as I ready myself for the last dregs of the last brunch on the last full day on Aruba. Weston washes up in the bathroom, using his own toothbrush that has been living in my bathroom for the past two days, because somewhere along the line we became a married couple, and then we head out into the brilliant Sunday morning. He scoops my hand into his, bringing my knuckles to his lips.

But the smile that graces my face is sad. I feel like a ghost as I drift through brunch, greeting and chatting with Amelia's and Rhys's families. I'm here, but I'm not really. Because all I can think about is that I have less than twenty-four hours left with Weston before we part ways for the rest of our lives.

We manage to scoop up the last plates of the brunch buffet before the servers clear the food. Somewhere between my first mimosa and inhaling an entire plate of eggs, I remember the business card Edward pressed into my hand yesterday.

I lean into Weston. "Should we go find that guy from the resort?"

"Let's do it." He's carrying something morose with him today like I am. His gaze lingers on me extra long each time. He's got my hand in his nearly permanently, to the point that my hand is sweating. But I don't want to give this up. I don't want to give *him* up. And our predicament seems just as impossible as Romeo and Juliet themselves.

Except it's not our families keeping us apart. It's the gig economy. Romeo and Juliet, the twenty-first century edition.

Once we finish eating and say our goodbyes to the family members who are headed to the airport, Weston and I beeline for the resort lobby. It isn't long before we're directed toward an office door labeled *MR. DE VRIES.* Edward opens the door with a big smile on his face, his blue eyes sparkling as he gestures for us to come inside.

The air is cool and leather scented. Two big arm chairs face his enormous desk. We sink into them, exchanging a curious look.

"I'm so glad you stopped by. Perfect timing, too, I was just about to go get a massage."

"That's the life," I say with a laugh.

"It really is. It's one of the hundred or so reasons why I love working at a resort." He flashes me a grin that reminds me of a car salesman. "So, listen, I won't keep you held up here. I trust you both had an amazing night."

"Stellar," I confirm.

"Outrageously good," Weston adds.

"One for the books," I tack on. I'm watching Weston to see if he'll add another one, and he almost does—but Edward butts in.

"That's great. Listen, you two work *really* well together. That was probably the first thing I noticed. But more than that, it seems the two of you work really well with the resort itself."

"Are you talking about the flowers we stole?" I ask.

Edward pauses. "No. What I mean is your adaptability. Going with the flow. There were a series of hiccups in the"—he checks some papers on his desk—"Bradford/Baker wedding yesterday, but you helped find solutions. You really went above and beyond your role as a photographer."

"Well, thank you," I tell him, grinning over at Weston. "I couldn't have done it without my second shooter."

"I notice these things. I see weddings every day of the week, practically. Which brings me to my main point." Edward laces his fingers together, leveling us with a professional look. "I want to offer you both a job."

"A job?" I squeak.

"Head wedding photographer." Edward gestures toward Weston. "Second shooter. Steady salary. Plenty of perks. And enough weddings to keep you occupied for the entire wedding season." Edward tilts his head, lifting a brow. "What do you say?"

My eyes have gone so wide that I think they might pop out of my head. "Are you serious?"

"This isn't an offer I make lightly. But also, it's not something you should decide lightly, either. Take some time to think it over. I have a contract here, which you're free to peruse at your leisure. I have just one small request."

"What's that?"

"I need an answer by tomorrow morning."

A breath whooshes out of me. I receive the packet of papers that Edward has pushed my way. Weston hasn't said anything in what feels like a millennium, and his face is totally devoid of emotion as Edward hands him a packet, too.

"I know it's short notice. But we're working on a deadline here. These weddings stop for nobody."

"I understand," I tell him, gazing at the cover page of the contract with reverence. "We'll take some time to think about it and let you know."

Edward smiles and thanks us, and we all shake hands before we're ushered back into the lobby and Edward is on his way to his massage.

I don't even make it ten steps before I begin flipping through the contract, looking for anything related to pay.

On page seven, I find it.

Because really, there's only one thing that matters here. Will they pay me enough to support myself and my gram?

And the answer is yes.

The pay is just a smidge higher than I've been making with senior portraits. It's not a huge pay increase, but it's enough to keep both me and Gram fed, housed, and happy from our different corners of the globe.

Which means that I already know my answer.

I'm ready to fucking sign the contract.

CHAPTER TWENTY-SIX

WESTON

I'm losing my shit over here.

With a job offer in my hand, a potential long-term girlfriend at my side, and more feelings than I want to fucking admit breathing down my throat, all I can think is, *I fucked up.*

I fucked up.

I caught feelings. And now I might not be able to catch my flight tomorrow.

"This is incredible." It's the tenth time she's said it. She's holding the contract to her chest as we sit on a big bench looking toward the ocean. She'll probably go to sleep with it clutched there, and I can't say I blame her.

This is exactly what she needs.

For her life.

Not for mine. *Right?*

She's blinking and holding the contract out in front of her again, as if checking for the umpteenth time that it's not a mirage.

"It's not going anywhere, babe," I tell her, pressing my lips to her temple. Because I can't *not* still treat her like this while she's near me.

I might have fucked up, but when she's sitting next to me, I want to keep fucking up. Which means that the only way I can get my head straight is to get the fuck off this island.

"Can you believe it?" It's the fifth time she's asked me that.

I laugh despite the repetition. "I couldn't the first four times you asked me, but I now I can."

She giggles, bringing the contract back to her chest. She sighs, eyes glittering as she looks out over the beach. Amelia and Rhys show up a moment later, squeezing our shoulders. As soon as Amelia asks what Nova has in her hands, it starts off a chain reaction of *Oh my god*s and *Can you even believe it*s.

Rhys listens intently as Nova shows off the contract, nodding and looking over at me. I can see the question marks in his eyes. They're the same ones in my heart.

Of course I can stay here and do this job with Nova. The question isn't even if I *want* to, because I already know I do, deep down. The question is: *Should I?*

"You really did *such* a good job," Amelia is saying. "They'd be stupid not to have someone like you on staff."

"Though I bet the other couples won't get wedding-crashed by the wild pigs," Rhys adds, elbowing me.

"Unless that's a feature you two chose and paid for beforehand and never mentioned?" Nova asks with a laugh.

"I don't remember selecting the wild pig add-on," Amelia cracks. "But who knows? The wedding planning process was a blur, so maybe I did add the 'get sniffed by a feral pig' option without realizing."

"If you blow up any picture to make into a quilt, please let it be that one," Nova says.

Keko and Elliot arrive next, which sets off another round of good news sharing. I smile and try to focus, but I can't stop thinking about Thailand.

I'm supposed to be there in two weeks. I've been fantasizing about the hustle and bustle of Chiang Mai for too long to remember. Mountaintop temples have been whispering in my dreams for months. Cliffhangers hasn't confirmed anything yet, but I have the surest bet of making something of myself if I go there.

And that's how it has to be. Every tug on my heart telling me to chill in Aruba for a little bit longer feels like a betrayal. I wasn't supposed to fall for someone in Aruba. I was supposed to see my best friend off into the next chapter of his life and then continue on my way. Because true success lies just over the hill. I can practically taste it. I haven't been working this hard, this long, on my influencing career just to let it evaporate on Eagle Beach in Aruba.

The sad truth is that if I don't make influencing work, then what the fuck else do I have to show for myself?

I can already imagine the my father's scorn as I tell him I've decided to *try on a photography gig* in Aruba. The sidelong looks from my brothers. The quiet snort from Grayson as he asks me for the fiftieth time in my life, "What do you do again?"

I'm so fucking sick of coming in last. But only one place will turn that around: Chiang Mai. As my friends joke and chat around me, I pull up my email one last time, refreshing for the millionth time over the past week. Still no email about the promo tour.

Fuck.

"Don't you think?" Rhys asks me, clapping me on the back.

I look up at him. I didn't hear a word of the conversation around me. Everyone laughs at the joke I'm not in on.

"Sorry guys," I say. "Zoned out."

"I said the two of you should wear matching outfits," Rhys repeats.

"For what?"

"For the photography gig," Rhys says. He's had to repeat himself, so the joke isn't funny anymore. But it wasn't funny to begin with; he doesn't know that I can't stay.

"Right." I force a laugh. Nova's smile dims slightly. After less than a week, she can already read my fucking thoughts, which is yet another sign I need to leave.

One more day. Flight is tomorrow.

It's supposed to be a relief, but it's not. Not entirely, at least. I'm a jumbled mess, and I can't tell if I need to dive headfirst into the ocean or just spend these last hours buried inside Nova. Rhys and the gang head off to the pool for the last time, leaving Nova and I alone on the bench once more.

"You okay, Weston?" she asks.

"I'm fine. Let's go back to the huts."

"Don't you want to go to the pool with them?"

I shake my head. "I'd rather spend these last hours with you. *Inside* you, specifically."

She tilts her head, something unreadable flashing across her face. I don't get the laughter I was expecting. Instead, she nods and stands up.

"Yeah. Let's just go fuck."

"I mean...it's not a bad idea, right?"

She shrugs, avoiding my gaze. "No. It just lets me know where I stand with you."

I can't help the sigh that escapes my lips. "That's not what I mean. But you and I are parting ways in less than eighteen hours. Why wouldn't we want to be with each other as much as possible?"

Finally, her green eyes drag up and find mine. There's hurt and confusion and so much more shimmering there. And I know I've caused all of it. "This doesn't have to be the last night, you know."

I clench my jaw, looking out over the ocean. I don't want to have this conversation. I just don't. There's no easy way to explain the acid knot in my chest. I want to stay here, and that's why I can't. Because if I'm going to carve out meaning for my life, it has to be on my own. Otherwise, none of the other pieces will fall into place.

"Don't you want to do something like this?" she presses. "I mean, you haven't even looked—"

"Nova," I snap. "You need to give a guy more than a half hour with something like this. This is a big deal. I know you're over the moon, but I'm not you. Can't we just enjoy our last evening together and talk about it later?"

She bites her bottom lip and nods. "Yeah. I'm sorry. I—I didn't mean—"

"It's fine. Let's just forget about it." I drag a hand through my hair, eager to recapture anything related to feeling lighthearted or horny. But right now, both are mere concepts. I hate how worked up I am, how unsettled this has made me, and even more than that, I hate that it's getting in the way of these precious last hours.

"Promise." Nova pushes up onto her tip-toes to give me a kiss, then offers a reassuring smile. "I want to enjoy this evening too."

"Yeah?" I slide my hands over her hips, jerking her against me. Tendrils of lust curl through me, reminding me of that lighthearted state I'm trying to reach. "How much?"

"So much that there isn't even a word to describe it." A smile curls at her lips, and when she looks up at me again, I coax a deep, hungry kiss out of her. Horniness: activated. I grunt, squeezing her hips.

"Well that's convincing." I press my forehead to hers, one last flash of reason searing through me. *You should start detaching now. Run away. This is ending, which means it's already over.*

But I can't. Not when she's in front of me. Not when she's looking at me like I'm the only man she's ever fucking wanted in her entire life.

She makes it too hard to stay away. Which is why I need to make the plane do the heavy lifting come tomorrow morning.

"I can do plenty of convincing once we're alone in a hut," she says with a smirk.

We lace our fingers together and walk back to the huts, going to mine because that's where the condoms are. Once we're inside, she shuts the door behind her, eyeing me like she's starving and I'm the best damn piece of cake she's ever spotted.

"You're looking at me like I'm dessert," I crack. She strides toward me, her gaze stuck between my legs. tugging my shorts down in one swift motion. Once my cock is freed, she pushes me at the chest so that my butt hits the bed. I bounce softly, watching expectantly as she falls to her knees.

"You *are* dessert," she says, eyeing my cock. The mere attention has me stiffening, as if that gaze alone is made of sexy whispers and firm strokes. "One I've never tried before."

"I don't think that's true," I say as she presses kisses up the tops of my thighs. My cock has gone fully hard now, the tip bulging and waiting for the heat of her mouth. I swallow hard, tilting my head to watch as she grows closer, closer to the prize. "You've had dessert plenty while we've been here."

"No. I've never *tasted* dessert," she clarifies, and then suddenly dips down and takes the entirety of my cockhead between her lips.

My fingers knot in her hair. "Oh, fuck."

She presses soft kisses up and down my shaft, looking at me with amusement dancing in her gaze. "Good fuck?"

"Excellent fuck."

She does it again, which makes my thighs rock hard and my abs turn to stone. Nova wraps her lips around me and takes a long pull—well, as much as can fit into her mouth without gagging. Fingernails scrape up my legs as her head bobs between my legs, and I'm not sure I've ever seen a prettier sight.

She sucks my cock until my balls tighten and I'm fucking close to blowing it in her mouth. But that's not exactly how I want this to go. She'll choke; I'll feel bad. I can already tell it won't end well.

Really what I want to do is get her on top of me again. That moonlight fuck was so epic for so many reasons, but the best part of all? Seeing her ride me like a motherfucking goddess.

I need that again. So yes, she can suck me off, but I need her on top as many times possible before my flight tomorrow morning. Which means this might very well be the last time ever.

Just thinking the word *ever* makes my chest tight. I groan and cup the back of her head.

"Babe," I say through gritted teeth. Even though I want her on top, it's hard as hell to make her stop slurping and slobbering.

"What?" She looks up at me, her lips puffy. "Is it okay? I mean—"

"Get on top of me."

"What?"

"I want you on top. Riding me." I pull her to standing and then gather the skirt of her sundress at her waist. "Also need this off."

"Okay, okay." She's smiling as she tugs her dress off, and when she's in the full, glorious nude, I take a second to admire her.

"What?" she asks, pushing on my shoulders. But I don't fall back on the bed. I just drink her in. All the soft curves and lines of her. Her belly and thighs and those breasts that I would one hundred percent choose to asphyxiate in if someone offered me a chance to play select-your-own-death.

"Just looking at you."

"Haven't you seen enough?"

I press a soft kiss to the swell of her belly. "Nope."

I can tell the attention makes her uncomfortable, and I'm not trying to make her not enjoy this. But I've never been with someone like her before. Someone who turned me on so completely, so effortlessly. She's a babe in every sense of the word, and maybe even more so because she barely fucking realizes it.

"Come here." I scoot back onto the bed, guiding her to climb on top of me. My thumb finds her clit, and she inhales sharply as I massage the tight bud. Once she's bucking and her nipples are hard as diamonds, I slip the condom on, and then she's crashing down, down, down around me. My cock is enveloped by the unyielding silk of her pussy, and everything goes hot and loud inside me.

The view from below is too sexy. The feel of her clenched around my cock is too sexy. And because her lips around my cock were too sexy, I have to use every last bit of restraint not to end this within the first thirty seconds. I grab big, juicy handfuls of her ass as Nova rocks and rolls against me. Her eyes flutter shut. Low moans escape her, the type of sound that tells me she's fucking *loving* this.

When I see the first shudder of her orgasm, I know it's safe for me too. I drill up into her until that throaty whimper blesses the air, and then my abs go rock solid and I'm groaning so long and loud that surely someone from the resort is going to come investigate.

By the time I'm done being bitch-slapped by the pleasure, Nova has collapsed on top of me, her chest sweaty against mine. I wrap my arms around her, pressing lazy kisses to the top of her head.

There are so many hours left in this day, but they're not enough. I want more.

And the fact that I want the remaining hours to bleed into weeks and months means that this needs to be the last time between us.

Or else I'll never be able to walk away from this woman.

CHAPTER TWENTY-SEVEN

NOVA

Weston and I float between galaxies after our orgasms, laying naked on his bed, staring up at the ceiling of the hut as we laugh and tease and talk.

The truth is, I wish I could stay in this spot forever. Not necessarily this hut—surely they'd start trying to kick us out by tomorrow afternoon once the wedding reservation ended—but *here*. With Weston at my side, his easy energy and his quiet, clever barbs, and oh so many of those soft, passionate kisses. Sometimes when the man looks at me right, it's like everything I've known up until that moment comes crashing to the ground. The cells of my body prepare themselves to rewrite my history, because none of what came before matters anymore. As long as I'm here with Weston...that's all I need.

And I want this to continue being the case. I know we got a huge offer and he needs time to think it over, but I can already see how amazing it would be for *both* of us. How much of a chance this could be for us to stay together and satisfy all our needs—like paychecks and Caribbean sunsets and frequent stargazing sex—all at once.

But every minute that goes by without addressing the big issue of *will you stay or won't you* feels like an interminable wait.

My phone rings. It's my gram. I hurry to answer it.

"Gram! How are you?"

"Waiting for your cute tush to get back home!" Her laughter is crackly. "Aren't you on the plane yet?"

My heart sinks. In all my blinding excitement, I forgot about the part where I'd have to let my grandma down gently. How it might not be even half as exciting for her as it is for me. Maybe she'll encourage me to nix the idea altogether.

"Not on the plane yet," I say, coming to sitting so that I can reorient myself in the regular world. Weston stands and begins dressing. "Actually, you know, there's something I wanted to talk to you about. Just promise me you won't tell Mom and Dad yet."

"Oh, lordy," she groans. "You found the shark, didn't you?"

I snicker. "Or was it a pirate?"

"Either one is dangerous. Or is that the whole point? Ohhh, I don't know! You tell me! What's the secret? You know I can't keep my chops quiet for long, so I'll give you a day before I start blabbin' it to the neighbors."

My body shakes in silent laughter. I can envision her perfectly, on the couch in her favorite gray sweat suit, slapping her knee right as she says "blabbin'." Most Sundays, she's sitting on the porch and watching the wildlife and occasionally shouting directives at my dad that he almost always ignores as he mows the lawn or putters around in the garage.

"Fine. I'll accept the twenty-four-hour promise of silence." I draw a deep breath, looking to Weston for some sign of encouragement before I spill the beans. He's not facing me, instead tugging his shirt over his head. "I got a job offer while I was down here, Gram. From the resort. They want me to be their official wedding photographer."

The piercing hoot from my grandma's end is so loud I pull the phone away from my ear. Weston twists to look at me, an eyebrow arching.

"Iiiiiiii knew it!" Gram shouts.

"Oh my god," I say, because my ear drum might be bleeding.

Weston jerks his thumb toward his backpack on the floor. "I'm gonna pack, okay?"

My mouth parts as my world splits in two. A ravine opens up inside of me—my home and past whispering in my ear, with my future and possibly greatest love story walking away from me. I must give something like an affirmative look, because Weston gives me a thumbs up and begins rummaging in his long backpack. I am devoid of air or thoughts while my grandmother celebrates my job offer.

"I think I'll crack open a beer," she's saying, and then dissolves into a fit of smoker's cough. "Are you serious, Nova? Is my granddaughter about to be an *official resort photographer*?"

I force a laugh. Weston's move was the least funny and relieving thing he could have done. Was there a clearer way of saying "I'm not going with you"? Maybe I was a fool for thinking he'd seriously consider it. But I feel like he just told me his answer. "I really want to accept the job, Gram. But—"

"But what? I'm about to open this beer, so if you tell me there's a reason to say no, I better hear it now."

I bite my lip as all sorts of emotion wells up inside me. "There's no reason to say no. They'd be paying me a little bit more than I make at the senior portrait agency. I'd have a room and meals included here at the resort, so no rent. And, well, I'd be living on Aruba."

"*Living on Aruba*," my grandmother says with a sigh, right as I hear the *crrrack* of the beer can opening. "Lord almighty. I never thought I'd hear you say those words."

I swallow hard, watching Weston as he empties the contents of his bag on the bed nearby. He rifles through clothes and begins folding things into small piles. "Does it sound crazy?"

"Of course it does! Don't mean you shouldn't do it."

"I don't want to leave you," I admit. "But with this salary, I can still send money back to you."

Gram lets out a long, raggedy sigh. "Nova, sweets, I'm not your responsibility. If I'm anyone's responsibility, it's your father's. But even not his. I'm the only one who can look after me, even if I don't have a damn cent to my name. And you know what would make me feel poorer than ever? If I kept my granddaughter from living the crazy life she was meant to live."

Tears are welling up in my eyes as I listen to her. She's right. And she's saying the words that I so desperately needed to hear. The words that I believe on the inside, down below all the layers of loyalty and submission and small thinking.

"Thank you," I manage to say. "Because I wouldn't accept it if you didn't think—"

"Don't even say that! I don't want to figure into this decision at all. You just promise me you'll make those crazy brides look good, you send me a picture of yourself every day, and you find yourself some incredible stories that you can't tell anyone about when you come home for Christmas. Unless it's me. You can tell me the stories."

Her excitement makes me incredibly warm and fuzzy. But watching Weston actively pack his things is like cold water down my back. This was supposed to be exciting for both of us. But right now, I'm the only one left standing.

"I haven't signed any papers yet, Gram," I go on, trying to swallow the strange, acid swirl rising in my throat, "but I'll let you know tomorrow morning what the next step is. And don't tell my dad!"

"I promise, sweet cakes. Keep me updated. And now, I'm gonna get drunk for no apparent reason, according to your father, at least. Because I won't be telling him why I'm celebrating!"

"Not for twenty-four hours, at least," I say, forcing another laugh as my gram whoops with more laughter.

After promising to call her tomorrow with more updates, I hang up, and I'm left in the thick, echoing silence of Weston's hut. I watch as he wordlessly piles up underwear, swim shorts, sandals.

"So you're leaving tomorrow." Really, the statement is a test. Questioning this version of reality I don't want to be true.

Weston twists to look at me. "Of course. I have a plane ticket."

"So do I. But plane tickets can be changed."

There's another long, unnerving silence that makes me painfully aware of how naked I am. I push off the bed and hunt down my sundress and panties that we discarded earlier in our haste to make love. No, to *fuck*. Because that's all we've been doing here. It's been nothing more than simple, basic sex.

My hands form fists as I attempt to make that thought true inside of me. It's hopeless. Nothing has been simple or basic with Weston. Least of all the sex. I can't act like I haven't fallen head over heels for this man—especially with myself.

"You know, the job offer included *you* in there," I remind him.

"I know," he says.

"This doesn't just affect me."

He shakes his head, avoiding my gaze as he turns the backpack upside down one last time, a few last items tumbling out. "Maybe it does. The only person who is truly invested in this offer is you."

I blink rapidly as I pull on my finally located dress. The thin layer of fabric bolsters me, but only slightly. "What does that mean?"

"You're the only one looking to change their life," Weston says, louder this time, like I'd also told him to speak up in addition to clarify himself.

"But…I thought…" I can't even find the words to follow up with.

"You thought what?"

"I thought you liked doing that sort of thing. Being artistic, social, *and* getting paid for it." I press the tip of my middle finger to my forehead, trying to organize my thoughts. But it doesn't work. There has been an explosion inside my brain, and I might never clean up the mess. "The contract is for two employees. If you don't sign with me, then you'll be leaving me high and dry."

"Oh, so this is just so *you* can get the job," Weston says, turning toward me. There's an edge in his voice and a fire in his eyes, neither of which I've experienced before. I can't tell if we're about to fight or fuck again. "Be honest, at least. You just want to use me to get to this job."

My mouth parts again and I sputter, trying to find the right words with which to cut him like he cut me. But nothing comes. Nothing, except, "You're so wrong."

"Am I?"

"Yes! Listen, I get this is a big leap. But isn't that what you love doing? Taking leaps?"

"Leaps to places where I want to land," Weston clarifies. "And I'm sorry, but Aruba just isn't where I want to land."

I swallow the knot that has cropped up in my throat, like a malignant tumor. "Then where do you want to land?"

He's quiet, the sizzling kind of pause that promises an answer I'm not going to like. When he finally speaks, so much time has passed that I wonder if I even asked the question. "Far away from here."

"So just anywhere that I'm not," I spit.

"Why are you trying to make this about you?" Weston shoots back. Now I know where this dangerous energy was heading: toward *fight* territory. "I have my own life, you know. What you're asking me to do is insane."

"How is it more insane than asking me to just pack up and go to Thailand?" I ask, my voice barely passing my lips. "Or is it only okay to ask *me* to uproot everything?"

His mouth turns into a thin line as he shakes his head. "See, that's your problem. You have roots to begin with."

His words hang in the air like an admonishment, and I can't figure out why. Everything inside me is sad and breaking and heavy. I'm getting my answer in sharp, painful bursts, over and over again. While I'm reeling, trying to find which was is up—and forward—Weston moves a pile of clothes to the side of the bed. Glittering jade catches my eye.

My mouth parts as I recognize the delicate, possibly ancient necklace. I reach out for it. "Did you take this?"

Weston barely glances at me. "What are you talking about?"

"How did you find this in my room?"

"I didn't find that in your room," Weston snaps. "It's mine."

I blink about a hundred times, trying to process this information. "Are you serious?"

"Why would I lie about that?"

I turn it over in my hands, already noticing small differences from my own. First of all, this necklace doesn't look like it's been traveling the world for years stuffed unceremoniously into the front pocket of a backpack. It looks fresher, sturdier somehow. There aren't the same well-worn nicks in some of the stones. I set it down, a strange lump forming in my throat.

If there's ever a time not to cry, it's right now. Weston and I are actively breaking up. He's choosing to stay his course, even though I've chosen to take a leap and build something in Aruba—preferably with him. And of course, this had to be the exact moment my sign from the heavens showed up.

So help me God, I will not cry because of this necklace.

"I have the same one," I say, fortifying my voice so he won't catch the waver there. I set it back down, forcing myself to look at anything other than him as he continues to pack up his life. Searching for something inside the hut that will reinforce the idea that the necklace means nothing. "That's really weird you have it, too."

He picks it up, turning it over in his hands as the silence creates a rift between us. It shouldn't mean anything. The fact that the most amazing, beautiful, inspired man in the world carries the same good luck charm I do shouldn't mean anything. It shouldn't feel like a sign, the same type of sign that Amelia got from Rhys's tie, but fuck, it does.

This is my sign.

If it's my sign, then I need to follow it. Even at the expense of my sanity. Even if it makes me look like a fool.

Because I didn't come this far only to keep doing the same old thing. If I can accept a crazy job offer, then I can admit the craziest thing inside my heart. Bolstered by tropical air and the intoxicating power of potential soul mates, I draw a deep breath. "Weston."

"Nova."

I open my mouth to speak but nothing comes out. Weston looks at me expectantly. I almost decide against it, and then I blurt out, "I think I'm in love with you. Like, for real. And I want you to stay. Will you stay with me?"

There. I asked it, point-blank. I looked down the barrel of the gun—the firearm of my future, let's say—and faced my fears. The space between my ears is throbbing as I await a response. I'm giving Weston the power to mold my future, to break my heart, to do any damn thing he wants with me.

He watches me for what feels like an eternity, his face a neutral mask. He didn't even flinch at the words. Didn't soften a bit. And with each eternal second that ticks onward, another sliver of my heart flakes off and floats to the ground.

Finally, he yanks his attention back to his bag. He scoops up the necklace and shoves it back into the cloth bag, burying it deep inside the backpack.

"You don't even know me, Nova. You can't be in love with me."

My throat turns into a vice, and tears fill my eyes. He's good at giving me answers without saying *yes* or *no.*

"How do I not know you? We've been up each other's butts for the past week. We've been traveling together for years—"

"You don't know me," Weston repeats, more firmly. "If you knew me, you wouldn't be asking me to stay."

His words just add to the cyclone of hurt inside me. Tears leak from my eyes, and I hurry to wipe them away. I don't know where to go from here. I've laid everything bare, and he's given me nothing in return. Nothing except rejection.

"Okay. Yeah. I guess when you said you wanted to stay with me, I took it the wrong way," I say bitterly.

Weston says nothing. And since I'm now fluent in his silences, I take it for what it means: *This is over.*

I swallow another knot in my throat, trying to focus on the room around me. One foot in front of the other. There's nothing else to say.

So I'll leave.

Each step toward his door feels like a mistake, but there's no way to fix it. I'm walking away from the best man I've ever met, the most explosive love story I've ever lived, and the clearest sign I've ever received.

Except the sign wasn't the same as Amelia's. The sign didn't point toward a magical-ever-after that would unfurl like the outrageous bud of a peony.

The sign led to heartbreak. The magic is gone.

Weston is leaving, I'm staying, and this painfully important and consuming thing we discovered between us has flatlined.

CHAPTER TWENTY-EIGHT

NOVA

I awake with a jolt. I have no idea what time it is, other than I'm pretty sure I've been in a coma for possibly several days or a year.

I grope blindly for my phone on the nightstand. I hear birds already, the morning variety, which confuses me further. I lay down to take a cry-nap after saying goodbye to Amelia and Rhys last night. They'd wanted to go drink at the bar, but I told them I needed to pack, when in reality I needed to continue licking my wounds and waiting for Weston to show up at my hut with a change of heart...or at the very least, a hard-on.

That obviously never happened, and instead I fell asleep.

I gasp when my phone comes to life. It's eight a.m. Motherfucking eight a.m.

Thoughts cram together inside my head trying to process this information. I am as confused as if I'd woken up back in New York

State. How can it be eight a.m.? That means it's Monday morning. That means that basically everyone is gone.

And worse yet?

It means that Weston left without saying goodbye.

My eyes burn from bleariness and repressed emotion as I fumble around my hut, trying to find anything resembling clothes. Since I fell asleep waiting for Mr. McYouDon'tEvenKnowMe to show up, that means I'm still in the middle of packing. All my shit is in weird little piles in the stupidest spots, per my bizarre organizational method.

I find a bra and then leggings, but no shirt. As seconds tick on, I grow more desperate to find out if reality really is as grim as I suspect. I finally spot a sundress and throw that on overtop of the leggings, which allows my sports bra to show, but at this point, I don't care.

The sun is blinding as I push out of my darkened tiki paradise and hurry toward the teal hut. There's a chance he didn't come to say goodbye because he *also* fell into a cry-sleep. He might have missed his flight altogether. There's *no way* Weston would leave the island without saying goodbye...right?

His flight was at seven-fifty sharp that morning. If he left already, he's been gone for at least an hour. I knock on the door, everything pulled tight and foreboding inside me.

There's no answer. I knock again, more urgently this time, and listen closely for any sound on the other side. A groan. Rustling sheets. Even just the zip of a bag.

Because maybe he changed his flight. Maybe I remembered his flight time wrong. *Maybe he decided to stay.*

I knock for the third time, though my knuckles sound desperate against the wood. I wasn't sure there was a way for a knock to sound desperate, but I've achieved it. Because each *thud* reminds me of my own desperate wish. My own insane dream that Weston himself inspired me to go after. The very same dream that has been slowly crumpling to the ground around me since yesterday.

I wait for a few moments, forehead pressed to the door, as the sticky, uncomfortable truth settles in the air between the crashing of the ocean waves.

I try the knob just to be sure. Or to violate Weston's personal space if he's actually inside, hiding from me, I guess. The knob turns. The door swing opens.

A completely empty hut awaits me. The bedsheets are rumpled. There's still a hint of Weston's scent in the air, which nearly brings me to my knees.

He's gone. He fucking left.

Tears spring to my eyes, and I close the door, hurrying back to my own hut. I look around for something—anything—that he might have left me. A note. A drawing. Even just some memento from our whirlwind time together.

But he's left me nothing to offset the ghosting, which makes it sting worse. All I have are pictures and the last wisps of my completely misplaced hopes.

What a fucking asshole. The words vibrate inside me on repeat as I crawl back into my bed. I put up a good front for a few minutes, staying angry, but then the tears come in full force and I'm crying into my pillow. Because he wasn't just an asshole. He lied to me about wanting things to continue. By just disappearing, he was colder and more callous than I ever could have imagined. Maybe what we shared meant nothing to him. Here I was, ready to dive headfirst into the unknown for the first time in my life because of him, and he was able to walk away without so much as a goodbye.

He could have left the door open for things to continue. We could have done long-distance while I stayed here in Aruba or gone back home. While I'm disappointed that he didn't want to jump into this opportunity with me, I still feel like we could have worked something out.

But now? He slammed the door shut on that. Showed me what he really felt about us.

If this is the nomad approach to flings, then I never want to do this again. I went out on a limb with Weston, because he'd shown me just how unique and worthwhile he was. But maybe I'd been the bigger fool to believe those icy blues. A man with a set of abs like his can't be trusted. That has to be the takeaway from all this.

This isn't exactly the glorious end to my vacation that I imagined. But somewhere in the painful crush of heartbreak and loss, I decide that I need to purge all of it and move on.

So I sob and cry and weep like the heartbroken fool I didn't want to be, and approximately two hundred tissues later, I sit up with renewed focus.

I'm alone on this island. Completely fucking alone. All my friends have flown back to their respective corners of the world, and the one man I briefly—psychotically—thought I could create a future with has not just left but *ghosted* me.

I could choose to see this as a sign for me to slither back to my comfy little snake hole back in upstate New York. My flight is still booked for two p.m. But no. For how stupid and childish and avoidant Weston has proven himself to be, he did instill some good lessons into me. I won't go into all of them now, because I'd like to continue hating him for the time being, but his words on living the life I've always dreamt of didn't go unheard.

And the truth is, I don't need him to create that life. I don't need anybody but myself and my own damn motivation. I thought that my life might have been *better* with him in it, but if he doesn't want to be there, then all I can say to him is, *fine, bye,* and maybe in a few weeks also, *Why can't I stop thinking about you; this is really gonna bother me for the rest of my life.*

Permanently bothersome or not, I'm not going to let this detract me. Weston will only prove to be a wobble in my path, not a complete detour. At this point, the detour to the life I've always dreamed of would involve going back home.

So after I take the morning to finish packing, shower, and compose myself, my first stop is Edward's office. Signed contract in hand.

His eyes light up as he pulls open the door, and when he invites me to sit down, the first question out of his mouth is, "Where's the second shooter?"

"He's, uh…" Shit, I didn't rehearse in my head how I'd handle this. "He's not able to accept the offer due to a personal emergency."

His personal emergency being his own nomad heartbreaker tendencies.

Edward nods tersely, gaze falling to the contract I've placed on his desk. "This position does require two photographers. The normal workload throughout the year is…substantial. There's no way you can do it on your own. I mean, it will literally involve being in two places at once."

My heart races. I'm not going to let Weston's decision affect my own. I want this job. Not only that—I *need* it. It has become the beacon of my commitment to lead an outstanding life. Even if it fizzles and goes nowhere. I want to at least *try.*

"I totally understand. Which is why I'm already lining up a different second shooter," I say. It's a lie. Well, I'd like to call it a *white lie,* so it sounds less intense, but truly, this is false information. I *will be* lining up a second shooter. As soon as I get the green light from Edward to begin building a life in Aruba.

His brow arches. "You have someone in mind?"

"I have a few different routes I'm pursuing," I tell him, looking down at the contract while the words tumble past my lips. "But I can assure you that I will have the second shooter confirmed by the end of the week. I don't take this responsibility lightly. I understand that the smooth functioning of the photography sessions depends on both of us. And my high standards and eye for perfection will ensure that I don't let you down."

I'm talking like the mission statement of my own damn resume. But if I'm making this up as I go along, then why not see where it leads me?

I have to at least try.

Edward nods slowly, lacing his fingers together. When he pins me with a look, I can see question marks there. But at last he says, "Well, for some reason, I think you'll make good on that word. Our current schedule allows for just a single photographer this upcoming week, so it might work out. As long as you can find your second shooter by Monday, it will be fine."

He offers me his hand, a smooth grin on his face.

And while fireworks explode inside me, I shake his hand.

Here we go.

CHAPTER TWENTY-NINE

WESTON

When the email from Cliffhangers Gear arrives a half hour after my plane lands in Ohio, I'm not surprised. The only thing I feel less than surprise is excitement when the email tells me my account has been accepted as a representative.

My upcoming stint in Thailand officially has purpose. My life has meaning again. I can now officially brag to my family that I know what I'm doing with my life.

Whoopty fucking doo.

The days in Bayshore churn beneath me. I don't leave the bedroom of my parents' house most days, and if I do, I go get lost in the woods. My father and I have exchanged barely twenty words since I got home, and my mom knows something is wrong, but I don't give her the chance to probe.

The Friday after I fly home, I'm starting to feel stir crazy. Just before lunch time, I pack up my notebooks and pencils, toss on my satchel, and start walking downtown. I can hear Nova teasing me about my bag in my head. Every time I look at it, I think of her. Which is ridiculous, because I had this bag for *years* before Aruba. She should not be the primary memory associated with this bag.

But damn near everything she touched has now become Nova-centric. She is a catchy tune I cannot stop replaying in my head. The type of song I sing even when I'm upset, or trying to have a conversation, or doing literally anything other than think about her.

Nova didn't just crawl into my insides, she stained me. Which is exactly what I was afraid of.

I don't know where I'm going, other than I'm heading there. Once I hit downtown Bayshore, the scents of the lake breeze become overwhelming and inspiring. I decide to keep walking. I don't stop at Hazel's realty office, though I see her car out front. I swing out to hit the boardwalk that runs along the shore. It lines the entire northern edge of town, and I'm hoping the lapping water will help pull me out of this funk I've been festering in for five days.

Five entire days. I've never needed so much time to stop thinking about someone. I need to get my head right, and fast. My flight to Thailand is in eight days. I can't go there still hung up on Nova. I don't include regrets in my luggage, much less heartbreak. I can't even believe the word is crossing my mind.

I did not fall in love with Nova.

No matter how many times I repeat these words to myself, I don't entirely believe them. And I can't stop thinking about when she confessed—twice—that she was in love with me.

Fuck it all, I almost told her, *I love you, too.*

But that can't be true. Because that's not who I am. That's not Weston Wanders. Women grace my feed as momentary delights, pretty sparkles to adorn the tapestry of my travels. None of them stay. I do not let them stay.

And more than that, I myself do not stay.

So why am I still imagining a major redo on the ending of that Aruba trip?

What I need is time. And, of course, a flight to Thailand, plenty of new sights, and maybe a new lover. Even though the thought of being with anyone who isn't Nova is totally unappealing, it still seems like the right medicine for me. And who *loves* taking medicine? You force it down, even if it doesn't taste good.

I'm lost in my thoughts—the same thoughts since the second I left Aruba—and walk for so long that suddenly I realize I'm on the east end of town, standing at the back of Dom's clinic. I look up at the big bay windows overlooking the lake, spotting London on the other side of the glass in her back office. She waves at me. Shit, I've been spotted. I wave back, and when she gestures for me to come inside, I can't imagine any reason not to. I have nowhere I need to go, other than away from my own head, which is the one impossible destination. Why not distract myself a little bit at the clinic?

London pulls me into a fragrant hug as soon as I come into the back office. I can hear the low murmurs of Dom's voice from inside one of the exam rooms, which tells me he's seeing patients.

"How are you?" London gushes, gripping me by the sides of my arms as she looks me up and down. "God, you got tan."

"Living in the tropics for a week will do that," I say, scratching the back of my neck.

"Did you come to work? I'm in the middle of writing, and your spot is still open." She grins, waving me toward the table. And that's when I realize—it's *Friday*. I always come on Fridays to work with her. I've been so lost in my head, it feels like a millennium has disappeared beneath me.

"Actually, yeah." I take off my bag, heading to the long table where I always spread out.

"So how was Aruba?" Her chair creaks as she settles in front of her laptop.

"It was good." It was so much more than good, but I don't know where to begin, so I won't.

"Did you end up catching any proposals while you were down there?" she teases. Her enormous engagement ring glitters on her fourth finger. Would I ever buy something like that for Nova? I doubt she'd even like it. She seems more like the type of girl who would want to tie a palm frond around our wrists and call it a day. As an homage to the time I fixed her light stand. If she were here, she'd laugh about that. But wait. Why am I thinking about getting Nova an engagement ring?

"Actually, no," I say, yanking my gaze off her ring. "But I helped out with the wedding pictures a little."

"See? I told you—you're perfect for that stuff. I can see you having a business like that someday."

Her comment doubles as a spear to the heart. I won't tell her that I was offered that exact opportunity. I don't know how the story will sound to anyone on the outside. Besides, it'll involve telling her about Nova, and I just can't go there yet. I bring out my sketchbook and open it to a blank page. I begin sketching idly, not really knowing what I want to draw yet.

"Maybe someday, once I'm done traveling the world," I tell her. My pencil goes *skritch skritch skritch*.

"Where next?"

"Thailand." *Skritch skritch.* "I leave in eight days."

"Just for fun?"

She has no idea what I do, either. Nobody does. And it's not their fault. It's because *I* have no idea what I'm doing.

"My brand was accepted to represent a company on a promo tour," I tell her, trying to sound as casual yet self-important as possible. Because this is my ticket to knowing where I'm going in life. This is my career, however much it doesn't feel like it. "So I'll be traveling Thailand, Morocco, and a few other countries on up to Ireland."

"Oh wow." Admiration shines in her voice. "Doing what?"

"Just…whatever I feel like. Taking pictures along the way. They'll have some company-specific trips I'll need to go on, and some equipment I'll test out and promote. But other than that, it's just…" *Nothing at all.* The words echo inside my head. That can't be the truth. I'm not doing *nothing.* This is *everything.*

As in everything I've ever wanted. Everything people dream of. Everything I tell myself I need in life.

So why does it feel like the opposite?

"They pay you to travel for them?" she asks with a small laugh. "Wish I could find that gig!"

This, right here: this is the reaction I dream of. Thinly veiled awe. The *wow, how do I get your life* response. I must not be hiding my confusion very well, or maybe London is just exceptionally astute, because she asks, "Are you not looking forward to it?"

"Of course I am," I lie.

"Oh. You just seem a little…" She shrugs. "Down."

I nod, staring at the page without even seeing what I'm drawing. I just need the therapy of the output. I don't even care what it looks like. "Yeah. True. I am."

"Do you want to talk about it?"

Skritch skritch skritch. "I do but I don't."

"Oh. Well, it's up to you." London offers a small smile. "I won't probe if you don't wanna go there."

Silence settles between us, and I continue drawing. London takes the hint, and soon she's tapping away on her laptop. Minutes float by. I enter into that coveted Zen focus state. When London pauses in her writing next, she gasps.

"Oh my god. Weston, that's amazing."

"What?"

"Your picture! She's beautiful."

I stop drawing and push the notebook away from me so it sits in the middle of the table between us. Who is she? She's Nova, of course. My subconscious is drawing Nova. It will probably continue to draw Nova for the next decade.

"I met someone in Aruba," I begin. London rests her chin on her curled fists, leaning in closer.

"Is she the girl you're drawing?"

"Yeah." I frown at the picture, then look up at London's eager eyes. "London, I don't know what to do."

Her brows draw together. "About what?"

I expel a deep breath and rub my face. If I'm going to admit this to anyone, it can be London. Because London is safe. I feel the closest with her out of any of my brother's girlfriends—sorry, *fiancées*. And I know that if I ask her not to say anything to Dom, she'll honor that.

"I'm supposed to go on this trip. It'll last at least three months, possibly six if it goes well. I don't even have a return flight to the States," I tell her. "I don't know when I can see her again."

"Can you two meet up around the world? She seems like a traveler if you met her in Aruba."

I shake my head, staring at the flowing outline of Nova on my page. "She can't live like I do. And I don't think I can stay in one place."

"Why not?"

I grit my teeth as the reason bubbles up inside me. I'm not sure I can say it. Admitting it feels too big, too wrong. But there's something about the past week that's unlocked something inside me. So maybe I can say the words. After all, I shared a part of myself with Nova and the world didn't collapse.

"I'm not good at long-term things," I say carefully. "I can't hold a steady job, much less a steady girlfriend."

She snorts like this is ridiculous. "Why would you say that? There's no reason you can't do those things if you want them."

I swallow a knot in my throat. "Well, I've tried before. And I didn't end well."

"You did?"

I sigh, indecision streaking through me. I could just clam up and leave and not go there. But I feel like I've come this far. Why not just a little further now? "Right after I graduated from college, I got a job at this huge advertising firm. Well, I was fired two years later."

Her face softens. "Fired?"

"Yeah. I've never told anyone about it, so maybe you could keep it a secret for me. It won't go over very well in this family," I say bitterly.

She reaches out to squeeze my wrist, her bracelets jangling. "I won't say a word. I just don't see the link between that and what you're talking about now."

"How could you not? I'm not fit for long term. I wanted to keep that job. Believe me. I'm just..." I falter as the words escape me. "I'm unfit, because I'm a failure."

London laughs, which is not the reaction I'm expecting. She presses a hand to her mouth, like trying to suppress it, but more laughter leaks out, and finally she says, "I'm so sorry. I've just never heard you say anything so absurd."

I narrow my eyes. "I'm being honest."

"You are the opposite of a failure, Weston," she says, lowering her chin to look me in the eye. "You and your entire family are the biggest bunch of competitive work horses I've ever seen in my entire life. I'm sure it might feel like failure if you don't keep a regular nine-to-five job like the rest of the modern world, but believe me—that's not your path. And that didn't happen to you by chance. There was a reason you were set free from that. Even if goes against your father's expectations or what you feel like you should be doing."

Her words stun me into silence. My gaze drifts back to the page.

"I'd actually be disappointed in you if you told me you'd found some boring office job like you used to have," she says, straightening her back. "That life isn't the Weston I know."

"I don't want it," I admit reluctantly. "But I don't want what I have, either."

As soon as the words escape me, it feels like Zeus himself has sent down a crack of thunder. Something about the words and the revelation and London's intense honesty has me cracking all the way open. There are no limits anymore. I have nothing to hide behind.

"Then what do you want?"

Nova. I look down at the page. "I wanted to stay on Aruba, but I was too afraid to try."

She tosses her hands up with a smile, like everything has become crystal clear. "Well, there we have it! Isn't that exciting?"

I laugh in spite of how heavy it is. Because yeah, it's exciting. But it's also terrifying. It's also inconvenient. Because I've set everything up to continue doing the thing I don't want to do. I've structured my life to favor the nomad lifestyle.

I have a flight in eight days that precedes a guaranteed paycheck.

I have a promo tour to complete.

And worst of all, I didn't just leave Nova, I hurt her. Whatever bridge existed between Nova and me, well—I made sure to torch it upon exit.

"Hey, brother!" Dom's bass rumble startles me out of my thoughts as he comes into the back office. He approaches me, arms out for a hug, which is one of those things about *New Dom* that I'm still getting used to. I come to my feet and let him pull me into a quick brotherly hug. He claps my back and then eases into the seat next to London. She leans over and kisses him on the cheek. A dopey grin crosses my brother's face, and all I can think is, *I know that life.*

I must have had that smile on my face a hundred times in Aruba.

"You just get back from your trip?" he asks, unbuttoning the cuffs of his shirt.

"Earlier this week. I've been laying low." I rub my forehead. My thoughts are turning dark again, which means I just need to take the plunge. "Hey, so, if I theoretically decide to move to Aruba in the future, do you think Dad would think even less of me than he does now?"

Dom's brow lifts. "That came out of left field. Are you planning on moving to Aruba?"

"No, no, I'm just thinking about it."

"I can't keep up with you," Dom says with a laugh. "You've been more places in the past year that I've been in my entire life, real life and dreams combined."

I smile, but it fades quickly. "I'm just thinking I might shake things up. Again. For like, the millionth time."

"Then do it," Dom says simply. "That's what you do, after all. Why would it be different now?"

I feel that same tug inside my chest, the one that always precedes thinking about or looking at the shame that lurks inside me. "Because it's been too many times. I feel like all Dad does is make fun of his lost, drifting second-to-last kid. The second-to-last who is actually in last fucking place."

Dom frowns, his gaze not wavering from mine as my words hang in the air.

"That's not true," Dom says. "I know Dad was harsh on all of us, and we had a helluva competitive childhood, but we're all adults now. We can do what we want with our lives. And you aren't obligated to live a version of life that he wants for you. Trust me, it's a lesson I've learned." When London lets out a little *hm*, Dom adds, "Am *still* learning."

Watching my mid-thirties brother admit this same struggle is somehow relieving. It's one thing to be in a quarter-life crisis and not know what you're doing—hello, hi that's me—but when the white-coated doctor admits it, suddenly there's legitimacy. And thank God. Because I've felt like the textbook definition of *a fucking joke* for way too long.

"You're doing what you want and making it work. What's wrong with that?" Dom adds.

"Nothing, is the answer," London says.

"But I have nothing to show for myself," I say, scooping out the last dregs of my doubts from the bottom of my heart. "Look, you've started this clinic. Grayson started his own business. Connor started his own business. What have I done?"

"Are you kidding me? You've been living outside the margins, which is basically the impossible option for any Daly offspring," Dom says with a disbelieving laugh. "Don't overlook that achievement."

The comment feels like a high honor coming from my eldest brother. I contemplate my drawing, and after a moment, Dom asks, "Who is that?"

"Nova." My chest tightens again, but not for the same reason as before. Now, it's just reminding me of how badly I hurt her. What I walked away from. How glorious things could have been. "We've known each other for a few years, but I fell in love with her in Aruba. And then I didn't just leave her, I hurt her."

Dom frowns. "Why'd you do that?"

"Because I'm not good at the long-term. What happens if I fail? It's better not to try, right? Avoid the pain."

Dom smirks. "That's interesting, coming from you." Of course he'd think that. He doesn't know just how deep my secret runs. Before I can even think about sharing the details, he adds, "You've done everything, gone everywhere. You're essentially fearless. But you're too afraid to fall in love. You can break your bones in a parachuting accident, but your heart is too precious?"

When he puts it like that, it's hard to refute.

"I'm not criticizing," Dom hurries to add. "I was in that boat with you. But let me tell me you. The risk of heartbreak is worth what you find in the process."

He's got a point. London and Dom share a sparkling look. Which reminds me of our last conversation a few weeks ago.

"Well, then, I guess you'd like to know you were right, Dom," I tell him. "About the inheritance. The necklace that Grammy gifted me. It turns out Nova has the same one."

London gasps, and Dom just looks supremely satisfied.

"Is it a common necklace?" London asks.

"It doesn't matter," Dom interjects. "She has the same one. What are the odds of that?"

Part of me is right there with him. Another part of me is deeply worried that I am just distracting myself with fanciful stories and the temporary insanity of lust disguised as love.

"I don't know what it means," I say.

"I do," Dom says decisively, crossing his arms. London is grinning into her palm like this is a big secret that everyone has known about but me. "It means follow the inheritance."

"You mean move to Aruba?" I ask him, trying to sound like it's outrageous when it's not. It's the only thing I've been thinking of for the past five days.

"Maybe. But only you know." Dom gives me a wink and stands, giving my shoulder a squeeze. "But if it *does* mean that, then I'm going to insist you have lunch with us. Because maybe your time in Bayshore is limited."

I smile despite the swirling uncertainties. The idea seems too big, too wild. If I go to Aruba, there's a high chance Nova will say *fuck you* and never speak to me again.

But when I think about Thailand, it doesn't feel half as right as giving Aruba—giving *Nova*—another shot. Not just giving it a shot, either, but a deeply invested *attempt*. Something I plan for. Something I fucking invest my time and heart and future into.

And maybe what Dom and London are getting at isn't exactly about following inheritances or signs.

Maybe it's about following love. Even if it ends up in a broken bone, or heart.

If that's the case, then there's only one place I can go.

CHAPTER THIRTY

NOVA

Three weeks into my brand-new Aruban life, I'm pretty sure it's actually been three years instead.

For being on island time, things sure move fast. It only takes a couple days on the job to realize why Edward was so eager to hire someone. Resort staff members quickly fill me in during gossipy breaks on the beach about the last wedding photographer and why he fled the island so quickly. Believe it or not, the wild hog family that lives in that stand of palms on the north end of the resort *isn't* the cause. But even if they hadn't told me, I would have found out for myself.

The resort wedding schedule is *breakneck*. They don't just need me and a second shooter. They need triplicates of us. This resort crams in as many weddings as possible, while understaffing as much as possible. What felt like happy luck running into another bridal party at that yoga class the first night on the island is actually a carefully curated dance of housing multiple destination weddings at once and still maintaining the image that each group is *the only wedding group of its kind.*

In just three short weeks, I've shot fifteen weddings. Which seemed like a mathematical impossibility until I realized the resort is actually much larger than the section I saw as a guest. It's like a house of mirrors, except with beaches. Just when you think you've reached the end, there's just one more doorway that opens into a new tiny community of tiki huts and pools. It's never-ending paradise. And I've traversed the length of this resort-of-mirrors a hundred times since I officially became an employee.

What doesn't help is that I'm doing most of the work myself. If I could call my second shooter an idiot to his face and have it improve his work performance, then I would. Unfortunately, I think if I called Matias an idiot to his face, he'd just take it as a challenge to be worse.

"Hey. Matias. I said *over here.*" I jerk my chin toward the dining room for the second wedding we're shooting for the day. "We need the place settings and the detail shots."

He grimaces as if I've asked him to clean toilets and saunters off toward the area. If Matias could be replaced by a mannequin who knew how to take photos, I'd do it in a heartbeat. The only credit to his name is that he knows how to take photos. That doesn't guarantee that they come out great all the time. There's a fifty-fifty chance he'll fuck it up, and one time, he even took a picture of his dick and claimed it was an accident. I can't wait to fire him—I just can't find a replacement quite yet. He was the only respondent on my search for the emergency second shooter, and every day that Matias sucks is another day that I miss Weston just a little bit more.

It's not because I only value Weston for his helpfulness and ingenuity. His last words to me—that I'm just using him to get this job—still burn through me, and I wish I could stop hurting long enough to consider reaching out to him to set the record straight. But whenever I consider that, I remind myself that reaching out to him is strictly not allowed.

I will not reach out to a ghoster.

He made his choice clear. The least I can do is forget about him and move on.

While Matias lazily takes photos of the dining room, I head for the altar. The florists aren't missing today, and everything is very much on time. Still, I think the altar that Weston and I rigged up last second looked better. But maybe I'm just biased.

Biased to everything Weston has touched. And I'm definitely *trying* to forget about him. It's just that Weston has somehow become baked into the very fabric of the universe. Everything I do reminds me of him. And whenever I'm working on this side of the resort—where Amelia and Rhys got married—of course every last nook and cranny reminds me of that insanely hot and ultimately heartbreaking week of my life.

One week shouldn't have affected me so much. But it did. And all I can do in the aftermath is keep moving forward and focus on my job. After all, I've got a lot back home riding on this decision. Namely, the outrageous shock and disgruntlement of my parents, the lofty scorn from Jimmy I've heard about through the grapevine, and the endless excitement and beer-drinking of my gram.

This needs to work out, or else my gram will have celebrated in vain. And I can't have that.

Sunshine beats down on me, and I smile despite the stressful schedule ahead of me and the fact that Matias sometimes actually falls asleep standing up. All things considered, I'm glad I took the leap. Even though working with these bridezillas from all corners of the world is a type of torture I didn't know existed. Edward did a pretty good job of acting like every wedding was as fun and easygoing as Rhys and Amelia's, which I learned by day three was *not* the case.

"Are you fucking kidding me?" a sharp, feminine voice asks from behind me. It's the type of voice you hear in nightmares. The sort of haughty, condescending question they make movies about.

I turn around and find Bride #1 for the day. I did her hair and makeup shoot four hours ago, and let me tell you, she asked that same question in that same manner about fifty times during the forty minutes I took photos for her. Yes, more than once a minute.

"Is everything okay?" I ask as sweetly as I can muster through gritted teeth. She had been openly criticizing her own maid of honor's dress size when that "best friend" was out of the room, so I can only imagine what sort of insults she hurled my way once I had left the room.

"Your 'second shooter'"—she makes exaggerated air quotes—"touched my centerpiece."

"I'm sorry, your—"

"My centerpiece," she says in a slow drawl. This woman can go from bitchy to intolerable in two seconds flat. "You know, the big decorative arrangement that's been placed in the center of a room or table for people to enjoy?"

If I could roll my eyes right into her throat, I would. But it would only hurt both of us, and right now, I only want to hurt *her.* "Is it broken or damaged in some way?"

"His *fingerprints* are on it," she says with an acid tone.

"Okay. We'll clean that up. I think you need to get back to your area right now, because you don't want—"

"Jenna?" A male voice calls out from down the boardwalk. Jenna twists and gasps, holding up her hands to shield herself.

"Damien, don't look at me, you can't look at me, I swear to fuck you have to get *out of here!*"

While Jenna keeps berating her own fiancé for using his eyes in a common area, Matias saunters up to me like he's using a slo-mo filter. He raises his camera, oblivious to the bridezilla meltdown happening. It's awe inspiring, really. Maybe this is another point in his favor: his immunity to drama happening around him.

"So I got all the pictures," he drawls.

"Thanks, Matias," I say, watching as Jenna swears out her husband-to-be and then eventually bolts back up the sidewalk toward the main building. "I don't think these two are gonna last. So the fact that you touched her centerpiece probably isn't a big deal."

"I didn't *touch* touch it," he says, as though there are varying levels of touching. We begin walking toward the wedding patio.

"Whatever. Are we ready for bridal party entry photos?"

He rolls his eyes. "You tell me."

I grab his camera, feeling a lot like the mother of a petulant child. I scan the photos quickly. He did decent work. At least there are no dick pics this time. However, there *is* a photo of his hand touching the centerpiece. I'm not sure if he took that as part of a personal vendetta against the bride or just out of sheer luck.

"Great. Let's get into place." The groom and groomsmen have been filing toward the altar, along with the officiant and some of the guests. As we near the wedding patio, I hear the muffled sounds of someone crying. There's one thing for certain: Amelia and Rhys's wedding was by far the most chaotic fun, but every other wedding is its own brand of chaotic stressful. Every bride-and-groomzilla has held its own treasure trove of surprises, and this Jenzilla is sure to surprise me yet again.

But I couldn't have counted on just *how* much of a surprise she had in store for me. When I near the veranda where the bridal party is gathering, I see Jenna crumpled into the arms of...a man. A man who, at first glance, on an instinctual, visceral, completely unfathomable level, makes my veins turn electric and every inch of my skin goes on high alert. A man who, from the back and from a distance, reminds me of Weston.

If I ever thought three weeks would be enough time to get over Weston, I already knew I was wrong, but this happening right here would convince me I'm extra wrong. Except I'm not stupid enough to think that it would only take me three weeks to get over Weston. It might take me years. Possibly a lifetime. So at least I'm mentally prepared for the long road ahead of me.

The man is quietly shushing the bride. He's not her fiancé, because I passed him fifty yards back, and because her fiancé never had the same hair style as Weston Daly. Besides, he's dressed in street clothes, not formal wear, with a black shirt stretching across strong shoulders and gray board shorts. Jenna's mother and bridesmaids—including the one she made fun of—are gathered around her, cooing softly and sending discrete looks of confusion to one another.

"I just don't know if I want to go through with it," Jenna is wailing as I approach.

"Honey, you don't even know this man," her mother gently chides.

"But he helped pick up my bouquet," Jenna insists. The man extracts himself from her grip, something in his movement looking a little too familiar. When he steps away and turns toward me, all the air inside my body departs in one graceless puff.

Because that man doesn't just *seem* like Weston Daly. He *is* Weston Daly.

His gaze lands on me, and we both freeze. It's only been three weeks, yet he looks so different. I swear his hair is longer, his face somehow different. More chiseled. Almost more worn, like he's been living the past few weeks in a personal hell because he's had to be away from me.

That's what I'd like to believe, at least. But it can't be true. Even though maybe it is true, because he's here now.

I can't make any sense of his being here. None at all. So all I do is gape and stare and get jostled by Jenna.

"Don't take a picture of me," she warns, even though I'm physically unable to operate my camera right now due to *Weston*.

"Weston?" I squeak.

He takes careful steps toward me. Our gazes lock, and the heat that zips through me tells me I am farther away than ever from reaching my *get over Weston* goal. All the repressed longing and love I feel for this man suddenly bubbles up and spills over. Tears are pressing to escape, and I can't even say why.

"Don't leave," Weston says. "Please."

"I..." My brain short circuits. I forget entirely what I'm supposed to be doing here. "I'm not going to. I mean, I can't. I'm working. Do you know the bride?"

"I ran into him when I was coming back from being *observed by my fiancé*, which was *your* fault because you sent that stupid oaf to fondle my centerpiece," Jenna accuses me in a tear-clogged voice. There is so much to say right now to Weston—so many questions to ask—but this bridezilla meltdown makes both of us perk up in a special way. I can see Weston's fixit-guy gears turning. He turns toward Jenna.

"Stupid oaf?"

"That stupid shooter of hers!" Jenna jabs her finger at some point past me, where I can only assume Matias is standing behind me, fast asleep while holding his camera in his hands. Or maybe exposing himself. Or better yet—taking dick pics *while sleeping*.

"Jenna, dear," her mother begins.

"He's stupid, but he's not an oaf," I say, out of zero loyalty to Matias and negative five loyalty to Jenna. "Well, maybe slightly an oaf. But not a *totally* stupid oaf."

Weston's icy blue gaze slides past me, landing on Matias. His eyes narrow, and something goes tight in the air. "Are you...?"

"What?" I ask. We have so much to talk about, so much to catch up on, so much left to argue about, it seems ridiculous to address *this* of all things in the middle of Jenna's wedding. The violins begin playing from the ceremony area, which makes Jenna burst into tears.

"I caaaaan't," she wails.

Weston steps closer to me, so close that I feel his breath against my ear as he says in a low voice, "I'm here to make things right. And that will include fighting for your honor again. So just tell me if Stupid Oaf is one of my foes."

It's not fair. He's been here for thirty seconds and already he's got me en route to a puddle on the floor. I try to suppress the giggles that are so ready to slide out of me, willy-nilly. "Not a foe. Just unfortunately the only available second shooter on the island."

He lifts a brow. "Actually, there's suddenly a new second shooter who became available. Not sure if you're interested in his services, but..."

My heart starts racing, because part of me is convinced this is all a mirage.

"Are you even listening?" Jenna demands. "*I'm* getting married, not *you two!*"

I sigh tersely, looking around for Matias. When I spot him lingering in the bushes, I bark, "Matias! Give Weston your camera. You're off for the day. Have fun."

Matias doesn't even question the directive, just mumbles something and hands off his camera to Weston and leaves. Weston dons the camera, and I click into work mode. I'll deal with his surprise appearance later. For now, we've got a bridezilla to marry.

Jenna manages to safely wipe away her tears from the thirteen layers of makeup, and her bridal party assembles in front of her. The bridesmaids begin walking down the white-carpeted aisle. Weston and I scatter further along the walkway, snapping pictures. Every so often I catch his gaze waiting for me, and my heart flutters so much that I feel like I'll need to call for a physician.

I can't believe he's here. I just hope it's to stay.

The rest of the wedding goes off without a hitch, though I think some of that is due to Weston's bizarre powers of calm and organization. When I brush his arm during group photos, I nearly have an orgasm. So the sexual chemistry is still alive and well. Possibly more alive than ever.

Which means that I need to proceed carefully. He's left me before. He could leave me again. Working alongside him for an entire evening without talking things over is a weird way to reopen this story between us, but there's not much we can do. And for however weird it is, it's somehow right. By the time our duties wrap, I feel like we've solved everything without having said a word. I've acclimated to his energy again, and I can never be away from him.

I *need* him. The previous three weeks away from him have proven this, I only realize now that he's back.

While Jenna and her new husband are grinning at each other on the dance floor, Weston and I excuse ourselves from the party. We walk side-by-side down the brick path leading toward the beach, the silence bloated between us.

"Can we—" he begins.

"Let's go—" I start at the same time. We both shut up, and then I try again. "Where are you staying?"

"At a hostel down the road."

I nod, looking out at the dark ocean. "How long are you going to be here?"

"I don't know. I don't have a return ticket."

Hope springs to life inside me, though it shouldn't. But before I can begin counseling myself on that, Weston takes my hand in his. His rough thumb goes back and forth over my knuckles as he speaks.

"So you just came back since I need you for the job, right?" I can't help the snarky comment that flies out of my mouth. Weston crumples visibly, squeezing my hands.

"I fucked up when I left. I wasn't nice, and then I left without saying goodbye—"

"Yeah, that was extra not nice," I confirm.

"When I was home thinking about things, I realized that I really had fallen head over heels for you even though I hadn't wanted to. And I started reevaluating everything and..." He trails off, looking out at the ocean. "I realized that if I'm going to chase after anything, it should be to build something epic. With someone I love."

My heart is racing so fast I feel like I might pass out. Because these words are the stuff of fantasies. "Yeah? Build what?"

"Build an empire...or enterprise...or an inground pool in the back of our little Aruban cottage...I don't know. Those are just some ideas."

My smile is nearly splitting my face in two, but it's fun to play dumb a little longer. "Oh. And who is the someone you love?"

Weston's smile grows wider. He drops my hand so that he can slide his hands over the swell of my hips. Feeling him enveloping me again is almost too sweet to bear. My throat is tight as he presses himself against me, his lips brushing against my forehead as he speaks.

"It's you, Princess Nova. I fell so hard for you I split my front teeth, but still denied it even when I had blood running down my chin."

I snicker. "That's both romantic *and* gory."

"It's in the graphic novel I started about our love story," he whispers, dragging his lips across my forehead. "I'll show it to you. I brought it."

My eyes flutter shut. "Stop. I can't handle too much more good news."

"Oh. Well, just let me know when you're ready for more good news then. I don't want to overwhelm you, and I have a ton of additional things to tell you about."

His fingertips travel down the side of my face and along my jawline, tilting my head back. When I open my eyes, his intense gaze is waiting for me. I fist the back of his shirt, rooting myself in him, waiting for the surge of passion to happen.

Because lord, I know it'll happen. It's inevitable with him. With *us*.

"Okay, I might be ready," I say, and then he presses his lips against mine in a long, slow kiss that stops time altogether. "But tell me first: did you bring the necklace?"

"Of course." His voice is a sexy rumble, one that provokes as much as it calms.

I don't know how he does it. Weston is laid-back and fast-paced at the same time. He makes the world spin faster yet will also point out things that stop time, like the constellation-gazing while we fucked on the beach. This kiss is no different. It's like someone pressed fast-forward and reverse at the same time, so in response, the DVD player just exploded. Except I'm the DVD player.

I whimper, and he kisses me again. His tongue presses against my lips, urging them open, and of course I comply. Our tongues meet in the middle, tentative yet hungry. His hand slides to my neck, fingertips digging into the back of my head. Claiming me. Possessing me. Utterly completing me.

We kiss so long and so indecently that it takes a random passerby commenting, "Didn't you rent a room for that?" before we break the kiss and come to our senses. From the way his jaw flexes, I can tell he's battling impure thoughts that might make it hard for him to be seen in public.

"I want to build something with you, Nova. If you'll still have me."

My throat tightens. "I don't know. I've got a really good thing going with my second shooter." Weston's fingertips dig into my hips. "He's barely functional most days and actually fell asleep once while I was talking to him."

Weston's grips relaxes. "Ah. Yeah, that sounds really hard to top."

"Super hard. Matias set the bar high." I look out at the ocean again, pretending to consider his offer. "Even higher when I accidentally saw his dick on the camera reel."

Weston's grip goes tight again. "Okay, so this means I can fight for your honor again when I see him next?"

I giggle, unable to suppress it any longer. "You can do whatever you want, Weston. I'm just so damn happy to see you again."

He scoops me up into a tight hug, and we stay like that for a long time. When he finally releases me, he says, "I've had time to think. And plan. And dream. Those are the things I'm good at, I guess. And I don't want to interrupt what you've got going on here. But I've had some ideas for the future. For *our* future."

"Like what?"

"Like a little business called NovaWest Deigns," he says, pressing a kiss to the tip of my nose.

"Hmmm. Sounds great. What do they do?"

"Wedding and event photography. Special sunrise sessions. And, in a surprise twist, boudoir photos."

I laugh, slapping at his chest. "Oh, come on."

"I'm serious. I've got a whole business plan drawn up. Three of them, actually. I never wanted to put down roots, Nova, but since I met you, I'm ready to fucking stay."

I've never heard better words in all my life. The truth is I don't know where our future leads, but it doesn't matter. As long as I have someone at my side who wants to collaborate, who wants to envision the next best thing?

That's all I need.

"I love you, Nova," Weston whispers against my lips. "I love you so much that it doesn't make sense."

"I love you too, Sir Weston," I say, tears pricking my eyes. And then we kiss, for the first of what is sure to be a billion times in our conjoined lifetime.

Aruba just got so much better.

Because we'll be in it—creating, living, and laughing—together.

EPILOGUE

ONE YEAR LATER

NOVA

"Oh my goodness," I whisper, peering out the passenger window of the car. We've been driving for an hour and just passed the WEL-COME TO BAYSHORE sign. "We're finally here?"

Weston nods, looking proud and sexy-as-fuck as he steers our over-the-top rental sports car. What can I say? We've had an amazing first year of business on the island. Weston wanted to opt for the sports car, and I couldn't say no to the idea of zipping around in this sexy black coupe for the next month.

He pulls off the highway, the humid lake air filling the car with a fresh, intoxicating scent. The streets turn tree-lined, and as we pull onto side streets and head toward the heart of downtown, I can hear birds chirping and kids playing in the distance.

It's a big difference from what I've gotten used to over the past year. Since Aruba is technically a desert island, it has forests of spiky cacti instead of maple and oak trees. We have to water our little orange flowers in front of our Aruban cottage three times a day just to keep them alive. I found out the hard way when I killed all our pink flowers the first time around. I'm not sure they'll still be alive by the time we get back. Even though we've asked our amazing elderly neighbor, Annamiek, to water those babies each day, I'm just not sure they can survive without my constant worry and attention. I guess I'll find out when I get back.

I gasp, pointing at a stately brick building with a big sign reading BAYSHORE HIGH SCHOOL. "Is that where you graduated?"

"Every single one of us," Weston says, downshifting as we come to a stop sign. Swear to god, my panties get wet just from witnessing that little maneuver. We haven't had a car on Aruba, though we have had plenty of other things—residency visas, checking accounts, our own business, tons of sex in front of our own little slice of Aruban cottage ocean access.

Weston's little reminder of the fact that I'm about to meet *the whole family* sends butterflies through my guts yet again. I've been looking forward to this trip since we realized it could become a reality about six months ago. That's when our own photography business, NovaWest Designs, really took off and became profitable. Not just profitable as in, *we can feed ourselves*. But *holy crap we found our niche* profitable, where we can eat, and rent a sports car on our actual vacation, and help pay my family's debt, *and* live permanently on a tropical island without issue.

Oh, and did I mention? Gram lives in *my* backyard now. That's right. Our Aruban cottage comes with its very own mother-in-law suite, which in this case is the Gram suite. She lives with us half the year, and in New York half the year. When I seriously presented her with the idea of spending some of her year in Aruba with us, she bit the bullet and swallowed all her pressurized cabin fears. Turns out, she loves flying now. She just flew back to New York—by herself—last week and sent me a selfie from the VIP lounge because she somehow managed to sneak in.

Most days, I can't believe this is real life.

"We're almost there," Weston says, excitement shining in his smile. I love seeing him like this. Excited to share his life with me. Actually, I'm not sure which one of us is more excited. This is our official meet-the-family tour—two weeks in Bayshore, two weeks in upstate New York. I have already met one of his brothers, Grayson, when he and his fiancée Hazel visited us a few months back for a winter getaway. Hazel and I spent most of their trip drinking wine spritzers and trading stories about dating a Daly boy. Well, and I gifted her a boudoir shoot. Because that's the other exciting part of life with Weston. He's always innovating. Not only do we schedule wedding packages, there are add-ons that include personalized graphic novels created by Weston and bonding sunrise packages, where we take intimate, gorgeous photos and even top it off with a little partner yoga.

And yes, Weston and I have mastered the art of standing up together. *Finally.*

We pull into a neighborhood of tightly packed cottages and lush, manicured lawns. He slows and pulls into a driveway that is already mostly full with SUVs and BMWs. We take the last open spot, and before we can even get out of the car, there's a shout from the front door.

"Weston's here!"

I step out just as Weston's mother rushes toward me. We've video chatted a few times, and she's all smiles. She wraps me in a big hug, cooing, "Hellooo, Nova!"

Weston appears at my side a moment later. "Jeez, Mom. Make it obvious who you love more."

She tuts and releases me, all smiles for her son. "You stop it. I love all my boys and daughters-in-law equally."

Weston shushes her. "We're not married yet," he says as he pulls his mom into a tight hug. My eyes widen slightly. *Yet.* What an invigorating and promising little addition. We've talked about marriage, but only briefly as a someday thing. But still, I've known since day one—well, maybe day *three*—that this man is the best match for me in this world. I, too, have a perma-grin as the three of us make our way into the Daly home.

Their house is warm, inviting, completely Midwestern lake chic. Voices drift from deeper inside the house, and once we cross into the kitchen, I realize this is already a *party.* The entire backyard is full of people. I spot Grayson and Hazel, but Weston swoops me along with him and begins making introductions. There's London and Dominic. Connor and Kinsley. Their dad, who is grilling hamburgers with a serious face, offers his hand for a handshake. Maverick lurks in the far corner of the backyard, wearing a tight black T-shirt and black jeans, even though it's mid-July and hot as hell. When a blonde waif slinks into the backyard and links her arm through Maverick's, Weston explains to me that she's less *girlfriend* and more *flavor of the week,* but Maverick felt like he should fit in for this Daly couples' party.

Appetizers sit on the picnic tables and everyone is lost in jovial conversation and catching up. I'm whisked away into conversation with Hazel, joined by London, and eventually Kinsley, who is wearing the cutest sunflower print shorts I have ever seen. We try to involve Maverick's gal pal, but she seems uninterested in leaving his side.

When the next round of drinks is brought out, Weston appears at my side. "Hey, let's video call Gram."

"Right now?"

"Yeah. Can you?"

I fumble to extract my phone from the back pocket of my denim shorts. "Yeah, I mean…I guess. What's the urgency?"

"Just call her. Make sure it's video."

I'm perplexed by the urgency, but I do as he says. Gram picks up immediately, almost like she was ready and waiting for the call.

"I'm here," she says. "Actually, we all are."

"All of you?" I ask. She fumbles with the camera, swearing under her breath as she struggles to flip the camera. My mom and dad are sitting in chairs in my gram's living room. "Oh, hi, Mom and Dad! What is this all about?"

"Don't say nothing," I hear Gram warn my parents.

"Weston," I start, looking over at him, but he's gotten everyone gathered into a group behind me. "Uh, what's going on?"

"Let me put this over here." Weston deftly swipes the phone from my hand and sets it up on the picnic table nearby, angling it so that it captures me and the family behind me. He comes back over to me, draws a deep breath, and then looks toward the phone.

"Is this good?" He offers a thumbs-up to the camera, and my gram shouts, "Perfect!"

"Weston—" I try again, but my reason and abilities are slowly unraveling as the seconds tick on. This was pre-planned. Everyone is smiling and anticipating something, and I am somehow the only one left out. All signs would point to some sort of big question, but I can't force my brain to synthesize this, so it just cycles in the same broken loop.

"Nova," he says, his fingertips sliding down the length of my arms. "I really wanted all of our loved ones to be here for this."

"For what?" I ask breathily, but I already know. Tears have already sprung to my eyes, and I will absolutely dissolve as soon as he asks that *lurking big question.*

Weston slowly drops to one knee, holding my hands in his. He kisses the knuckles of both hands, looking up at me with so much tenderness that I start crying. Already. Before he's even said anything.

"Nova," he begins.

"Yes!" I shout.

Weston dissolves into laughter, wiping away a tear. "I didn't even ask anything!"

"Then why are you crying?" I'm openly crying now. And I feel like this is just so indicative of our relationship. We're so close—closer than I've ever been to anyone, closer even than my gram—so of course I'd accept his marriage proposal without him technically making it.

He laughs into his hand for a moment, then wipes at his face and starts again. "Nova. This is supposed to be serious."

"Fat chance of that," Gram cackles from the video call.

More laughter escapes him, but he pushes ahead. "I think we just demonstrated for both of our families that we are completely, hopelessly perfect for each other. A year ago, I was terrified to dive into what we had between us, because I thought that falling in love would disrupt my life. But I was so, so wrong. Falling in love with you made my life epic. Living with you, growing with you, starting a business with you, has been the adventure I didn't realize I needed. Tell me we can be on this adventure for the rest of our lives, babe. Marry me."

I throw my head back and laugh wildly, some mixture of insane, profound glee and happy tears. I am equal parts shocked and not surprised at all. I throw my arms around him and squeal. Applause erupts around us, and I can hear my family cheering from the video call.

"Oh, my God, I forgot the ring!" Weston exclaims. He digs in his pocket and produces a simple silver band with glittering green inlaid stones. He slides it on my ring finger, his hand shaking slightly. "It matches our necklaces."

"I love it so much," I whisper as he kisses every square inch of my face. "I love *you* so much."

I relish it all. The love, the attention, the way our lives fit together like puzzle pieces now. Because this is a big love. This is the type of love I never thought I'd find in my life. This is the type of love that even I was ready to write off.

Until Weston came along and reminded me that I could dream bigger.

"You didn't technically answer after I asked you," he tells me, scooping my hands into his between our chests.

"Oh, was I unclear?"

"No, I just want to hear it again," he says, expelling a deep breath.

"Yes, Weston. I will marry you. Gladly. Over and over again."

"Can we not get married on a beach, though?" He asks with a laugh. "I feel like I'm a little burnt out on beach weddings."

"Let's get married in the Himalayas," I say offhandedly. From behind us, a champagne cork goes *POP*. Everyone around us is celebrating and chattering and whooping. For us. For our love.

"Or what about Australia?" he asks.

"Mmmm. Sub-Saharan Africa?"

He grins and then presses a kiss to my lips. "Actually, I take it back. We can get married on the beach. Hell, we can get married in a trash can. I don't care. I just want it to happen. With you at my side, I know it'll be epic."

"Careful, this is starting to sound like a Dr. Seuss rhyme," I tell him, before snagging another juicy kiss from his lips.

"We can hammer out a few stanzas for the graphic novel," he says. The graphic novel that he's been adding to slowly over the past year. And if that wasn't the sign that this man was for me—beyond owning the same gorgeous necklace for *no apparent reason*—then I don't know what would be.

Dominic appears at our sides, holding two champagne flutes, which he presses into our hands. "You two ready to join your own damn party? Or are you just going to be stuck in your own world all evening?"

"Probably more the latter than the former," Weston says with a laugh.

And isn't that just how it goes? From day three onward, Weston and I have been living in our own world. Full of our own jokes. Our own sunrises. Our own bliss.

"Don't worry," Dom admits in a low voice. "I get it." He squeezes his brother's shoulder. "I'm happy for you two. You both look insanely happy. And that's all that matters. I wish you both a thriving, happy future." Dominic squeezes my arm. "Sister-in-law."

Weston's eyes are shining as he looks back at me. More tears are coming now, and I can't even stop them. Because this is so much more than just finding the most amazing man. He comes with a great family. I now have new people to turn to. More amazing people that constitute my trusted network of awesomeness.

Because holy hell. I found the life of my wildest dreams.

No, scratch that.

I found a life better than my wildest dreams.

THE END

Need more Daly moments? We've got one last brother to meet in Make Me Hot (http://books2read.com/make-me-hot): a friends-to-lovers rom-com featuring the youngest brother Maverick as he joins a cutthroat food competition with his best friend, the aspiring silks performer Scarlett. Keep reading to find the entire FIRST CHAPTER of the next book...

Want even MORE brothers? Get to know the Fairchild brothers in an intense and steamy billionaire romance series, *The Bad Boys of Wall Street*. Start with the first book, *The Price of Revenge (htt p://books2read.com/price-of-revenge)*, as Axel Fairchild reunites with his first—and only—love, Cora Margulis, 8 years after she broke his heart and married someone else.

READ 'MAKE ME HOT'

CHAPTER ONE of 'MAKE ME HOT'

(Book 5 in the Bayshore series)

SCARLETT

"Excuse me, is this seat taken?"

The soft question from my right makes me jump out of my internal thoughts. I've been nursing this chardonnay for far too long. It's warm. My hand hurts from gripping the stemmed wine glass. And honestly, I've just been fiddling with it as a way to keep my hands busy so I don't reach across the table and strangle one of my more annoying table mates here in the middle of the Bayshore Theatre's reception hall.

I twist to look at who's asking me. A middle-aged woman I don't know is grinning down at me, gesturing to the open chair to my right as if there's any question. She could be an aunt or a distant second cousin. Not *mine,* of course, since this isn't my wedding. This is the Daly wedding. Grayson Daly, to be exact. I squint at her, trying to place some Daly features in her face. She might have their nose. I peg her as an aunt.

"No, no, seat's not taken." I make a shooing motion to show her how fine it is that she steal the one open chair at my round table.

"Are you sure?"

"Absolutely." I move the chair toward her as a gesture of how okay it is. The seat represents the plus one I'd planned on coming with...until we broke up three months ago and I'd forgotten to alter my RSVP. "It's just the ghost of my ex-boyfriend, so I'd be happy for you to take him off my hands."

Mrs. Probably-Their-Aunt titters nervously and drags the chair to a neighboring round table. The reception is full of an astonishing number of Daly family members who I never heard about growing up. Not that I hold a PhD in Daly Genealogy or anything, but I should have at least received some sort of honorary-Daly award by now.

I've been hovering around the Dalys for damn near two decades. Tagging along on pool days. Going to the same school, elementary through high school. Hell, I've been Maverick's closest female-friend-he-doesn't-fuck since we were twelve years old.

"Ahhhhhh." It sounds like gas escaping a vacuum chamber, but actually it's the most annoying of my table mates. Veronica. The girl that Maverick came with. His "date," even though everybody and their brother—especially his own brothers—know that Maverick doesn't date. This girl absolutely will not stop making these long, drawn-out noises as she critically assesses some aspect of the reception. "I really disagreed with the peony selection. They could have put some thought into the color scheme." Now she's shaking her head, grimacing while she leans over her half-eaten plate of food to sigh about the flowers with the other woman at our table, Maverick's cousin Betsy.

There aren't many instances when I wish my ex could actually be near me these days, but I wouldn't have been upset if he rolled up now just so I could stop feeling like the odd woman out among this impromptu trio at our dinner table.

It doesn't help that Maverick got swallowed into the Daly crowd, and Betsy's date has been using the bathroom for approximately a half hour. I wouldn't be surprised if it was related to the weird collard-and-kale dish that we were served tonight. One look at that limp pile of greenery and I felt sorta queasy, too.

"It's like, who was behind this? Who puts peonies with carnations?" Betsy scoffs with incredulity, and I'm feigning intense interest in the people milling around post-dinner so I don't have to critique the flower selection along with them. As if I'm looking for someone and just can't seem to find him.

Definitely not looking for my ghost ex-boyfriend. After two lackluster years together, breaking up with Tom was the hardest thing I've ever had to do. I'm pretty sure he still thinks we're getting back together, too. At least, that's what Maverick reports. Because thanks to the tiny-town effect in Bayshore, Maverick and Tom are coworkers. Of course.

A belly laugh that I would recognize anywhere, even beyond the grave, drifts through the air. I snap my gaze around and find the source. *Maverick.* He's halfway across the reception hall, his head tossed back in laughter as he and his older brother Weston are looking dapper and fit for a fucking modeling contract in their black-on-black suits.

I don't know Hazel, Grayson's new wife, very well, but I know *of* her plenty. And this woman would only have a wedding decked out in mauve and black-on-black, with owl centerpieces surrounded by white peonies—and, apparently, carnations, though I never would have noticed if it weren't for my lovely tablemates. Hazel is the only one in Bayshore who could pull off this slightly morbid yet wildly elegant theme.

I'm certainly not complaining—the look is perfect for Maverick. I might be Maverick's platonic bestie since the time puberty rolled around, but I haven't been blind all these years. The man's hot enough to make lava seem palatable. Hot seeks out hot. Which is why Veronica, for all her irritating gaseous sighs and peony complaints, looks like a next-gen Kardashian with lips so plump they could only be destined for Hollywood.

But you know what hot doesn't seek out?

Me. Which is why I'm on the outskirts of this carnation-calamity conversation, the laid-back sidekick stuffed into a skintight dress, second-guessing all my eyeshadow decisions and wondering what, exactly, Maverick and Veronica would be getting into later, and whether or not he cares at all about her personality.

"Lettie." Maverick's raspy baritone floats through the air, settling inside me with pinpricks. I smile up at him as he comes around the table. His longish tresses, so dark brown they're almost black, are slicked back in a trendy yet formal look. His jawline could cut glass, and his normal stubble has been replaced with a freshly sheared face. Not that I notice or care about these things ever. He jerks his chin at the space beside my seat. "You get rid of Tom's chair?"

Helpless laughter cascades out of me as he settles in beside Veronica. Finally, the table feels right again with him here. Now if only Betsy's boyfriend would come back, so I could resume blending into the male shadows like I'm used to.

"Your aunt needed the chair," I tell him. He's scooting in his chair, returning to his half-finished plate. Veronica's is half-finished out of concerns for her figure, but Maverick's is half-finished because he got interrupted by a call for an impromptu family pic. And let me tell you, seeing all those Daly sons side-by-side takes a certain type of willpower. Especially when Maverick insisted on scaling Grayson's shoulders in a precarious tower with their brothers leaping in the air beside them for a photo op.

"He'll be pissed when he shows up and finds out you let Sally have his chair. And she's my *cousin*, by the way."

He still hasn't formally acknowledged Veronica since he sat back down, and she still hasn't blinked in his direction. Not like they're required to. Hell, I don't know what the rules of flings are these days. I never knew to begin with. You could probably search the entire United States for a more loyal, commitment-focused twenty-something than me and not find her. Which just makes mine and Maverick's friendship all the more hilarious.

He's Mr. One-and-Done. And I'm Ms. Hunting-for-Forever.

Yet somehow, we pinky swore a BFF pact back in sixth grade and never looked back. He and I bonded over playing basketball, which blossomed into an easy sort of camaraderie centered around jokes and simply being present for each other that hasn't changed since. I'm pretty sure he sees me as a feminine-looking dude...one he can both share a beer with and talk about life's conundrums with, without the typical dude ridicule.

"Do I at least get some credit for knowing that she was on the Daly side?" I return to my plate, even though nothing here interests me. I'm quite content with the entire steak I consumed, less content with the warm chardonnay. I'm extremely physically active, so I need my protein. As in, *all* the protein.

He grimaces and shakes his head. "Max, three points. But only because my brother got married today."

"Wow." I let out a low whistle. This is the type of shit that Maverick and I are known for. Bullshitting, pure and simple. We could spend an hour splitting hairs about this imaginary score card we're about to invent, believe me. "Woulda thought that you'd be more generous with the points dispersal, considering that I was only one family tree limb off, but whatever."

"Hey. Those limbs are separate for a reason."

I stifle my laughter. His date is now looking at us like we're speaking Arabic.

"What happened with a tree outside?" she asks, her brows drawn together.

"Nothing." Maverick wets his bottom lip, finally swinging his gaze toward Veronica. He's got a plastic sort of smile on, the type I see him use all the time with his flings and hookups and one-night stands. The type of smile I'd call him out on. But Veronica doesn't know him well enough to realize she's being played.

Or maybe that's what she's there for in the first place. To be with the player.

"I gotta go to the bathroom." Veronica offers an even more plasticized smile and stands. Betsy follows her lead, sending Maverick a look that I don't understand, and the two saunter off through the bustling reception hall.

"Those two became fast friends," I say, now that it's just us here. Betsy's date either is having a bowel emergency forever or just snuck out on her. Based on her preoccupation with the carnations, I'm thinking they're heading for a breakup.

Maverick stabs at what little remains on his plate. "Yeah?"

I watch him move around the potatoes for a moment. "You're not that enthused about the food." *Or the girl.*

"Looked way better sitting in the pans than it tastes, but hey." Maverick drops his fork and leans back into his chair. "I'll give Gray shit about it for the next five years, so I don't mind."

"You could have done a way better job," I tell him, crossing my arms over my chest. My cleavage has been on display tonight, which was my plan as a recently-single woman, but also uncomfortable. I wear dresses twice a year, if that.

He smirks, and for a tantalizing moment his gaze drops to my cleavage. "Sometimes I forget you have boobs."

My body shakes with silent laughter. This is how not interested in me sexually he is—he doesn't even remember I'm female. We put the *pal* in *platonic,* if you misspelled it intentionally.

"Consider this your annual reminder." I point to my chest. "I've got knockers."

"Yeah, but you can't really knock anyone out with them," he chides.

"Don't sit there and criticize the potential of my *breasts*," I say. "Just because they aren't as big as your date's doesn't mean they aren't secretly trained as MMA fighters."

He snorts, turning his fork over, but some of the humor has drained out of him. Maybe it was too weird to compare me to his date. He's probably going to go barf in the toilet just imagining me naked, which is what I've assumed his response would be since we were teens.

It's not what my response would be to seeing *him* naked. No, my response would be way different. I'm not going to lie and say I haven't imagined it already, but that scenario will only ever live in my imagination. Besides, it would be too weird to finally know exactly how long or thick his *unmentionable* is—also things I've imagined once or twice *only*, I swear. Friends shouldn't see friend's naughty bits, much less imagine them.

"But seriously," I barrel on, determined to steer the conversation back to safe territory where my boobs aren't the center of conversation. "You could have made a better meal than this."

"Probably."

"Grayson should have hired you."

He huffs, shaking his head as if it's an absurd idea. "I'm not *that* good."

"Well, you're good enough to feed large groups of people, that's for sure." I jerk my chin out in the general direction of the bathroom doors. "Look. Here comes Edward E. Coli."

Our long-lost table mate is heading our way, looking haggard after his extended journey into the bathroom stall. Maverick twists, the start of a smile playing at his lips. "Who?"

"Your girlfriend's new best friend's boyfriend," I say with a *duh* tone.

"She's not my girlfriend. You know this."

"Fine. Gal pal. Whatever."

A moment later, Betsy's boyfriend sits back down at the table with a sigh. His tie is loosened slightly, and I can't tell if he just got back from a secret make-out session with *another woman* or if his body really was rejecting the dinner. This is how unexciting my life is. I spend most of my time theorizing about the exciting aspects of other people's lives, because my daily existence is spent doing one of three activities: working, exercising, or babysitting my niece and nephew.

I'm really rocking at being twenty-six. I'd have a quarter-life crisis if I could get the time off from my serving job. Instead, I'll just tack on a few extra push-ups and work out my stunted life aspirations at the Cleveland gym where I practice aerial silks. It's my one solace in life. Well, that and bullshitting with Maverick.

"Man," the guy says with a sigh as he crosses his arms. "I'm ready for beer."

Maverick lifts his half-drunk glass of brew in salute to Edward E. Coli. No, that's not his name. *Patrick*. That's it.

"Always time for another beer," Patrick-not-Edward says.

"Especially when the beer is going the be the majority of your dinner," I say, nodding toward his plate. "You didn't eat much."

"Tasted like bleached cutting board," Patrick says with a grimace. "They shoulda brought one of those food trucks out."

"Bayshore has food trucks?" Maverick says dully, like he's only half-listening. But I know it's his defense mechanism. He's pretending he's not interested, because he doesn't want to talk about it, even though he knows he should. I know this man too well.

"Bayshore has one food truck hidden away," I say pointedly, pulling a face at him. I try to kick him under the table for good measure, but I only reach the middle leg of the table, jostling the whole thing. Maverick narrows his eyes at me.

"No it doesn't," he says. "It's not a food truck yet."

"You do food trucks?" Patrick says, a brow lifting.

"No," Maverick says.

"Yes," I say at the same time. "He's been building one for the past couple of years as slow as a snail."

"It's just a little side project I've got going on," Maverick tells Patrick, his tone dripping with *it's seriously nothing*.

"What kind of food you gonna sell?" Patrick asks. I could kiss him. I make needling Maverick about his unexplored culinary talent an official hobby, so I'm happy to pass the baton to Patrick.

"I don't have a menu set or anything," Maverick says, smoothing his palm over the slicked side of his hair. "But I make a lot of burritos, rice dishes. I've got a plate I want to make called the Hot Mess..."

"Dude, did you hear about that food truck competition happening soon?" Patrick jerks his chin toward Maverick. "You should enter! At least for the fun of it."

Maverick smirks just as Veronica and Patrick's girlfriend come back. Something hard slides over his face, and he shrugs noncommittally. "Eh, we'll see."

"What's going on, guys?" Veronica asks as she sits down next to Maverick, sending a conspiratorial smile toward Patrick's girlfriend. "Anything fun happen while we were gone?"

"Just about to get another round of drinks," Maverick says before Patrick or I can say anything about the food truck.

"Ooooh, get me another *blanc*," Veronica purrs in the way in an actress would in a bad porno. She wraps her arm around his, leaning in to plant a sloppy kiss on his lips. Maverick seems surprised at first, but he melts into it. I admit I spend a little bit too much time side-eyeing their kiss, because A) it's a train wreck I can't look away from and B) I spend too much time wondering what it would feel like to kiss Maverick.

It's not like I *want* to kiss Maverick, even though I'm pretty sure if he asked me at this point, I'd say yes. As long as we could establish that it was for science, because I wouldn't do *anything* that would disrupt our decade-long friendship. It's a long-simmering curiosity that I wasn't aware of until recently. I know everything about this man—I should know how his lips taste too, right?

Again, for *science.*

Despite how well I know Maverick, there must be plenty I don't know about him. The way Maverick looks when Veronica breaks the kiss is a look I've never gotten from him, not even after fifteen years of knowing him. The type of look a girl like me could never coax from him, either.

A familiar, aching heaviness stretches across my chest, something I know well but don't often pry into. It's easier to look away, to offer a smile, to watch him cycle through women from afar and tell myself I don't care.

But when Maverick's gaze drags back to find mine, there's something electric there that pins me to my spot, reviving the recent question that has circled dangerously inside my skull like a shark after fresh blood:

What would it be like to be the girl on his arm?

KEEP READING

(http://books2read.com/make-me-hot)

AUTHOR'S NOTE

The choppy waters of Lake Erie in the summertime are a special sort of haven, shrieking sea gulls and all. This series is set in a fictionalized mixture of my hometown and a neighboring town in northern Ohio. Writing this series has become a love song to my homeland.

Even though I grew up mostly critical of my little slice of the world (like most moody, dissatisfied teens—HA!), I now recognize it for what it is: a gorgeous spot in the Midwestern landscape, one that is capable of producing all the love and emotion and depth that a romance author could hope for.

I sincerely hope you enjoy this visit to Bayshore...and I hope you'll continue this journey with the brothers of the Daly family!

LET'S STAY CONNECTED!

Stay connected with me via my newsletter (http://bit.ly/EL-news letter), where I share teasers, sales, and other exciting news. (Plus, if you haven't heard, I have an MMA romance series available, and **you'll get the prequel novella FOR FREE** when you sign up to my newsletter).

Or join my reader group, EMBER'S BLOSSOMS, to hang out up-close and personal! Early looks at new covers, exclusive access to ARC sign-ups, and more.

FACEBOOK
INSTAGRAM
GOODREADS
BOOKBUB
http://www.emberleighromance.com/

And before you go...

Please consider leaving an honest review about this book! Even just a few words or a line mean so much to us authors.

ALSO BY EMBER LEIGH

THE BAD BOYS OF WALL STREET
The Price of Revenge
The Price of Passion
The Price of Infamy
The Price of Forever

WINTER HARBOR
(co-written with Whitley Cox)
The Bastard Heir
The Asshole Heir
The Rebel Heir
The Matchmaking Heirs

THE BAYSHORE SERIES
Make Me Lose
Make Me Fall
Make Me Yours
Make Me Choose

Make Me Hot
Make Me Smile

THE BREAKING SERIES
Breaking the Rules
Changing the Game
Breaking the Sinner
Breaking the Habit
Breaking the Fall